IDEAL LIFE

ALSO BY EVELYN SKYE

For Adults

Ideal Life

The Incredible Kindness of Paper

The Hundred Loves of Juliet

One Year Ago in Spain

Damsel

For Young Adults

The Crown's Game

The Crown's Fate

Circle of Shadows

Cloak of Night

Three Kisses, One Midnight

For Children

Princess Private Eye

IDEAL LIFE

A Novel

Evelyn Skye

EMILY BESTLER BOOKS

ATRIA

NEW YORK AMSTERDAM/ANTWERP LONDON
TORONTO SYDNEY/MELBOURNE NEW DELHI

EMILY BESTLER BOOKS

ATRIA

An Imprint of Simon & Schuster, LLC
1230 Avenue of the Americas
New York, NY 10020

First Emily Bestler Books/Atria Paperback edition August 2026

EMILY BESTLER BOOKS/ATRIA PAPERBACK and colophon are registered trademarks of Simon & Schuster, LLC

Interior design by Esther Paradelo

Manufactured in the United States of America

1 3 5 7 9 10 8 6 4 2

Library of Congress Cataloging-in-Publication Data has been applied for.

ISBN 978-1-6680-8201-0
ISBN 978-1-6680-8203-4 (ebook)

To Tom & Reese

When you hold out for a perfect future version of yourself, you turn the present into a mere dress rehearsal for something more important later on.

OLIVER BURKEMAN

There is the strange attitude and feeling that one is not yet in real life.

PSYCHOTHERAPIST MARIE-LOUISE VON FRANZ

Talia

You deserve a better life—your Ideal Life.

Talia Morgan's heart was racing, but she smiled at the motto above the receptionist's desk. Ever since she was fifteen, she'd known she wanted to find a way to make people's daily lives better, and now, twenty years later, she was on the cusp of truly achieving that.

"You ready, boss?" Erin Berg, a bright-eyed Stanford undergrad who was interning at Ideal Life this summer, came into the reception area from the offices behind her. It was just past 8 p.m., and they were about to attend a celebration dinner with some of tech's biggest investors downstairs in a Michelin-starred Japanese restaurant.

"Almost ready," Talia said, but she nearly snorted at herself. She didn't look like a CEO of one of the country's hottest startups. She was just a generic thirty-five-year-old woman: generic brown hair in a practical ponytail, generically average body of someone who didn't exercise as much as she should. And she was still dressed for work—that is, the Silicon Valley uniform of T-shirt and jeans with a company-logoed hoodie (in this case, Ideal Life's purple star).

But no matter. The great thing about a place like Palo Alto was they cared more about your brains and work ethic than how you looked. Talia started to turn to go back to her office. "I just, uh, need to swap out my hoodie for my blazer—"

"Already got you covered." Erin handed over the navy jacket Talia kept on a hanger behind her office door. There was a joke that you could tell who the boss of a tech company was because they dressed like everyone else, except they threw a blazer over their T-shirt.

"I grabbed your heels, too," Erin said.

"You're always a step ahead," Talia said as she slipped out of her hoodie and into the blazer, kicked off her sneakers, and stepped into the pumps.

"I learned from the best," Erin said, grinning.

Talia laughed. But it was true that she'd taken Erin under her wing. Silicon Valley was still largely a boys' club, and tech women had to stick together. Talia had learned the hard way not only how to work harder and ideate better than the male engineers, but also how to get credit for her brilliance. It's why she was no longer a worker bee behind the scenes and instead was the founder and CEO of a startup about to be acquired by tech behemoth OmnisZcience. (Which everyone just called Omni, partially because nobody could remember how to spell it with the extraneous Z in the middle.)

Her phone rang. It had to be Sam. He was the only person she knew who didn't preschedule calls or just text.

Talia picked up. "Are you here?" she asked.

"Wow," Sam said. "No preamble, no hello, *straight* to business." There was an undercurrent of teasing in his voice, though. This is how Talia and Sam had always been, ever since they became best friends at Stanford during their freshman year. He was the easygoing beta to her idealistic, mile-a-minute alpha.

"Samuel Jason Chang, *please*," Talia said. "I can't take banter right now. I'm all nerves. Are you downstairs or are you not here yet?"

"Hey," he said softly. "It's okay. I got you. I'm here."

Talia exhaled. "Okay. I'll send Erin to let you in." The building was typical of downtown Palo Alto, where shops and restaurants lived on the first floor, while offices populated the higher ones. You needed a company badge to get access to Ideal Life on floors two through four.

A couple minutes later, the elevator doors opened, and Sam stepped out alone; Erin had gone on to the restaurant. He wore a tuxedo jacket he'd found at a thrift store and altered so the edges were stylishly roughened up, paired with a black T-shirt and black jeans. Unlike Talia, who had no sense of style, Sam had an effortless young-professor aesthetic—complete with slightly tousled black hair—that he seemed to just roll out of bed with. It probably had to do with being around books all day; he owned a bookshop half an hour away on the coast.

"Congratulations," Sam said, drawing Talia into a hug. He was several inches taller than her, even when she wore heels, and his arms enveloped her completely.

"Thank you," she said, allowing herself a moment to close her eyes and sink into the familiar comfort of him. "I'm happy—really happy—but also nervous. Is that weird?"

"No," Sam said. "Omni is one of the biggest tech companies in the world, and they're buying *your* company. For a hundred million dollars. Of course you're happy and nervous at the same time."

"I think I'm also anxious because we didn't actually get the acquisition papers signed this morning. There was some small appendix that the lawyers needed from their colleagues in France that didn't come in on time. Supposedly, though, the document will be done tomorrow morning, and we'll sign everything then. But we decided to go ahead with the celebration dinner because we'd already booked out the whole restaurant downstairs." She grimaced. "I hope we're not tempting fate."

The thing was, startups like Talia's company skated on thin ice. So often, they were six months away from going under, even the ones with great technology and reputations. They needed either constant infusions of cash from venture capital investors, or to catch the eye of a bigger company with deep pockets that could acquire them. That was certainly the case for Ideal Life, and Omni's desire to buy them came just as Ideal Life's bank accounts were getting low on funds.

Sam released Talia from the hug, but he smiled. "The French document issue sounds like a minor delay, and everything will be fine. Omni wouldn't be sending their execs to the party tonight if the acquisition wasn't already a done deal."

"Yeah . . ." Talia said, beginning to pace Ideal Life's reception area, her heels clacking unevenly on the floor. She was more accustomed to sneakers, and she didn't quite feel like herself when she had to adjust her gait like this. "It's just . . . we *really* need this deal to happen. And the acquisition contract is only the first step. After we sign tomorrow, Omni will get to send their teams of lawyers and investment bankers and software engineers to sift through all of Ideal Life's stuff—contracts, source code, everything—and if they find anything during due diligence that they don't like, they can walk away. It's like selling a house, where the buyer signs a contract but is free to bail if they discover that you have termites or asbestos."

"Does Ideal Life have termites or asbestos?"

"No, but—"

Sam took her by the shoulders and looked straight into her eyes. "Then it will be fine. More than fine. So let's go downstairs to this fancy-ass restaurant and shovel fifty-dollar sushi rolls into our mouths, okay?"

That broke Talia out of her spiraling, and she laughed. "We can't eat like the animals we really are, and you know it. I have to look *professional*. The Omni execs and Ideal Life's venture capital investors will be there, and some journalists, too."

"What a shame," Sam said. "I was looking forward to eating sushi with my hands." He smiled as he offered his arm to Talia. "Regardless, shall we?"

She took a deep breath, then pushed the elevator button before slipping her hand into the crook of his elbow. "Thanks again for being my 'date,' even though you have to hop on a flight in a few hours. I really appreciate you taking a red-eye to your poker competition, just so you could be here tonight."

He said something quietly that she couldn't quite make out because the elevator dinged and the doors opened, and then it was forgotten as they stepped inside.

Ideal Life was Talia's brainchild. She'd conceived it in the fourth year of her neuroscience PhD at Stanford. She was supposed to have been working on her dissertation, but one afternoon while at lunch with Sam, the conversation had drifted to Talia's memories of her mom and dad, who—to be frank—had been terrible parents. They were the kind of people who had partied hard when they were young, but then they didn't outgrow it even after they'd had kids. Vera and Dave had gone out with their friends almost every single night, and *Talia* had been the one to make sure that groceries were bought and that the laundry got done and that her little sister, Libby, understood her homework and went to bed at a reasonable hour.

If only their parents had had some kind of scaffolding around their lives to gently intervene whenever they got a call from a friend to come out for "just one drink." If only there had been something to nudge them to ignore the FOMO and stay home with their little girls instead. Because when they *had* been present, they had showered Talia and Libby with love. If only they'd had some guidance to teach them to prioritize.

That memory was how Ideal Life was born.

Talia's concept was this: Using a combination of brain activity readings and customers' personal histories and habits, Ideal Life's AI created personalized profiles of what behaviors each customer was likely to act on in the future. Ideal Life would then help them optimize their positive lives by heading off their negative tendencies.

For example, if a former alcoholic's friends invited her to a bar, Ideal Life would gently suggest that she offer to meet up with them earlier for dinner at a restaurant instead.

Or if someone had previously suffered a heart attack and needed to be on a heart-healthy diet but had a penchant for Kentucky Fried Chicken, Ideal Life could help redirect them when their cravings began to steer them toward the drive-through.

These recommendations showed up in whatever form the customer preferred—they could be notifications on phones or a voice inside earbuds or a customized avatar "Friend" that popped up on Omni 3Ds, augmented reality lenses that looked like regular plastic-framed glasses.

These Ideal Life "Friends" were inspired by Sam's favorite book from childhood, *The Golden Compass*. Each character in the series had their own distinctive daemon, which was like the person's "inner self" in the form of an animal. Sam had always wished for his own daemon and daydreamed what form it would take.

This is what Talia thought of when she wanted to create a virtual assistant for Ideal Life users. After all, why shouldn't everyone have bespoke software, tailored especially for them?

Her Ideal Life Friend was a cartoon bee wearing a crown with a personality inspired by Queen Elizabeth, who would buzz into her Omni 3Ds' field of vision when it wanted to help Talia. Other users had created photorealistic versions of their grandmothers, or an anime version of a favorite teacher. Ideal Life was hoping to make licensing deals in the future with Disney for their Marvel superheroes and animated movie characters. In any case, Ideal Life's customers loved being able to design their own virtual Friends—it made the suggestions to remediate their lives so much more palatable and felt truly personal.

That popularity of Ideal Life Friends in augmented reality was what had piqued Omni's interest.

When one of Talia's early investors had called to tell her that Omni was thinking about acquiring Ideal Life, Talia had literally fallen out of her chair. She'd nursed the bruise on her hip for over a week afterward, but it had been worth it.

Because if—*when*—Omni bought Ideal Life, it wouldn't just

be one of many third-party apps on the smart glasses. Omni would integrate Talia's technology through all of Omni's global social media and communications functions. That was 3.5 *billion* people.

Which meant Talia's childhood dream of making the world a better place was finally coming true.

Sugiyama—the eponymous restaurant of the world-famous chef—was sleekly elegant, all white marble floors and high ceilings and gold accents on the wall sconces. Deep, cream armchairs surrounded tables made of dark walnut. And in the center of the restaurant on a raised platform was a glass sushi bar, where all the diners could watch the chefs slice perfect slivers of fatty tuna and delicate yellowtail that had been flown in overnight from Tokyo's famous Toyosu Market.

The second Talia and Sam walked into the restaurant, glasses of champagne were put into their hands. She would only fake-sip tonight—male business leaders were allowed to drink heavily and slur speeches and still be declared geniuses, but women were held to a higher bar. Whether fair or not, Talia had learned that her success depended, in large part, on understanding what the unspoken rules were, because what mattered the most to her was expanding Ideal Life's reach so she could help more people. If she had to sacrifice a few glasses of champagne along the way, so be it.

Sam, on the other hand, took a long gulp of his.

"You doing all right?" Talia asked. "I know this is a lot of people."

"I *like* people. It just takes a minute of adjustment."

"We can hover here together as long as you need." Talia had been dragging Sam out to events their entire friendship, so she was very familiar with the brief transition phase he needed to shift from living in his own head to being in the real world.

If allowed to, Sam could spend a lifetime happily lost in thought, pondering philosophical questions or logic puzzles or immersing himself in the fictional realms of books he read. He was neither introvert nor misanthrope. It was more that his extreme intellectual curiosity made him introspective, and he spent the majority of his time thinking or having debates in his head. Shifting into "public mode" with *other* people for company (besides himself) required a minute, and Talia had always been the best facilitator of this because she understood him.

Sam drank a little more of his champagne but left about half in the flute. "Here," he said, reaching for Talia's glass. "Let's swap."

"Aw, an almost-empty flute," she fake-cooed. "This is the best celebration gift you could have gotten me."

"Oh, hush," he said. "It's just the right amount so that no one will try to refill it, but not so full that you'll get teased for not drinking."

Talia shook her head and smiled. "Sam Chang, you are my favorite person."

He shrugged. It was effortless between them. Always had been.

Ryan Higashi, general partner at Luminary Innovation Fund and the very first investor in Ideal Life, approached them. "Ah, the woman of the hour!"

"Sorry," she whispered to Sam. "Incoming, and I can't stop him."

"Don't worry," he said. "I'm good."

"You sure?"

"Yeah."

"Then let's do this party thing," she said. These moments with Sam had helped Talia shake off the last of her nerves. Now she put her game face on, the one that said *I am a strong, confident, brilliant—but not bitchy—woman.* It wasn't an easy face to perfect, because the conflicting demands and "requirements" on women these days were myriad. But after much trial and error over the years, Talia had the formula down:

1) Smile just enough that it met your eyes but didn't crinkle them. (Too big a smile was interpreted as ditzy. Too little of a smile and you could be labeled cold.)
2) Hold eye contact for two and a half seconds. (Two seconds or less made a woman seem flirty or subservient. Three seconds or more was much too intense.)
3) And always say your conversation partner's name warmly in greeting. (Saying their name would make their subconscious feel validated and, therefore, important, and the goodwill would transfer back to you.)

"Ryan, hello! I'm so happy to see you here." Talia shook his hand—firmly but gently. (Limp fish hands signaled a weak woman unworthy of leadership. But too hard sometimes scared men away, although Silicon Valley was more forgiving—here, the merit of your ideas carried more weight than your gender. Usually.) "May I introduce you to my friend Sam Chang?"

"Sam, a pleasure. I know you just got here, but do you mind if I steal Talia from you? We're doing photographs for the press over in the corner with all the investors and the Omni team."

"No worries," Sam said. "I want to go watch the sushi chefs anyway. Have fun."

As Talia and Ryan crossed the restaurant, they were stopped half a dozen times by people who wanted to congratulate her. Finally, though, they made it to the far side of the room, where a backdrop with Ideal Life's purple star logo alternated with OmnisZcience's name, written in simple blue font. Omni was so well known they didn't even need a symbol. The name was logo enough.

Ideal Life's investors chatted over glasses of wine with a couple of Omni executives and several people Talia didn't know.

"Hey, Talia, good to see you." Raj Banerjee, head of Omni's artificial intelligence division, shook her hand. "Let me do introductions. You know Melanie Goldschmid, product lead for Omni 3D."

"Of course; thank you for coming tonight." Talia smiled and gave Melanie a warm-yet-professional hug. During undergrad, they'd overlapped for a year in Kimball Hall, one of the upperclass dorms. It wasn't unusual to run into classmates in Silicon Valley; Stanford students often didn't go too far after graduation.

"This," Raj said, gesturing to the man next to him, "is DeVon Robinson. He's head of media relations for Omni. And he's to blame for this circus of journalists getting invited tonight." Raj and everyone else laughed as he pointed at the three other people with them. "That's Jesse Fogarty from *TechCrunch*, Kristin Santos from *The Wall Street Journal*, and Rich Zherdev from *Wired*. Laura Owusu from the *San Francisco Chronicle* was supposed to be here, but she got stuck in traffic on 101, so she'll be here late."

Everyone groaned in commiseration at the mention of Highway 101. If it wasn't rush hour, it was something else, like a new pothole that suddenly cracked across three lanes or construction . . . again. Frankly, it was more of a surprise when there *wasn't* a snarl on 101.

DeVon waved over the photographer he'd hired to snap photos of the event, and she shot some pictures of Talia, Raj, and Melanie in front of the Ideal Life / Omni backdrop, with some variations that also included each investor group. Then the reporters were given the opportunity to ask them a few questions.

"Why did you create Ideal Life?" Jesse from *TechCrunch* asked.

Talia talked about her parents' past struggles and their recent transformation, thanks to Ideal Life.

"Omni has been on a startup acquisition spree," Rich Zherdev from *Wired* said. "Why is Omni interested in this one?"

Raj—who was well versed in corporate jargon—said a bunch

of specific yet vague stuff about "pushing technological frontiers" and "forward-looking innovation" and "integrative, collaborative synergy."

Kristin from *The Wall Street Journal* leaned in. "It's unusual to celebrate a potential acquisition at such an early stage, when there is still a lot of due diligence to be done and the deal might fall through. So why are we doing this tonight?"

DeVon laughed and clapped his hands together. "Well, I think it's important to celebrate important milestones. Plus, Omni truly believes in Ideal Life, and we want the world to know about it."

Talia read between the lines. All the major tech companies had been neck and neck in competition the last few years to continually demonstrate their superiority and ability to expand into new fields. Omni was using tonight's party as another way to broadcast that they were still on top of their game, despite being a dinosaur in the industry, having been founded in 2004 (which might as well have been the Mesozoic Era in Silicon Valley time).

The PR work didn't bother Talia, though. Publicity people were going to do what publicity people did. As long as Talia got to work on her technology and improve lives, she was happy.

"Speaking of celebrations," Raj said, "I think we've monopolized enough of Talia, and it's time to get on with the party. Shall we?" With the ease of someone used to steering others, he ushered them all into the main part of the restaurant, where servers floated around and Ideal Life employees mingled, eating spicy tuna hand rolls and sipping on sake from pale-green porcelain cups.

Talia found Sam easily. He was, as promised, at the sushi bar platform in the center of the restaurant.

"Hey, there you are!" He smiled and held out a small glass plate with picture-perfect slices of sashimi on it. "You have to try the salmon. It's like butter—it just melts in your mouth."

She took the plate and borrowed Sam's chopsticks. Their

friendship was uncomplicated like that—all comfort, no pretense. "Mm, this *is* good."

"Arigato gozaimasu," one of the sushi chefs said, thanking her from behind the bar.

Talia and Sam wandered through the restaurant, chatting with employees from Ideal Life and investors from the various venture capital firms that had given Talia money early on to start and grow the company.

A couple hours in, it began to sink in that this was really happening.

"I actually did it, Sam. I made Ideal Life real. And now . . . Oh my god. Omni's buying it."

He squeezed her arm. "I'm so proud of you, Tal."

"That means everything to me. I know you wish people would read more books rather than be online, and I know you hate how everyone's attached to their phones. You don't like Omni glasses, or Omni at all, which makes the fact that you're here, that you support me, even more special—"

"Talia, stop." He took her by the shoulders and looked straight at her. "I really, truly, couldn't be prouder of you. You're driven by such unselfish, good-hearted instincts that it doesn't matter if you partner with Big Tech—you're going to make a difference in people's lives. It's what you've always wanted, and you're doing it. You amaze me."

She looked away, simultaneously relieved, grateful, and embarrassed by his praise.

"I couldn't have made it this far without you," Talia said when she'd recovered herself. "Oh, but I'm the worst friend! I haven't even asked about your poker tournament tomorrow. How are you feeling about it?"

Sam shrugged. "I can't control luck, but I can control numbers, so we'll just see how it goes." High-level poker was part chance, part game theory, and Sam was able to use his winnings as a way to balance out his bookstore, which bled money.

Over on the raised sushi bar platform, Raj and Melanie began clinking their glasses. As everyone crowded together and the room hushed, Melanie said, "Thank you for inviting us here to celebrate with you. We at OmnisZcience can't tell you how excited we are about the work you're doing at Ideal Life, and we see a bright future ahead for all of us. And we'd like to invite your visionary founder and CEO, Talia Morgan, up here to say a few words."

"That's my cue," Talia said.

"I have to jet soon," Sam said, "but I'll stay for a minute while you give your toast."

"Thank you again for being here tonight." She gave him a quick hug, then made her way through the restaurant. Meanwhile, waiters passed out a fresh round of champagne to everyone.

Raj handed Talia a glass as she stepped up onto the sushi bar platform. Erin, the summer intern, stood at the front of the crowd and beamed up at Talia, bouncing on her toes and ready to drink in every word.

"Oh gosh, I don't really like speeches," Talia said, already feeling the blush spread across her face. "You all know me—I'd rather be actually making things better than just talking about it."

The Ideal Life employees laughed. She had uttered the phrase "let's make it better" in so many engineering meetings that it had become a meme on the company's internal Slack chat.

"The one thing I *will* say is this. The headlines tomorrow are going to talk about Omni acquiring Ideal Life, and a lot of focus will be on Omni. But I just want you to know that the most important part of all this is *you*. *You* are the ones who created this incredible technology. *You* are the ones who made my grad school daydream a reality. *You* are the ones who are making real lives better, one decision at a time. So this toast is for *you*."

Talia lifted her glass, and being on a raised platform, she felt like she was being buoyed up by the wave of champagne flutes as everyone else in the restaurant lifted their glasses, too. Near the door, Sam tilted his toward her.

"To you!" Raj toasted, and the room burst into cheers and clinking.

Joy fluttered in Talia's chest. This was really, really happening.

"Excuse me, Talia?" Below the sushi bar platform stood a woman in a skirt suit, her dark hair in long box braids. "Hi, I'm Laura Owusu from the *San Francisco Chronicle*. I'm sorry I'm late, but I was wondering if I could have a few minutes of your time?"

"Of course!"

Talia led Laura back to the corner of the restaurant with the Ideal Life / Omni photo backdrop.

"Omni's photographer took some pictures of us earlier that I'm sure they'll send to you, but I'm also happy to do a couple shots now for your piece if you want." Talia grimaced, second-guessing how narcissistic that sounded. She blamed it on still riding the high from the toast a few minutes before.

"No thanks, that won't be necessary," Laura said.

Ugh. Now Talia definitely felt like a narcissistic ass. The people-pleasing part of her immediately wanted to make up for it.

"Well," she said, "Ideal Life is really excited about our future with Omni. Everyone at the startup believes we're on the forefront of innovation and that the synergistic outlook is . . ."

Forefront of innovation?

Synergistic outlook?

Gah—this is why Talia preferred just doing the actual work to talking about it!

Laura frowned at her.

"Sorry," Talia said. "I'm not good at this PR stuff. Why don't I let you ask me questions and I'll answer them?"

"Okay, well . . ." Laura glanced over her shoulder, as if making sure no one else was in hearing range.

How odd.

"I must confess it wasn't traffic on 101 that made me late," Laura said. "I have a scoop about Ideal Life that no one else knows yet, and I was working late on the story. But I wanted to give you a chance to comment before I publish my article tonight."

"A scoop? What do you mean?" Talia was the founder of Ideal Life. It was her job to know everything, and she wasn't aware of any news besides this Omni deal.

Did Laura know the acquisition documents had been delayed and hadn't actually been signed yet?

But a minor bureaucratic French holdup wasn't newsworthy. In fact, the French attorneys would be in the office in a matter of hours and send the paperwork so that Ideal Life's and Omni's lawyers would have it first thing in the morning, Pacific time.

"I have a very reliable source in the Los Angeles Police Department who informed me that a few hours ago, they arrested a woman for murdering her Tinder date. The accused—Rebecca Lawrence—claims her Ideal Life Friend told her that her Tinder date, Gabe Marques, was the same kind of man who had made for bad relationships for her in the past, and Ideal Life recommended that she 'eliminate him'"—Laura used air quotes—"as an option. But Rebecca Lawrence took it literally and killed him."

"What?" Talia's stomach went into free fall.

No. This couldn't be true. Talia created Ideal Life to make things better for people, not to hurt them.

Laura, in full investigative journalist mode, didn't stop. "How could you let something like this happen?"

"I . . ." Talia's palms started sweating.

If something like this was possible once, would it be possible again?

Or—oh god—had it already happened twice, three times, more . . . but no one had connected the dots yet?

Have I murdered *people*? Talia started hyperventilating.

Her panic seemed to egg Laura on. "Why didn't Ideal Life

take into account that the accused had restraining orders filed against her in the past for violence against her exes?"

"W-we have over a million users, and we don't do background checks on our customers. We only ask . . . Everything they tell us is voluntary."

"Don't you think that's irresponsible?" Laura asked.

Beyond flustered, Talia started pacing, counting to herself to slow her breathing and completely tossing out the window the role of calm, collected CEO.

"I'm sorry . . . what?"

"Don't you think that's irresponsible?" Laura repeated. "Not running thorough background checks?"

The reporter's backward perspective shocked some composure back into Talia. "No! It's not irresponsible; it's the opposite," she said. "We respect our customers' privacy. This is a critical, foundational principle of Ideal Life. We're not scraping the internet for everything about them. We promise to keep their data private and only use it to *help* them."

"And do you believe that this policy 'helped' Mr. Marques?"

"I . . ." Talia looked frantically around the room for someone to save her. But they were all busy drinking new rounds of sake and oohing and aahing over the desserts, which looked like sushi but were actually quenelles of ice cream topped with slices of colorful mochi.

In her pocket, her phone buzzed. But when she looked, it wasn't a phone call that would allow her to excuse herself for a few minutes. It was her 11:11 wish alarm.

At the beginning of freshman year, Sam had been homesick and made a wish at 11:11 p.m. for a friend, not only one who was good for late-night college debates over soggy fries, but one who could last a lifetime. Talia had knocked on his door a few seconds later because she had missed a lecture in Computer Science 106A and heard he was in the class, so she had hoped she could borrow his notes.

Talia and Sam had been making wishes at 11:11 p.m. ever since.

I wish I could rewind today, she thought. Then there might be a way to fix this, to add some kind of safeguard into Ideal Life's programming to prevent the murder from happening. Or Talia would fly down to LA and throw herself between Rebecca Lawrence and Gabriel Marques if she had to.

But she knew the 11:11 wishes weren't real. It had only been coincidence that she and Sam had met that way.

Talia's hands shook as she stuffed her phone back into her pocket.

Laura cleared her throat. "Talia? Any further comment on this story?"

"Hey, hey, hey," DeVon said, swooping in with three plates of mochi ice cream. "Glad you could join us, Laura. I'm DeVon Robinson, Omni's head of media relations; my office is where tonight's party invite came from. It's great to finally meet you. So, what are you two talking about? Anything I can help with from an Omni perspective?"

Laura's eyes glinted at the new prey. Or maybe it was a reflection from the sconces on the wall. Either way, it gave Talia chills.

"Great timing," Laura said. "I've just received a report from the LAPD . . ."

Talia

The Omni executives left in a flurry after DeVon told them about the breaking story.

"We have a lot to think about," Raj had told Talia. "But it's probably best that we haven't signed the acquisition documents yet."

And then he left. But she knew that "a lot to think about" was just the euphemism to tide her over until an official letter from the lawyers came in the morning to inform her that the acquisition was off.

All around Talia, though, the party continued, her employees totally oblivious. They had no clue that their joy would be crushed soon, that Laura only needed to add in Talia's bumbling quote and DeVon's "No comment," and then she'd send her article to her editor. It would be on the front page of the *San Francisco Chronicle* by morning.

How could this have happened? How could Ideal Life have led to *murder*?

Talia's idea for this technology had been so pure, so optimistic.

But a real person—not just an anonymous name or a series of 0s and 1s—had died tonight because of her.

"Hey, boss, are you okay?" Erin came over, her flame-red hair a little wilder after all the celebrating. She set down a glass of water for Talia. "Here. In case you've had a little too much sake. No judgment, of course. Those porcelain cups look deceptively small."

"Do I look that bad?" Talia tried to laugh, but it came out flat.

"Maybe a little tired," Erin said. "I honestly don't know how you do it. You're brilliant on the tech side of the business, but you can also talk to investors and do interviews with journalists."

If only you knew, Talia thought.

"Anyway," Erin said, "I wanted to check in to see if you needed anything else. Otherwise, I'm going to head back to campus and get some sleep before the big signing in the morning. I'll be in early to help set up."

"Um, about that . . . We've delayed it a little. No reason to make the Omni execs come to our office if we're not sure yet that we'll have that French document we need. So why don't you sleep in? You can come in late."

"Really?" Erin grinned. "Okay! I mean, not that I don't love work—I do—but I wouldn't mind a couple extra hours of sleep. Thanks, Talia!"

With Erin gone, Talia sank farther into the deep armchair in her corner of the restaurant. She wished Sam hadn't already left for the airport. He might not be able to change things, but at least he always knew what to say to make her feel a little calmer.

She pulled her phone out again to send him a message or maybe call him, but then she remembered that his phone would be off by now.

Like method actors, Sam believed in going deep into whatever he was working on. If he was writing a pitch for an author event at his bookstore, he worked in silence, with no music, no podcasts, just him and his words, connected by his intense focus. And if he had a poker tournament like he did tomorrow, he would shut off all his devices so he could get into a game theory mind frame; the process began in the evening before each tournament so that there was nothing for his brain to latch on to except poker before bed, poker during sleep, then poker all day long during the competition.

He had once tried to explain it to Talia like a very long, immersive meditation session. She hadn't been able to understand, because she was always juggling ten things at once.

Not that it stopped Talia from trying to call Sam now, but as expected, it went straight to voicemail. She didn't leave a message. After the tournament ended, he'd turn his phone back on and see the news anyway, and then he'd call her immediately.

Did Talia have any other friends she could call? It was getting close to midnight, though, and you didn't call someone this late unless it was an emergency.

This was, of course, an emergency. But she didn't *really* have friends outside of work anymore besides Sam. Startup life demanded eighty-to-one-hundred-hour weeks. Her entire world *was* Ideal Life. Honestly, she probably would have lost Sam, too, if he hadn't insisted on not letting their friendship die.

Not far from Talia, a sheet cake with Ideal Life's purple star logo sat mostly uneaten. She stood abruptly from the armchair, grabbed a fork, and took the whole cake upstairs to the fourth floor.

She walked quickly through the reception area, then wound her way in the dark through the cubicles. When she got to her office, she closed the door and locked it, leaning against it for a long moment, as if the physical barrier could shield her from the world.

But of course it couldn't.

Talia slumped into her chair and set the cake on her desk, where she shoveled giant chunks of it into her mouth, bite after bite, without stopping.

She got through about a third of the cake before the buttercream was just too much, and she threw it all up into her trash can.

Then she crawled onto the purple sofa on the opposite side of her office—the one she'd catnapped on many times during the all-nighters she'd pulled to build this company—and curled up as small as she could.

★

Talia hadn't meant to fall asleep—she wouldn't have thought it possible, given the circumstances—but she had. It was still dark outside her office windows, though, so she couldn't have been out for too long.

Groaning, she sat up and wiped the drool from the corner of her mouth, the glass face of her watch cold against her skin.

Wait, what?

She didn't wear a watch.

But there was definitely a watch on her wrist now.

It was an elegant analog clock with a silver link strap, black roman numerals on a white face, showing that it was one thirty in the morning. On the right was a blue knob—the crown—with two little arrows on it, one pointing up and the other, down.

Talia had never seen this watch before in her life.

She jumped up from the sofa and poked her head outside of her office door. "Hello? Are you guys pranking me?" Maybe some of her employees had come back upstairs, seen their boss passed out in a sugar fugue, and decided to play a joke on her.

There was no one there, though. And Talia was a light sleeper. Surely, she would have noticed if someone took her arm and strapped a watch onto it.

Also, she had locked the door to her office.

What if I *was the one who put the watch on and forgot*? But that was unlikely. Talia had had about half a glass of champagne the whole evening. She couldn't have procured a nice watch and then completely blanked about it.

Maybe she was too groggy to figure it out right now. She turned her attention instead to the watch itself—namely, the arrows on the crown.

"Why label it?" she mumbled. "Kind of obvious that the knob goes either one way or the other."

Still, she turned the crown in the direction of the down arrow.

Nothing happened. The knob didn't budge, and the hands on the watch didn't move like they ought to. It was like it was stuck on the current time.

She used a little more force, but the crown still didn't give.

So Talia turned it the other way.

The crown spun easily with an accompanying mechanical whirring beneath it as the internal gears moved the watch's hands backward.

But all around Talia, her vision whipped into a frenzy, too, like she was rewinding a movie at 4x speed.

"What the . . . ?"

She stopped turning the watch crown.

All of a sudden, she found herself not sitting on the couch but at her desk with a partially demolished sheet cake in front of her and a fork in her hand. Her stomach lurched a bit, as if she were on a roller coaster. In reverse.

What just happened?

The time on the watch said it was 12:30 a.m., a full hour earlier than it had been a few seconds ago.

Talia shook her head. *This has to be a dream.*

The watch still claimed it was 12:30 a.m.

If Sam were here, he would be giving her an "I've told you before" shrug. He was always wary of new technology and warned Talia against cavalierly adopting it. Usually, she laughed him off. But what the heck had she just done?

She reached over to her phone on the desk and tapped the screen. It confirmed the time—12:30 a.m.

Talia slapped herself across the cheek, then pinched herself really hard. *Wake up.*

She opened her laptop to check the time there.

12:31 a.m.

How is this possible?

Then Talia gasped. "No . . ."

At 11:11, she had wished she could rewind the day to stop the murder.

"Holy shit."

But that couldn't *really* be what had happened, right?

Talia was a scientist, which meant she never accepted the first result without deeper experimentation. So she took a deep breath and turned the crown upward again, just a little, but slowly this time.

Everything around her reversed. Including a bite of cake coming *out* of her mouth and back onto the fork, then back into the cake itself.

That was gross, but it also wasn't like spitting out food, because the cake reverted back to being uneaten.

She stared at the reconstructed purple-frosting star. This was very, very difficult to wrap her head around.

Still, the scientist in Talia persevered, and she verified the time on the watch itself, her phone, and her laptop.

12:25 a.m. She'd gone six minutes into the past.

Oh my god.

Her pulse sped up at the possibility that maybe she *could* go back and stop the Tinder murder from happening.

She wouldn't know unless she tried.

Talia spun the watch crown hard, and her vision and her body flew into reverse as if sucked into the past at hyperspeed.

Talia

She bolted upright in her bed. Her vision was still wobbly, though, and Talia had to brace herself against the headboard until her brain caught up with her body and where they were in time.

Speaking of time, she checked the watch—1:30 a.m.

Talia frowned. It had been 12:25 a.m. when she spun the watch crown. But she *had* turned it to go back in time.

She reached for her phone on the nightstand, and she exhaled as the screen came to life: 1:30 a.m. *Thursday*. She had gone back a full day.

Her brain immediately prodded at the boundaries of her impromptu science experiment. *Is that the limit*?

Because 1:30 a.m. was exactly twenty-four hours from when the watch had appeared on her wrist. Exactly twenty-four hours from the farthest point "forward" in time that she'd been.

Talia carefully turned the crown toward the up arrows.

The crown wouldn't move.

Okay, then. At least based on this small sample size of results, it seemed like Talia could rewind up to twenty-four hours max.

Then her eyes went wide.

Could she go forward again? Could she return to where she'd started?

Shh, don't panic, she thought. If she couldn't, it wasn't a big deal to redo a single day.

Still, her heart beat a little faster.

But the most important thing right now was that Talia was being given a chance to stop the murder of an innocent person. She shouldn't waste the opportunity with worrying about whether she could fast-forward, or how this was possible at all. You didn't look a wish horse in the mouth. (Yes, she knew that wasn't the actual saying, but close enough.)

First things first. She turned on the light, then crossed the room to get her laptop. Talia lived in a studio apartment—the bedroom, living room, and kitchen were all a single space—because she spent most of her waking hours in the Ideal Life offices anyway. It didn't make sense to pay astronomical Bay Area rent on a bigger apartment she was never in.

She also lived frugally because she took only a modest salary from Ideal Life; Talia wanted her startup to be able to use its resources for getting better, rather than paying her. And the Omni money wouldn't come through until the deal closed. So Talia didn't have much by way of furniture, either. There was a small Ikea dining table and chairs, a single bookshelf, and her bed. The only decoration in the apartment was a waist-high robot sculpture made of old computer parts that Sam had found at a flea market; it stood by the door holding a tray for keys and other miscellany.

Talia opened up her laptop and logged into Ideal Life. As CEO, she had access to everything on her dashboard. There were real-time performance metrics, including currently active users, server response times, and a panel on system health indicators like error rates and API status. Under the more technical section of the dashboard, she could see bug reports, cybersecurity alerts, and details about things like resource utilization. And of course, there were all the customer profiles.

Ideal Life's chief privacy officer, Sara Trankjaer, would be upset over what Talia was about to do. But what Sara didn't know wouldn't hurt her, and if Talia *didn't* do this, then someone would die.

She found Rebecca Lawrence's profile and double-clicked. A new window popped up, populated with the personal history Rebecca had provided to Ideal Life, as well as her brain-activity logs for the three months she'd been using Ideal Life's app. That invention—wireless brain monitors in the form of small circular stickers—had been Talia's innovation during her PhD.

But she wasn't interested in Rebecca's brain-activity log right now. What Talia wanted was the right side bar of Rebecca's profile, where a drop-down menu gave the following actions:

Export Data
Issue Warning
Suspend Temporarily

And finally, a red button that read Freeze Account.

"Gotcha," she said.

But Talia's cursor hovered over the red button without clicking.

Just a touch of her fingertip, and she would literally erase the past.

If it worked.

Her heart was trying to throttle itself out of her chest. Was this really happening? *Could* it really happen?

Her Ideal Life Friend, the cartoon bumblebee wearing a crown, appeared as an augmented reality image, overlaid onto what Talia was seeing through her Omni 3D glasses. The posh British voice came through tiny speakers in the Omni 3Ds.

Ideal Life Queen Elizabeth: Are you feeling all right? I am detecting some hyperactivity in your left amygdala, which may indicate heightened emotions.

"Dismiss!" Talia said. "And ignore my brain-activity indicators for the rest of the day." She couldn't have Queen Elizabeth piping up every two seconds when Talia was trying to do something that was obviously going to be stressful.

Obediently, the bee flew off the Omni 3Ds' display.

"Okay, focus," Talia said, eyes back on her computer. "I can do this. I *should*."

But what were the downstream effects of changing the past?

It'll be worth it, she told herself.

Talia clicked on the red button and entered her employee passkey to confirm the action.

ACCOUNT FROZEN.

"Holy shit. It worked." She let out a long breath. Thank god.

Rebecca Lawrence was now locked out of the Ideal Life app, which meant she would never see the suggestion later today that she should "eliminate" Gabe Marques.

Talia collapsed backward into her chair.

She had literally just saved a life.

And yet, she was still mortified that it had come to this. If Gabe Marques had died, it would have been Ideal Life's fault, which might as well have been Talia's own personal fault, as far as she was concerned. The startup might look like a company to outsiders, but to Talia, it was an extension of herself. She had dropped out of grad school before finishing her dissertation, lost touch with friends, and put every drop of her heart and soul into this desire to help people live better lives. So yeah, any failure of Ideal Life was a direct failure of Talia.

Had she done enough here in the past to ensure that harm like it wouldn't happen again?

Talia wanted to talk to the engineering team, but unfortunately, that would have to wait until regular office hours.

Unless she could simply turn the watch hands forward to 9 a.m.?

She touched her fingers to the crown.

But then she moved them away. She didn't want to risk it going forward, since she wasn't entirely sure yet how this thing worked. If she was wrong and something else happened . . . like time zoomed to the original starting point and erased what she'd just done, and she couldn't rewind again because it was a one-time wish.

It occurred to Talia that since she was here redoing Thursday, she might as well call the French attorneys to light a fire under them and make sure they sent over that missing document. Even though it was the wee hours of the night here in California, it was already the workday in France. And if Talia got that final French appendix before the lawyers here began their day, then Omni would be able to sign the acquisition documents on time, *before* the celebration party.

Oof, this mini rewound timeline was getting tricky to keep track of. To make sure she didn't screw it up, Talia wrote down the key times:

Thursday a.m. (French time): Get missing document.
Thursday a.m. (Pacific time): OmnisZcience and Ideal Life finalize and sign acquisition documents.
Thursday p.m.: Rebecca Lawrence does not *kill Gabriel Marques.*
Thursday p.m.: Celebration at Sugiyama restaurant downstairs.

Having confirmed Thursday, take two, Talia turned on the translation function on her Omni 3Ds. Then she called Jean-Marc Dubois, the partner of the French law firm, from her computer. He picked up on the third ring; he was also wearing Omni 3Ds.

"Good morning, Talia. How are you?" (In reality, he'd probably said something like, "Bonjour, Talia. Comment ça va?" but the glasses converted it in real time to English for her.)

"Hello, Jean-Marc," Talia said. "Apologies for bothering you, as I know that my attorneys have been pestering you as well, but we really need that technology-transfer preapproval letter today. It's the only thing we're missing for the appendices of the acquisition documents."

"Yes, yes, of course; don't worry—it will arrive."

But Talia knew for a fact that it would not. At least, not if Jean-Marc just waited in his office. She had already been through this part of the day before.

"I must respectfully disagree," Talia said. "However, Ideal Life will pay extra to send one of your junior attorneys down to the government office to physically retrieve the document from them. We *must* have it by the end of your workday. Everything else is set for Omni to sign the acquisition agreement today."

"Hmm, I do not know if we have anyone to spare—"

"Please, Jean-Marc. I'll send you a bottle of your favorite wine."

"Are you stereotyping me?" But he laughed. "Fine, fine, I will get one of our young attorneys to go down to the office. But don't send me French wine. Send me a bottle from Sonoma Valley. That's near you, isn't it?"

"You got it. Thank you, Jean-Marc."

That hopefully taken care of, Talia hung up. There was still plenty of time before she had to head into the office, so she took a long, hot shower, washing away the disaster of last night (which technically hadn't happened yet, but it still felt good to soap the memory away).

Then she brewed a huge pot of coffee and set to work making a list of all the things she wanted her engineering team to look at in order to head off problems with Ideal Life's suggestions in the future.

Talia was back in Ideal Life's offices at 8 a.m. It was peaceful at this hour, before everyone else came in. The startup had begun across the hall in a three-room suite; now they took up the entire second, third, and fourth floors of the building.

There were a handful of executive offices and conference rooms with doors, but everything else was an open floor plan.

Cubicle walls and desks were all on wheels so that the space could be reconfigured as needed. For example, the human resources department mostly worked alone, so they usually kept their cubicles as individual spaces. But the programmers often collaborated, so they could roll away some of their walls and move their desks next to each other, creating a wall of screens so they could look at code or brainstorm together. Talia loved the flexibility of Ideal Life's offices; it made space—both literal and figurative—for new ideas to bloom.

As she walked into her own office, she double-checked that her navy blazer was hanging on the back of the door as a way to visually verify that she was still in the right day.

Indeed, it was there, waiting for her to change into it later for the party downstairs at Sugiyama.

Right now, though, she wore her Ideal Life hoodie with the purple star logo. It had been waiting for her in her closet at home, even though the last time she'd seen it, Erin had been taking it away here at the office as Talia put on the blazer.

She supposed it made sense, though, if she thought of it like rewinding a movie. The character would go backward in time not only in action, but in what they were wearing, too. Like how Talia had woken up in her bed a few hours ago in her pajamas.

"Good morning, boss!" Erin singsonged as she poked her head in.

"What are you doing here so early?" Talia asked, right before she realized she knew exactly what Erin was going to say.

"Big day today, and I didn't want to miss a second of it! How many college juniors can say they were working at a company when it got bought by Omni?"

"I love your attitude," Talia said, which is what she'd said the first time this "scene" happened.

She could probably deviate from the script if she wanted to. So far, she'd frozen a customer's profile and called Jean-Marc to get him to accelerate their efforts to get that French document—

which had arrived, hurrah!—and yet she'd still ended up here with Erin coming in and saying and doing the same things as yesterday.

Early hypothesis: The replay is static except for the parts I try to change.

But like in any science experiment, it was best to limit how many variables changed. So Talia told Erin to ask the receptionist to order bagels for the whole office. When Erin asked what kind of cream cheese, Talia said, "Go crazy—get them all." Exactly like last time.

When the engineering team got in, though, Talia called a meeting on the third floor. She asked Erin to sit in, too, because she saw a lot of herself in Erin and wanted to give her as much experience as possible during her summer internship. Talia didn't want this to be a typical internship where the student was just an errands gofer.

There wasn't a conference room big enough for all of them, but since the entire third floor was programmers, product managers, and other engineering-related employees, everyone just moved the cubicle walls aside so they could see Talia at the front of the space, standing on a chair.

"You all remember when ChatGPT first became public, and ordinary people learned about AI for the first time, right?" Talia said. "Remember how nerds like us immediately started messing with it to get it to say all sorts of unexpected things?"

Everyone in the room nodded and laughed. You couldn't introduce a new technology like that to Silicon Valley and not expect it to immediately get poked and prodded at, hard.

"The ChatGPT team had to go back and do a lot of work to account for what humans would do to their system. They managed to fix most of the problems, like the chatbot declaring that it wanted to get married to the user."

More laughs.

"Well, I know that you have all worked hard at these kinds of elements for Ideal Life, and I think we've done an amazing job. But there is always more work to do, especially as we roll out new features. Also, Omni is going to sign the initial acquisition papers this morning, which means that over the next few months, they will be doing due diligence on our company to make sure that everything is airtight and that they're not buying a bag of random nuts and screws.

"So I would like us to take another look at Ideal Life. For example—and this is purely hypothetical—what if someone is about to go on a Tinder date, but Ideal Life notes that the guy is a lot like other men she's dated in the past who haven't been good for her. Suppose that our AI suggests that she 'eliminate' him, but instead of canceling the date, she takes the word 'eliminate' a bit too seriously and kills him instead?"

One of the engineers rolled his eyes. "That seems pretty far-fetched."

Erin piped up. "But it *could* happen. And I think that's Talia's point. If Ideal Life is trying to help everyone optimize and achieve the life they deserve, then we should make the suggestions as clear as possible, not only to benefit the customer, but also so that we don't accidentally cause collateral damage."

Talia smiled. What guts Erin had, speaking up in a room full of seasoned engineers when she was still in college. *This girl will go so far.*

"Right," Talia said. "It is, of course, impossible to anticipate everything. But I'd like you to run more simulations to stress test our system's AI. I want you to go hard on this—really push things to the extreme. Oh, and let's go ahead and remove the word 'eliminate.' Any questions?"

There weren't many, so Talia wrapped up and went back to the fourth floor. The rest of the day went quickly and smoothly. The e-sign versions of the acquisition documents arrived shortly before lunch. Before she signed, she skimmed the main agreement again. Her eyes stumbled on the termination provision:

Section 8.3 TERMINATION FEE

(A) In the event this agreement is terminated by OmnisZcience (by choice or through material breach), then OmnisZcience shall pay Ideal Life a termination fee of Five Million US Dollars ($5,000,000) ("OmnisZcience Termination Fee") by wire transfer of immediately available funds within two (2) business days after such termination.

(B) In the event this agreement is terminated by Ideal Life (by choice or through material breach), then Ideal Life shall pay OmnisZcience a termination fee of One Million US Dollars ($1,000,000) ("Ideal Life Termination Fee") by wire transfer of immediately available funds within two (2) business days after such termination.

In nonlegalese—Ideal Life could owe a million dollars to Omni if something bad happened that was Ideal Life's fault between the signing of these documents and the closing.

Something like Rebecca Lawrence taking an Ideal Life suggestion literally and murdering Gabe Marques.

"But that won't be a problem," Talia said to herself. She had taken care of that.

She hoped.

There was nothing more she could do now, though, other than shove the what-if away and continue onward.

Talia quickly signed the acquisition documents. An hour later, Omni had also signed them, and she had the fully executed versions in her inbox.

Whew . . .

And finally, huzzah!

Then there were, as usual, the normal fires to put out that constituted much of any CEO's day, but they were the same ones as Talia had dealt with the last time she did this day, so she handled them easily.

By early evening, though, she was exhausted. She realized

she hadn't slept more than an hour or so in the equivalent of two days. But there was still the big celebration party to get through, and then she'd finally get back to where she started.

She took a short nap on the purple couch in her office.

At 8 p.m., the alarm she'd set on her phone went off. She tossed a piece of gum in her mouth to dispel nap breath and walked out into the reception area, where she paused to admire the Ideal Life sign.

"You ready, boss?" Erin came up from the offices behind her.

"Almost," Talia said. She was still dressed in her jeans, T-shirt, and hoodie. "I just need to swap out my hoodie for my blazer—"

"Already got you covered." Erin handed over the navy jacket Talia kept on a hanger behind her office door. "I grabbed your heels, too."

"You're always a step ahead," Talia said as she slipped into the blazer, kicked off her sneakers, and stepped into the pumps.

"I learned from the best," Erin said, grinning.

Talia's phone rang.

"Are you here?" she asked.

"Wow," Sam said. "No preamble, no hello, *straight* to business."

But this time, she wasn't all nerves before the party.

"I'll send Erin to let you in."

A couple minutes later, the elevator doors opened, and Sam stepped out. Like the first time, Erin had gone on to the restaurant, so Talia and Sam were alone.

"Congratulations," he said, about to envelop her in a big hug.

"Wait," she said. "I had the craziest day, and I *have* to tell you about it."

In her office with the door closed, Talia recapped everything that had happened after Sam left the party (which, to him, hadn't happened yet). She told him about Laura Owusu, the *San Francisco*

Chronicle reporter, and the bombshell of an Ideal Life–prompted murder. She told him about running away to this office and falling asleep, then waking up to the strange watch on her wrist. And then she recounted the rewinding and everything she had gotten the chance to redo.

"So . . . yeah. That was my last day. Or more, technically, because I did it twice?"

Talia folded her hands in her lap, not touching the watch but not blocking his view of it, and waited for Sam's response. Her heart pounded against her ribs. He'd believe her, right? Sure, it was far-fetched, but this was Sam, and he knew how firmly based in data and science she normally was. Talia wasn't the delusional sort.

The right corner of Sam's mouth twitched. It was a nearly imperceptible tell that Talia knew meant he was caught off guard and trying to size up the situation.

She waited.

He didn't say anything.

Talia tightened her interlaced fingers against one another.

Finally, he cleared his throat. "Can I take a look at the watch?"

"Of course." In fact, Talia was eager for Sam's opinion on it. He was one of the most brilliant people she knew—he'd double-majored in physics and philosophy in college—and he had long been her most reliable sounding board. She snapped open the silver clasp and handed the watch to him.

Sam turned it over in his hand, inspecting it closely. He spent several minutes squinting at the crown and its little arrows while being careful not to move the dial.

"How do you think it works?" Talia asked.

He made a clicking sound with his tongue, the Sam signal for thinking. "Um, how much sleep have you gotten, Tal? You've been working so hard leading up to this acquisition."

"You don't believe me!"

"Talia—"

But she snatched the watch back from him and turned the crown, winding the hands on the dial back to the moment when she'd finished her recap. This time, instead of putting her hands in her lap and waiting quietly for Sam's response, she said, "Before you say anything, give me a second to write something down."

She ran over to her desk, grabbed a pen and a piece of paper, and scribbled down a few lines. Then she folded the paper in half and brought it back with her to the couch.

"Okay. I'm done. So . . . yeah. That was my last day. Or more, technically, because I did it twice?"

She folded her hands in her lap and waited for his response.

The right corner of Sam's mouth twitched as he tried to size up the situation.

She waited.

He didn't say anything.

Talia tightened her interlaced fingers against one another.

Finally, he cleared his throat. "Can I take a look at the watch?"

"Of course."

Talia gave him time to inspect it. Then she asked, "How do you think it works?"

He made that clicking, thinking sound again—or, rather, for the first time. "Um, how much sleep have you gotten, Tal? You've been working so hard leading up to this acquisition."

She nodded. "I understand why you'd say that. But read this, then tell me if you reconsider." Talia handed him the piece of paper.

Sam unfolded it, and a second later, his eyes went wide.

This is what she'd written:

Here is the conversation we're about to have:
Me: So . . . yeah. That was my last day. Or more, technically, because I did it twice?
You: Can I take a look at the watch?

Me: Of course.

Me, after you've had time to scrutinize the watch: How do you think it works?

You: Um, how much sleep have you gotten, Tal? You've been working so hard leading up to this acquisition.

Sam swallowed hard, his Adam's apple bobbing at the effort. He refolded the paper and gave it back to Talia while shaking his head. "H-how is this possible?"

She looked down at the watch in his hands. "Because I made a wish at 11:11, I guess."

He didn't say a word.

Then, still in shock, he passed the watch back to her.

"It allowed me to save a life, Sam."

He gathered her in his arms. "I don't know how that watch can do what it did, but . . . I'm sorry you had to go through that, Tal."

"So you believe me?" she said, muffled against his chest.

"I kind of have to, given the evidence, as nonsensical as this seems. But even if you were losing your mind, I'd be here for you." He tightened his hug.

"I'm just so relieved I could undo it. I don't even care how it worked. Just that it did."

When they broke apart, though, Sam's brow furrowed.

"What?" Talia asked.

"I just realized . . . it's not a one-time thing. Your watch didn't limit you to rewinding only once, for the purpose of stopping the Tinder date from happening, even though that was the intent of your wish. You just rewound now so you could replay our conversation and prove to me that it was real."

Talia's jaw dropped. "Huh, I guess you're right. I didn't even think about that—I wonder how much I can use it."

Now that the serious consequences of a murder had been undone, she allowed herself to think of lighter possibilities of the watch.

It would be like everyone's dream come true—the ability to go back in time and say all the witty things you thought of three hours after a fight. To undo spilling coffee on your blouse right before the meeting with your boss when you were going to ask for a promotion. To rewind and get a few more hours of sleep.

"Who knows?" Sam said. "Maybe the watch will just disappear. Maybe it'll vanish after tonight's celebration, like a twenty-four-hour Cinderella–fairy godmother wish that served its purpose. But if it's still here tomorrow . . ."

"Think about how productive I could be," Talia said. "I could optimize each day by analyzing it, then going back and doing it again but more efficiently. I could get twice as much done."

He laughed. "That's such a Talia thing to say." Then his smile fell away. "But hey, Tal, promise me something."

"Anything."

"This watch has the potential for manipulating people for personal gain—"

"I would never!"

"I know, I know," Sam said. "I just had to bring it up. But also . . ." He picked at a loose thread on the sofa.

"What is it?"

He looked up and held her gaze. "Promise me you'll tell me if you rewind and accidentally do something that changes my life. And promise me you won't change my life on purpose."

Talia took his hands in hers. "I promise, Sam."

Sam

Everyone's heads turned when Sam and Talia walked into Sugiyama, the Japanese restaurant where the Omni–Ideal Life celebration was being held. They were all looking at Talia, and Sam smiled privately to himself.

She had always had this kind of understated charisma. Whereas many people thought of "leaders" as the exuberant, extroverted student-body-president types, Talia excelled at *subtle* leadership. She constantly praised others' contributions, and because of that, everyone admired her and also wanted to work with her. In college, she started a fundraiser to help high school students in local, underprivileged communities get internships with Stanford professors, and what began as a small collection in their dorm ended up raising over $100,000 campus-wide. During her PhD, Talia convinced all the lab assistants to do things her way, without issuing a command or doing any kind of hard sell, simply by putting in the work herself and demonstrating how much better it was.

Talia wasn't infallible, though; she was human with plenty of foibles, and Sam knew most of them. Still, the measure of a person wasn't in their perfection. It was in the balance of their strengths and their flaws, and in how they managed to keep some sort of equilibrium between the two.

A waiter glided up to them. "Champagne?"

They each took a glass. Sam immediately took a long gulp.

"You doing all right?" Talia asked. "I know this is a lot of people."

"I *like* people. It just takes a minute of adjustment."

"We can hover here together as long as you need."

He loved that she knew this about him, that she had intuitively always known it.

Sam drank a little more of his champagne but left about half in the flute. "Here," he said, reaching for Talia's glass. "Let's swap."

"Aw, an almost-empty flute," she fake-cooed. "This is the best celebration gift you could have gotten me."

"Oh, hush," he said. "It's just the right amount so that no one will try to refill it, but not so full that you'll get teased for not drinking."

Talia's smile sent a glow straight through his core. "Sam Chang, you are my favorite person."

She had been *his* favorite person ever since the moment he met her. Seventeen years and counting.

"Ah, the woman of the hour!" An Asian American man in a well-cut plaid blazer and pressed chinos approached them.

Sam examined him. He didn't mean to, but being an immigrant from Taiwan and growing up in a very white community in Mississippi meant that Sam was still a little surprised—in a pleasant way—every time he came across another Asian person, even though they were plentiful in California. (He had actually loved Mississippi and still did; it's just that, growing up, the only other Asian face he knew belonged to the uncle he lived with.)

This man crossing the restaurant, though, was as far from Sam's absent-minded-professor uncle as possible.

Long, relaxed strides that showed an assuredness that the man belonged here among the Silicon Valley business set? Check.

A glimmer in his eyes that looked like someone about to win a huge hand of poker? Also check.

Sam's money was on this guy being one of Talia's early venture capital investors, who would reap a fortune when the Omni acquisition of Ideal Life was complete.

"Sorry," Talia whispered to Sam. "Incoming, and I can't stop him."

"Don't worry," he said. "I'm good."

"You sure?"

"Yeah."

"Then let's do this party thing," she said.

Sam recognized Talia's small inhale of breath, the way she steeled herself and put on her professional persona. In fact, it was observing her do this over the years that had taught him how to speed up his own shift from when he had to get out of his head and into the company of others.

"Ryan, hello!" Talia said. "I'm so happy to see you here." She shook his hand. "May I introduce you to my friend Sam Chang?"

"Sam, a pleasure. I know you just got here, but do you mind if I steal Talia from you? We're doing photographs for the press over in the corner with all the investors and the Omni team."

Bingo, Sam thought, about his guess that Ryan was an investor. Although Sam wasn't surprised; he was good at reading cues from physical details like clothes and body language. It was all part of understanding the other players in a game of poker or, sometimes, in life.

Like at his bookstore—he could tell who was likely to buy something and who wasn't. There were the casual browsers who were killing time before a tide-pooling tour, with no intent to leave the shop with a book (it would get in the way of tide pooling). There were people thinking of adding a novel to their nightstand if something happened to pique their interest. And then there were the readers who were truly on the hunt, who had a voracious need that was a mixture of doubt and hope that they would find a book that would change their life. *That* was what got Sam up in the mornings—the possibility of doing that for someone.

It was also why he understood Talia's drive and passion for Ideal Life—he and she both wanted to touch people's lives in however small a way they could to make them better.

Well, maybe Talia's way isn't small, he thought. Ryan stood waiting for Sam's response about stealing Talia for the press junket.

"No worries," Sam said to them. "I want to go watch the sushi chefs anyway. Have fun."

And that might be all the time Sam had with Talia tonight. But that was okay. He knew that what she needed from him wasn't constant presence by her side but just the knowledge that he was here in the restaurant. Their friendship was a give-and-take, where sometimes Talia gave, and sometimes Sam did. Tonight was his turn.

Besides, he was happy to take advantage of the fact that Omni was footing the bill for tonight—he would eat his weight in overpriced, fancy sushi.

"Excuse me," a woman said, coming in from the entrance behind him. "This is the Omni–Ideal Life party, right?"

Sam turned to her. "Yes. Are you a reporter?"

She blinked at him, caught off guard by his quick assessment. "How could you tell?"

He shrugged. "Just a guess." It hadn't been, though; he'd been 99 percent sure. Her suit was smart but off-the-rack—she was too dressed up to be a startup employee but not tailored enough to be a VC. Her heels were low pumps with rubber soles, practical for running around town after stories. Also, the notebook peeking out of her purse. "What outlet are you from?"

"Laura Owusu, the *San Francisco Chronicle*."

"Ah, good; you didn't get caught in traffic."

She squinted at him. "I'm sorry?"

Oh, right. She didn't know about what had happened in the last iteration of this party. Sam laughed his comment off as if it had been a joke. "You know, 101 is always a gamble. Could be thirty minutes from San Francisco to Palo Alto, could be three hours."

Laura laughed. "So true. Listen, do you happen to know where Talia Morgan is? We're supposed to be doing some press stuff."

Sam pointed to the far side of the restaurant where Talia and Ryan had gone. "You haven't missed anything. They're about to get started."

At the sushi bar, the intern he'd met earlier sat next to him.

"Could I have an Ideal Roll?" Erin asked the chef, ordering one of the specials for the night. "There's no nuts in there, right? I'm allergic."

"No," the chef said. "The ingredients are black sushi rice—representing 'dark mode' interfaces favored by programmers—wrapped with avocado, which is very Californian, Wagyu beef because OmnisZcience is the best, and topped with gold flakes as a nod to Ideal Life's incredible valuation."

"Sounds delicious," Erin said. She unsheathed a pair of wooden chopsticks and turned to Sam while she rubbed the wood splinters off of them. "So, I heard you and Talia met while you were in college. That's so amazing. Have you been in love with her all this time?"

Sam nearly choked on his sashimi roll. "What?"

Erin smiled. "Don't worry—I haven't told anyone. I don't think Talia knows, either. But I could tell by how you swapped your champagne for hers so she could carry a partially drunk one, and the way you looked at her when she walked away with that venture capital guy; it was like, I don't know, a sense of wonder was beaming out of you. It was really sweet."

"I think you're reading the signs wrong. Talia and I are just friends."

"Okay," Erin said, still smiling like she didn't believe him at all. "Then tell me how you met. Because I'm a rising junior now, and I'm hoping my soulmate—I mean, my 'just a friend'—is floating around somewhere on campus, too."

"You're very forward, you know that?" Sam laughed.

Erin did, too. "I know. It's something Talia's trying to soften in me. She says I have a lot of promise, but right now, I'm like the overly excited kid who runs straight into the flock of pigeons and scares them all away. Her goal is to teach me how to feed the pigeons instead."

"You've got time. Talia started out by scaring the pigeons, too."

"Do tell."

The sushi chef slid her Ideal Roll over the glass counter, but Erin ignored it, leaning in toward Sam instead.

"It's not that exciting of a story," Sam said. "Basically, I was kind of a recluse in college—not on purpose, but I tend to get lost in books or even my own head, and it's easy for me to forget to actually go out into the world. Well, Talia wasn't going to let that stand.

"She found out that the physics department hosted a regular Thursday-night poker game. So one Thursday night, Talia walked into my room, grabbed the novel I was reading out of my hands, and dragged me out of the dorm without telling me where we were going. Now, keep in mind she had her younger sister with her—"

"Wait," Erin said. "You know Libby?"

"Yeah. Talia's family lived about thirty minutes away, and since Libby was sixteen then, she'd often drive over and do her homework while hanging out with us in the dorm. Sometimes I'd go to Talia's room and she wouldn't be there, but Libby would—she used to climb in the first-floor window. We spent so much time together back then I basically adopted her as my own little sister, which was nice because I don't have any siblings. So, you've met Libby, too? I didn't think she was around this summer."

"No . . ." Erin blushed. "I've just heard about her."

Sam smiled softly. "Yeah, I guess everyone has. Pretty wild that that kid is all grown-up and world-famous now. Anyway, the poker game. Talia marched us from the dorm all the way across campus to the physics department building. Then she sat me down at the table without even asking me if I knew how to play."

"Did you?" Erin asked.

"Know how to play? No." Sam laughed. "But of course Talia did, and she was charming enough that she convinced the other guys around the table to let me, her, and Libby be a team so that Talia could teach us. I think the guys said yes partially because they thought Talia would be an easy mark—she was a psychology major, she smiled a lot, and she was a girl. Yeah, I know, I know—don't get me started on that last one.

"They told us the stakes and dealt us in. And before they knew it, she'd cleaned them all out and no one quite knew what hit them. That's Talia, running into the pigeons and scaring them all. But she kept showing up to every physics poker night after that, and I tagged along. Libby, too, if she was around. And soon enough, they all fell a little bit in love with her because she was clearly brilliant but didn't make them feel stupid for having underestimated her. And through serendipity—or more accurately, Talia's relentless will—I learned how to play poker."

"Damn, that woman is my hero," Erin said.

Mine, too, Sam thought, but he didn't say it aloud because Erin already knew.

"Don't put Talia on a pedestal, though," he said. "She'd be the first to tell you that she's not perfect."

"Hard to believe."

Sam kept his smile to himself. He wasn't going to divulge Talia's weaknesses to her starry-eyed intern. But he knew very well how her idealism could be so big that it consumed her. Talia's hopes and dreams of a better future sometimes drove her too hard—she would go an entire day without eating if she was deep inside a project, she rarely had time for friends, and she was hardly ever even at her apartment, spending all her time at the office instead.

"So if Talia's your best friend," Erin asked, finally pulling her sushi roll in front of her, "why aren't you wearing Omni 3Ds like everyone else here?" She tapped on her own glasses. "It seems, like, *de rigueur* at an Omni / Ideal Life celebration. Or are you one of those people who prefers Ideal Life on your phone?"

"I . . . don't use Ideal Life."

"What? No way." Erin's chopsticks stopped halfway to her mouth. "How are you going to make Talia fall in love with you if you don't even use her tech?"

"You are relentless."

"Did I run into the pigeons again? Sorry! But seriously, you don't use Ideal Life?"

Sam shook his head. "I have a complicated relationship with technology."

It wasn't always that way. Talia's idealism had rubbed off on him in college, but it lost its luster too soon after that. Straight out of school, Sam was hired to work for Nowhere Cat, a quantum computing startup (the name was a reference to Schrödinger's cat, a popular way of explaining the confusing here-but-*not*-here theory behind quantum physics).

Sam had been thrilled to get to work at Nowhere Cat, which at the time had just announced the development of a quantum computing chip that could create topological qubits—a shocking advance in technology that was at least two decades ahead of anyone else. And there were more exciting developments in the pipeline.

Unfortunately, that all came crashing down six months after Sam started work, when a whistleblower revealed that Nowhere Cat's management were lying. There was no breakthrough in topological qubits or in anything else. It was all just smoke and mirrors—masked in technical jargon—to get more investors in the hopes that *someday*, with enough money, they'd actually be able to discover what they'd already claimed to have done.

Disillusioned, Sam stumbled out of Nowhere Cat's offices with no desire to work at a tech startup again. He holed up in his apartment and buried himself in novels and books on various philosophies.

It was Talia who finally barged in and pulled him back into the world again. She coaxed him out of his paralyzed state of disappointment by taking him to his favorite place in the Bay Area, the misty cliffs of Pacifica. They would just sit there quietly on a bench together—him reading, her working on her PhD research on her laptop.

Then one day, he saw the old lighthouse on the cliff's edge was for sale, and an idea blossomed.

"What if I could turn that into a bookstore?" he asked Talia.

"Bookstores are notoriously hard businesses to turn a profit," Talia said. "But . . ."

"But what?"

"You could supplement by playing on the professional poker circuit."

They smiled at the same time. It was perfect.

And that's how Sam ended up as the owner of a bookstore in the middle of nowhere.

His 11:11 wish freshman year had been for a friend who could last a lifetime. And today more than ever, Sam felt the potency of 11:11.

"Oh my god!" Erin's phone had dinged loudly and she now had an article up on the screen. "*Your Gossipy Tech BFF* has already posted about tonight's party here!" She leaned over to show Sam.

Your Gossipy Tech BFF was like Lady Whistledown's Society Papers from *Bridgerton*, except about the people and companies in Silicon Valley (so a little less sexy). No one knew who wrote *Your Gossipy Tech BFF*, but apparently, they'd been here at Sugiyama tonight or at least had an informant who had.

Badass Ideal Life CEO Talia Morgan Showing STEM Girls Everywhere How to Get the Boys to Bow at Your Feet

Palo Alto, CA—Despite all the talk about progress, Silicon Valley bucks still largely flow to men. But earlier today, Omni signed a deal to buy startup Ideal Life for $100 million, and guess whose brainchild it is? Talia Morgan, who grew up a stone's throw away in San Bruno.

And they just threw a super-swanky shindig tonight to celebrate her.

Let me set the scene for you:

The restaurant: Sugiyama, the Michelin-starred bastion of marble, gold, and premium bluefin tuna flown overnight from Tokyo's famed Toyosu Market. Servers in rose kimonos with gold *obis* or navy *haori* jackets over crisp black dress shirts and a modern version of *hakama* pants.

The investors: identifiable by their Peter Millar plaid blazers and non-Rolex watches from "if you know, you know" brands that cost more than my car. The chinos are neutral and tailored, the cashmere socks are understated but Loro Piana.

The Omni execs: They arrive in dark jeans, the men in plain button-downs and the women in monochrome silk blouses, probably put together by a subscription-box service in that upscale-but-not-particularly-inspired way of accessible luxury. It still puts them head and shoulders above the way most of the Valley dresses, so B for fashion, but A- for effort.

Our star: Talia Morgan is too busy and impressive to dress up, and this is . . . refreshing. While most young founders would flip their shit to be wined and dined by the Titans of Tech, Talia clearly went to work today like she did any other day, then threw on the heels and blazer she keeps in her office and came downstairs (because oh, did we forget to mention? Ideal Life is headquartered just an elevator ride above Sugiyama).

Some might say her appearance is sloppy.

But here at *Your Gossipy Tech BFF*, we disagree.

Talia Morgan represents all the little girls who loved math and science and did the hard work but always worried about having to do extra to outshine the boys. But Talia's attitude is "Screw that. I'm brilliant and you'll pay for my genius, and then you'll pay for my dinner, too, and I'm going to be comfortable while doing it."

Hear, hear, Talia Morgan. We salute you.

"Wow," Erin said. "What an amazing write-up." She looked at Sam, whose expression must not have been as adoring. "Oh, *Your Gossipy Tech BFF* isn't your speed, is it?"

Sam gave her a half shrug. "I'm more a Carlo Rovelli or Neal Stephenson reader."

What he was really thinking, though, was how the article had painted today as just any other ordinary workday for Talia. Whoever the writer of *Your Gossipy Tech BFF* was, they may have gotten the scoop on the clothing of the night, but not the *biggest* secret. That was for Sam and Talia alone.

He stuck around the party as long as he could, but eventually, he had to leave to get to the airport. He located Talia with her marketing director in the ivory leather armchairs near the windows. There were groups of others hovering close by, all hoping for a minute of Talia's attention, but the lamp above shone on her alone like a spotlight, leaving everyone else a little in shadow. Sam allowed himself a few beats to appreciate her like this, the center of a visionary startup she'd created from scratch.

When a waiter tried to squeeze past him, though, the movement caught Talia's eye, and she looked up and waved Sam over.

"Hey, I just wanted to say goodbye before I head out," he said.

"Oh, already?" Talia got up and hugged him.

"Unless you want me to stay?" he said, his voice lowered. "To, um, you know, make sure things still turn out all right tonight, with the watch and all?"

"This is why you're my favorite person," she said, squeezing him extra tight.

He leaned in, holding her for as long as she would let it last.

Too soon, though, she pulled away. "I think it's all going to be okay from here on out, though, so you should go. Don't miss your flight."

"You sure?"

Talia smiled, and the warmth of it wrapped itself around him like another hug. Sam couldn't help but smile back.

"It meant everything that you were here tonight," she said. "Not only the party, but listening to me earlier and being there for me. But I have one more favor to ask of you."

"Anything," Sam said, and he meant it.

"Kick ass tomorrow at the tournament, okay?"

He normally slept on red-eye flights, especially when he had to play poker first thing in the morning. But Sam didn't sleep. Instead, he made sure his phone was connected to Wi-Fi, and he stayed awake the entire way to Cleveland, just in case Talia *did* need him. She'd always had more faith in technology than he did, and she was especially optimistic and excitable about *new* gadgets.

He wanted to be available if she was wrong that the evening would end well. If the watch didn't work the way she hoped.

Sam would play badly this tournament, he already knew. Besides missing out on sleep, he wasn't going through his usual mental immersion into probability and game theory.

But Talia didn't message him at all. And for once, he was happy about that.

When the plane landed, Sam was utterly exhausted. But it was worth it.

Talia

Talia woke up the next morning in her bed.

"What time is it? Wait, what *day*?"

She scrambled for her phone on the nightstand.

Friday, 7:03 a.m. Time had continued to march forward normally, past the initial point when she'd turned the hands on the watch dial.

Oh, thank god. Talia allowed herself to slump back into the warm covers. She'd gone back, stopped a murder, and gotten the acquisition papers signed. Maybe now everything would return to normal.

Except when she looked at her wrist, the watch was still there.

Did that mean she could rewind again? Not that she wanted to. Yesterday had been stressful enough once, let alone twice. No reason to live through it a third time.

A message from her mom popped up on Talia's phone.

Vera: Still on for meeting me and Dad for breakfast?

"Shit!" Talia jumped out of bed. She'd completely forgotten that her parents were taking her out this morning to celebrate the Omni deal.

Talia: Of course! Just running 10 min late. See you at Hobee's at 7:45?

Vera: We'll be there with bells on!

Talia grinned. She loved this new, more "grown-up" version of her mom. Her parents had always loved Talia and her sister,

Libby, but they'd been absent during the girls' childhood because there'd been too many happy hours and comedy clubs and parties to attend. But a combination of aging and Ideal Life's prototype had tempered Vera and Dave Morgan's compulsive need to go out. Now they did things like spending the day at the botanical gardens or getting up early so they could catch Talia before work to have breakfast with her.

Unlike Sugiyama, there was nothing glitzy about Hobee's. It was a family-owned breakfast joint known for its enormous slabs of coffee cake. Other than that, it was pretty ordinary in a cozy, wonderful way—French toast, pancakes, omelets, and unlimited mugs of coffee. On weekends, the line would be out the door, but on a weekday, Talia and her parents were able to get a booth right away.

"So, how was last night?" Dave asked as they slid into their seats.

"Tell us everything," Vera said. "Was it fancy? Did you give a speech? Did Omni present you with one of those giant checks that said one hundred million dollars?"

Talia laughed. "The deal won't close until they do their due diligence on everything, so no, there was no giant check."

"But it was fancy?" Dave asked.

"Yes, it was fancy."

"Good. At least they know how to treat my girl right."

That made Talia smile. The hollow feeling she'd carried around in her chest all her childhood was hungry for this kind of love, and she was proud at how Ideal Life had helped bring out the best in her parents. After two years of using the app, they'd totally changed their social patterns, and now they didn't even need Ideal Life anymore. Talia considered that a victory. Her investors hadn't loved that customers cycled in and out, but Talia *wanted* people to "graduate" from Ideal Life. It was like using training wheels—once you got the hang of it, you could bike off into the sunset of your improved life on your own.

"Well, I want to hear more about your fancy celebration," Vera said, "but first let's order some food. I've got a serious craving for chocolate chip pancakes." (She was the one Talia got her sweet tooth from.)

Talia adjusted her Omni 3Ds so they weren't sliding down her nose and picked up the laminated menu.

She wanted some of Hobee's famous coffee cake. And lemon-ricotta pancakes. And a Nutella stack, which was French toast layered with chocolate-hazelnut spread, bananas, and applewood bacon.

Her Friend, the crown-wearing British bumblebee, flew into her field of vision.

Ideal Life Queen Elizabeth: Would you like me to provide calorie and nutrient information on these items?

"God, no," Talia said.

"Everything all right?" her dad asked. He hadn't been able to hear Queen Elizabeth, since her little voice came through the tiny speakers in the Omni 3Ds, a neat trick of smart glasses technology that made sound audible only to the wearer.

"Yeah, sorry—my Ideal Life Friend was trying to help." Usually, the app really did improve Talia. (Or maybe it was just because it was hard not to feel that way when the suggestions were given to you by one of the most impressive female leaders in history.) But right now, Talia didn't want reminders that a calorie count was available, so she took off the glasses.

She returned her attention to the menu. It was all so tempting. How was a woman supposed to choose?

The corner of her mouth lifted as she remembered the watch on her wrist.

I don't have *to choose. I can eat one, then rewind as many times as I want!*

Heck, Talia could stay here all morning with her parents, basking in their warmth and indulging in every item on the menu.

She wondered if this watch had ever appeared to anyone else before. Then the scientist part of her brain started wandering into questions again about how the watch actually worked.

But before it could get too far, Talia squashed the line of thought in its tracks. She didn't get many occasions to be with her parents, and she wanted to focus on them.

She ended up ordering a tall stack of lemon pancakes with sides of sausage and breakfast potatoes. Calories didn't matter. She'd rewind them away in a little while!

Once the waiter finished taking her parents' orders and filled everyone's coffee cups, the questions began again.

"Start from the beginning," Vera said. "I want to imagine what it was like when you walked into the restaurant. Were you wearing a pretty dress?"

"Sorry to disappoint," Talia said. "I threw a blazer over my T-shirt and jeans. But Sam looked nice! He had on a great tuxedo jacket that he'd modernized."

"Sam was there?" Vera said, nearly spilling her coffee. "Why didn't you lead with that?"

Dave shared a conspiratorial smile with Talia. Vera had loved Sam ever since he came home with Talia (as friends) for Thanksgiving their freshman year, since the Morgans lived just half an hour from the university and he wasn't going to fly to Taiwan, where his mom and dad didn't even celebrate Thanksgiving (seeing as it was an American holiday).

While many parents would have made a lot of noise about making sure Sam slept on the sofa bed in the living room, away from their daughter, Vera was the opposite—she'd *tried* to get him to sleep in Talia's room with her in her twin bed, much to

Talia's horror (and Sam's amusement). Talia had apologized to him for her mother the entire weekend.

Seventeen years later, Vera was still on a mission to get the two together, every time Talia mentioned him.

"Yes, Sam was there, and he helped calm my nerves."

"And you walked into the restaurant together?" her mom asked. "Are there photos?"

"It wasn't prom, honey," Dave said.

"There *were* photos—" Talia said.

"See?" Vera smirked.

"But there weren't any 'grand entrance' photos of me and Sam, Mom. I meant there was a whole press junket thing where I took pictures with the Omni execs and the VCs."

"What a shame," Vera said. "I bet those executives and investors were all pasty from being in front of their computers all day. The reporters should have taken photos of Sam instead. He is a very handsome young man—strong arms from lifting boxes of books all day, nice tan from long walks on the beach . . ."

Dave was trying not to laugh out loud.

"Speaking of handsome young men," Vera said, "Jacob and Libby seem to be having the best time in the Maldives!"

Talia winced. Her sister was only two years younger, but she'd somehow managed to find the perfect husband while in college, which meant Libby and Jacob had already been together for over a decade. But even though Talia was still single, she never begrudged her little sister anything. She *wanted* Libby to have all the happiness in the universe.

Fresh out of school, Libby and Jacob had decided to backpack around the world and document it, and this hit at the time when YouTube and Instagram were really taking off exponentially. It didn't hurt that they were both gorgeous, too, and sponsorships and partnerships poured in so fast they were able to turn down all but the biggest.

They'd now appeared in ad campaigns for Patagonia in

Bhutan, Conrad Hotels in Tahiti, Loro Piana in Rome, and more. Libby and Jacob had a hundred million subscribers on Instagram and twice that on YouTube. And they were always being flown around the world and put up in luxury suites and sent on incredible expeditions, all on someone else's dime.

Vera pushed her phone in front of Talia and hit Play on Libby and Jacob's latest video.

"Hi, friends!" Libby was in a green sundress, and her blond hair was pulled back into a high ponytail. She stood on a dock with cerulean water surrounding her, a beach with palm trees behind her. Talia smiled at seeing her sister's familiar sunniness.

"Today Jacob and I are going to help with coral reef rehabilitation in the Maldives!" Libby was saying. "As you probably know, global warming has devastated a lot of coral ecosystems around the world. But here in the Maldives, a partnership of scientists and hotels has found a unique way to try to turn that around. Visitors—like you and me—can seed new coral reefs.

"So we're going scuba diving today, and we're bringing you with us. And even more fun is that after we leave, they'll send us updates on how our new baby reefs are doing!"

Jacob popped into the frame then. He wore a black rash guard and green board shorts that matched Libby's sundress. "But a quick reminder that if you're going to be in the sun a lot, you can protect yourself by covering up like I do. And use sunscreen—just make sure it's labeled coral-safe, without the chemicals that can wash off your skin and harm our oceanic friends."

"Aren't they so sweet?" Vera said.

Talia nodded. One of the many things she loved about her sister and brother-in-law was that even though they were beautiful and could have flaunted it, like some creators did, Libby and Jacob didn't want to build a business on boobs and abs, so there were never gratuitous bikini shots or videos of Jacob shirtless. And despite their fame, they were still earnest and principled, working only with companies they believed in and making sure the contracts they signed allowed them to speak their true opinions.

Sometimes when Talia watched their videos, she wondered if she was doing life wrong. Sure, she was building what she hoped was a company that could change the world. But Talia was young and single and childless. Shouldn't she be out traveling the world instead of just watching her sister do it? Shouldn't Talia *also* be scuba diving in the Maldives or dancing in the streets of Rio de Janeiro during Carnival or strolling through the cobblestone paths of small villages in Provence and drinking wine with the local vintners?

Her social media was full of not only Libby but also other women her age fulfilling their wanderlust and looking stunning while doing it. Talia looked down at her Ideal Life hoodie and jeans and frowned. *Your Gossipy Tech BFF* had liked her casual "confidence," but still . . . Maybe she ought to try just a *tiny* bit more. Talia could go over to the mall after work and pick up some better clothes? Also some makeup and skin-care products?

But then their breakfast arrived. Talia drowned both her pancakes and sausages in maple syrup. The potatoes, however, were doused in ketchup instead.

I'll buy myself a new wardrobe after the Omni acquisition closes, Talia told herself as she took a big, sticky bite. And she'd plan a vacation then, too. She could ask Libby for recommendations.

When Talia and her parents finished eating, she wasn't ready for their time together to end, and she did still want to order the other things on the menu that she'd been eyeing.

It was okay to use the watch for this, right? She didn't think she would accidentally cause war to break out on Mars if she went back in time an hour and ate some bacon.

Besides, it was a logical fallacy to think that any single event could change the future. This was something Sam had told her last year, when he was rereading *War and Peace* (yes, *re*reading).

Tolstoy had pointed out the human tendency to think of cause and effect too simplistically. When a player lost in chess, for example, he tried to identify *the* mistake he made. But in assuming a single causal relationship, he failed to see all the tiny little decisions that both he and his opponent made—not to mention external factors like how a cloud parted and let the sunlight glare directly in his eyes for a second, breaking his concentration near the start of the game, or how the barista had broken up with her girlfriend the night before and, distracted, accidentally put two shots of espresso into the chess player's opponent's coffee that morning, thereby increasing his mental sharpness.

This was probably an overly philosophical way to think about the question of rewinding (especially since all Talia wanted right now was a chance at some bacon), but the point was, picking something else to eat was an inconsequential change. Life was full of thousands of small choices every day.

She nodded to herself, okay with her decision, and turned the watch's dial.

Everything went in reverse until Talia and her parents were back to holding menus. There was no food yet.

She also had her glasses back on again, a fact she was quickly reminded of because the bumblebee floated regally into her field of vision, her crown sparkling but her face showing some concern, like a mother fussing over a child.

Ideal Life Queen Elizabeth: Are you feeling all right, Talia? Your body temperature is slightly elevated, and your resting heart rate is thirty beats per minute faster. I also notice theta wave fluctuations in your brain. Please let me know if I may be of assistance.

"I'm fine, just excited." Talia took her glasses off and turned to her parents and the waiter. "Sorry, I'm testing out some new software, but I'll put these away for now." She did, however, make a mental note to keep an eye on whether Queen Elizabeth reacted every time Talia used the watch. *If* she kept using the watch.

The waiter arrived at the table, and her mom and dad put in their orders. Then it was Talia's turn.

"I'll have the Nutella stack, please," she said. Pancakes smothered in chocolate hazelnut spread with bacon layered in between sounded like the perfect round two of breakfast.

Plus, Talia was starving. The last breakfast was no longer in her stomach, so there was no problem of already being stuffed even though she was pigging out again.

The waiter filled everyone's coffee cups, just as before. Then her mom's questions about the Omni merger celebration began again.

"Start from the beginning," Vera said. "I want to imagine what it was like when you walked into the restaurant. Were you wearing a pretty dress?"

"Sorry to disappoint," Talia said. "I threw a blazer over my T-shirt and jeans. But Sam looked nice! He had on a great tuxedo jacket that he'd modernized."

"Sam was there?" Vera said, nearly spilling her coffee. "Why didn't you lead with that?"

Dave shot his conspiratorial smile at Talia.

"Yes, Sam was there, and he helped calm my nerves."

"And you walked into the restaurant together?" her mom asked. "Are there photos?"

"It wasn't prom, honey," Dave said.

"There *were* photos—" Talia said.

"See?" Vera smirked.

Talia noted to herself that this conversation was going exactly like it had the first time around. Even though she'd invoked Tolstoy a few minutes ago to give herself some philosophical backup for rewinding, this repeated chatter from her mom still gave Talia some comfort.

"But there weren't any 'grand entrance' photos of me and

Sam, Mom. I meant there was a whole press junket thing where I took pictures with the Omni execs and the VCs."

"What a shame," Vera said. "I bet those executives and investors were all pasty from being in front of their computers all day. The reporters should have taken photos of Sam instead. He is a very handsome young man—strong arms from lifting boxes of books all day, nice tan from long walks on the beach . . ."

Dave was trying not to laugh out loud.

"Speaking of handsome young men," Vera said, "Jacob and Libby seem to be having the best time in the Maldives!" She set her phone in front of Talia and hit Play on Libby and Jacob's latest video.

"Hi, friends!" Libby was on the dock in her green sundress, her blond hair up in a high ponytail. "Today Jacob and I are going to help with coral reef rehabilitation . . ."

Talia settled in to watch her baby sister again, this time managing to shove aside that nagging feeling that she wasn't traveling enough or dressed well enough and instead just enjoying Libby and Jacob's success and joy.

"Aren't they so sweet?" Vera said.

Talia nodded. Their smiles were so genuine and contagious.

Breakfast arrived, and everyone dug in.

Talia's Nutella stack was divine. The sweetness of the chocolate contrasted with the rich saltiness of the bacon, all sandwiched perfectly between fluffy layers of pancakey carbohydrate goodness. God, Talia loved breakfast!

After they finished eating, she rewound the meal, and Talia and her parents ate breakfast together again, two more times (a veggie-and-cheese omelet with a side of coffee cake for round three, and Belgian waffles smothered in strawberries, candied pecans, and powdered sugar for round four).

And it was worth it, even if she did have to watch Libby and Jacob living a more perfect life than hers, and even though Vera tried to convince Talia to date Sam in each rewind.

Libby

While Talia was finishing breakfast with Vera and Dave, Libby emerged from the bathroom in the overwater bungalow she and Jacob were staying in. It was just after 9 p.m. in the Maldives, and it had been a long day of photo shoots for the resort. The life of a full-time creator was not as relaxing as it looked; when a hotel chain paid for your flights and your luxury suite perched on stilts over a cerulean-blue lagoon, your end of the bargain was producing lots and lots of content for them—photo shoots for their digital advertising; short, entertaining videos for social media; and long, detailed videos for YouTube. Every moment of your "vacation" was documented. So really, every moment you had in paradise was work.

Still, Libby was happy with her life. She had a sweet husband who was also hot and who didn't mind living out of a suitcase. She got to fly business class and stay in five-star hotels in far-flung locations and eat in the best restaurants in the world. It was not a life she could have imagined for herself, growing up watching her mom and dad, who still lived in the same town they'd grown up in, still partied with their friends from high school who had also never left, who never even stepped foot on a plane.

And yet . . . Libby now held a little ticking bomb in her hand as she walked out of the bathroom. It was a pregnancy test that very definitely confirmed what she'd suspected—beautiful, because her biological clock had started making itself known rather insistently last year, and the overwhelming desire to have a baby had consumed her. But also a bomb, because how did a baby fit into their jet-setting life?

She walked into the bungalow's bedroom. The suite was built out of light wooden planks and decorated with *thundu kunaa*—handwoven mats of dyed reeds in beautiful, intricate patterns—and lacquered vases and framed art made of seashells. Jacob sat propped up in their four-poster bed, working on some of the footage they'd shot while scuba diving today.

"Honey?" Libby said.

"Sorry, gimme one sec." Jacob dragged his finger slowly over the trackpad of his computer, barely a millimeter at a time. Libby recognized the movement from the thousands of times she had edited videos, trying to trim the clip at precisely the right tenth of a second.

"Okay, sorry; I'm done now," he said, looking up at her. "What's up?"

But the last bit was truncated, because Jacob's jaw dropped when he saw the pregnancy test in her hand. "Is it . . . ?"

Libby bit her lip and nodded.

"Oh my god!" Jacob jumped out of bed, nearly knocking his laptop onto the floor as he rushed over and cocooned her in a hug. "Really?"

Libby held him tight. "Really. Really! We're having a baby."

"We're having a baby!" Jacob echoed. The ability to articulate anything more eluded them in the immensity of the moment.

Instead, they held each other and bounced up and down. Jacob had to wipe away the tears trickling down his face that were beginning to soak Libby's hair.

After they'd collected themselves, he picked up the phone and dialed room service. "Champagne, please. We're celebrating! Oh, hold on—no, not champagne." He laughed at himself. "Something nonalcoholic."

"And something chocolate," Libby said, leaning into the phone.

Order placed, Jacob hung up and threw his arms around Libby again, bringing them both down together flat onto the bed. He pressed his forehead against hers, one of her favorite things in the world. Maybe it was because her parents had been absent so much in her youth that now, Libby wanted no personal space at all. But whatever the reason, Jacob loved being close to her, too, and that's why they were so good together. Not every couple could spend all day, every day, working in such proximity to each other and then spending their little downtime together as well.

"I love you," Jacob said. Then he moved down to kiss her belly. "I also love *you*, little bean. And the world is going to love you, too."

Libby froze. Because there it was again. This baby was a gift but also the thing that would blow up their lives.

"Jacob . . ."

"Hmm?" He was still nuzzled against her stomach.

"What if I don't want the world to know about our baby?"

He looked up at her, frowning. "I guess we can hide it for a while? But at some point, you'll start to show—"

"But what if I don't want to document the process of you and me becoming three?"

Jacob nodded. "I get it. It's a personal journey for us. Of course, honey. We can strategically shoot videos of you without showing your stomach later on in the pregnancy. Plenty of celebrities do that and then announce the baby *after* they're born. Not that we're celebrities, but you know."

"It's not only that," Libby said. "I'm not sure I want us to be a content-creating *family*. I mean, I know it works for some people. The Globetrotter Duo became the Globetrotter Trio and then the Globetrotter Quartet, and now their kids have even more sponsorships than the parents do. But . . ."

"But what?"

She thought again about how she'd held that pregnancy test like it was a tiny bomb. "What about the privacy rights of our baby girl?"

Jacob's eyes lit up. "A girl? We're having a little girl?"

"I don't know. I just have a feeling." Libby took his hands in hers. "But what I'm worried about is, what if our daughter grows up and resents that we put her online from the very start? We didn't have to worry about this when we were kids, because the internet didn't exist like this yet. But if we post photos and videos of the baby, she will never have gotten a choice. Kids these days don't get to consent. They just become props in their parents' lives."

"Whoa, back up." Jacob pulled his hands out of Libby's. "I promise we'll never treat our baby like a prop. If we put her online, that just makes us normal, proud parents. And we have the opportunity to show our child the entire *planet*. We are so lucky in this career we've built, and we can give that to her. But if you're saying what I think you're saying—that you want to quit all this—then . . . what have we been working so hard for?"

Libby buried her face in a pillow. She didn't know. This is what she'd been privately wrestling with while hoping to get pregnant. Would she really throw away what she and Jacob had made? Their audience of hundreds of millions had taken years to grow, and it's because of them that Jacob and Libby got paid.

Without their little media empire, who would they even be?

"I don't . . ." Jacob murmured beside her. "What would we do for a living? Our only marketable skills are being ourselves on camera."

Someone knocked on the bungalow door. "Room service!"

Jacob let out a long exhale before showing him in. The waiter set up an ice bucket with a bottle of sparkling mango juice and presented them with a decadent chocolate cake, sprinkled with deep-red pomegranate seeds.

"Congratulations on your celebration," the waiter said, before exiting with a smile.

Libby and Jacob stared at the cake, not sure what to say next.

So much for paradise-perfect celebrations.

Talia

After breakfast, Talia headed into the office. The first thing on her calendar was a meeting with the marketing team.

As usual, Erin was already in the conference room before anyone else, with a box full of donuts for everyone and her computer out, ready to take copious notes. She was also wearing her Omni 3Ds, which ran most of her apps, including Ideal Life. It was fascinating to Talia—who had grown up carrying a phone—how quickly the under-thirty set had adapted to smart glasses and how comfortable they were with visuals projected in front of them through lenses rather than on a screen in their hand. But that was part of why Omni wanted to buy companies like Ideal Life.

"I think you work harder than I do," Talia said, smiling as she set down her own laptop and the coffee she'd picked up in the break room.

"Not true," Erin said, "but I try to."

"First in—"

"Last out," Erin finished. "I know, I read that that was your motto in a *Palo Alto Weekly* interview last year. I've adopted it as my own, as well as your other one: 'Relentless pursuit of constructive criticism.' I thought it was so brave to open yourself up to constant feedback."

"How else would I know if I could improve myself or my product?" Talia said. "What's actually scarier to me than criticism is staying the same. I don't want Ideal Life to be mediocre. That's how we help make other people's lives better, too."

"One hundred percent," Erin said, nodding. "Oh, hey, before everyone else arrives, how did Sam like the party last night?"

"I think he enjoyed it. But even if he didn't, he'd never let it show. He's the kind of friend who's always there for you, you know?"

Erin pursed her lips, as if deciding whether or not to say something.

"What?" Talia asked.

"Nothing . . . I mean, it's not my place to—"

"I *want* you to be bold and speak up, Erin. I know that's in your core personality, because you demonstrated it in spades when you applied for this internship. So don't be afraid to talk here. There's a balance to strike, of course, but it's not good to be hyperaware of hierarchy."

Erin laughed self-consciously. "Yeah, I guess I don't normally have trouble speaking up. But this is personal, so . . . Okay, well, I was going to say that Sam is so great and obviously you two care about each other a lot, and I'm rooting for you."

Talia shook her head. "Not you, too. I just came from breakfast with my parents, where my mom wouldn't stop gushing about Sam. She's been not so subtly trying to get us together for, gosh, seventeen years now? It hasn't happened yet, though, so it's not going to."

"But why not?"

Talia shrugged. "I can't point to any specific reason why Sam and I stayed only friends or why we didn't become more. It probably could've gone either way, but sometimes life simply does what it's going to do. And we're really great as we are, so I'm happy."

Erin let it go. But a wave of sadness hit Talia as she remembered again that she had no real friends except Sam. There was something a little awful—and lonely—about the fact that it was a summer intern who asked Talia about Sam, rather than one of her old friends from college or grad school.

But Talia couldn't dwell on this because Lena Tahir, the director of marketing, came into the conference room then, followed by the two others on her team, George Jackson and Henry Carter.

All three of them looked a little hungover from the celebration last night. Staying out late was rough in your thirties.

"Morning," Talia said, putting on her CEO mantle again. "Sorry for calling a meeting first thing."

Lena waved it off. "Totally my fault for having three too many cups of sake. It was *so* good, though."

Talia laughed. She could understand lack of restraint like that. After all, she'd just come from multiple breakfasts. "Well, I wanted to get the conversation started about what marketing is going to look like over the next few months. There's going to be a lot more attention on us now that Omni has signed the acquisition papers, and I was wondering if we have plans to ramp things up."

"We've been brainstorming." George tapped on his tablet and woke up the projector. A short presentation appeared on the large screen on the conference room wall.

"It's a new wave of our millennial ad campaign," Henry said.

"Okay . . ." Talia chewed on her lip.

"Millennials are our biggest demographic." Lena started explaining their plan as George flipped through the slides. "We've got some designs for new digital ads in *The Wall Street Journal*, *The New York Times*, and other big media sites whose audiences have disposable income and are tech-savvy."

"That's the same as we've been doing, right?" Talia asked.

"Yes," Lena said. "But it's foundational and I think it's worked, so I don't want to give up on it if it can continue to give good results. Still, we're continuing to innovate. Tech podcasts are big, and Henry is doing research on ones where we could get you on as a guest. We can also look into sponsorships on some of them."

On the other side of the table, Erin touched her Omni 3Ds. A message must've popped up on them. Then her eyes met Talia's.

Talia nodded in support.

Erin sat straighter in her chair. "So, um, I was thinking, how about social media creator campaigns?"

George made a "meh" noise. "We haven't had much luck with influencers recently."

Erin winced, and Talia suspected it was because the term "influencers" was passé. Libby and Jacob used the word "creators" because it was more respectful of the time and work they put into creating content.

"Although . . ." Talia looked from George and Henry to Lena. "It's possible we're a little out of touch because of our age."

Henry groaned but agreed. "Being in tech in your thirties is like being an NFL player in your thirties. The Silicon Valley chapter of AARP is already sending me mail, and it's *snail* mail."

Everyone laughed. What Henry said was only partly true, because the Valley did value experience. But the younger generation was coming in fast on their heels.

"I'm sure you chose great creators last time," Erin said, "but I'd be happy to take another look and see if there are others we could add to the roster."

Lena smiled at her, then looked at Talia. "I like this one. She's smart *and* diplomatic."

Erin beamed.

"Okay," Talia said. "That all sounds like a good start. Anything else?"

George, Henry, and Lena shook their heads.

"Then I'll let you get to it—" Talia started to say.

"Wait!" Erin jumped up from her seat. "I had another idea I wanted to share."

"Oh. Yeah, of course. The floor is yours."

Erin touched her Omni 3Ds again, where her Ideal Life Friend was likely sending her a nudge of encouragement. Then she turned to George and said, "Mind if I use the screen?"

He disconnected his presentation, and Erin projected hers on the wall.

The first slide was a photo of Temple Dots, Ideal Life's wireless brain monitor stickers. They were currently transparent and nearly invisible on the skin; customers wore them on their temples, as the name suggested. Temple Dots mapped brain activity and correlated it with each person's individual history to help Ideal Life identify neural pathway patterns and make suggestions for better behavior and choices. They also kept track of other health indicators, like heart rate, blood oxygen levels, and sleep patterns.

"Obviously the tech is incredible," Erin said. "But like Lena was saying, our current biggest demographic is millennials, especially on the older end of that spectrum. And I know Ideal Life *does* do some Gen Z outreach, but I was thinking, what about doing more? We want to be our best selves, too, and I think it's a market that Ideal Life can expand.

"But to get to us, you first have to appeal to something other than the dry tech pitch that works on the *Wall Street Journal* and *New York Times* crowd. That's not where *our* attention is. Which leads me to this."

She flipped to the next slide. There were more Temple Dots, but instead of looking like boring transparent Band-Aids, they were colorful—primary colors, fluorescents, and pastels.

"Gen Z—and Gen A—exists in an age of *personalization*. We started with stickers and filters on our apps, then custom emojis. We want to personalize our water bottles, our laptops, everything. Ideal Life already allows us to design our own Friend avatars. So why don't we do that for Temple Dots, too?"

Talia leaned forward on the conference room table. "Tell me more."

Erin moved to the next slide. There, the Temple Dots grew even more varied, featuring floral designs, art deco, psychedelic swirls, and more. "Think nail art but of the high-tech variety. Customers can choose from predesigned Temple Dots or design their own."

Lena was nodding furiously. "Yes! And this will likely lead to an increase in sales, too. Currently, customers keep Temple Dots on for two to four weeks before they have to switch to a new pair, because the adhesive we use is top-notch medical grade and lasts forever. But if they had the option to change it up to match their mood, their outfit, or whatever . . ."

"I love it," Talia said. "Although I like it not because it's good for sales, but because it adds to the joy in people's everyday lives."

"So do you want us to run some numbers on cost, timeline, et cetera?" Henry asked.

"Yes," Talia said. "Let's do it."

Elated, Erin bounced in her seat and flushed bright red.

As usual, Talia's day was packed with meetings, but she never forgot that Sam was playing in a tournament today. Whenever she had a few minutes free, she tuned in to the live stream of the Cleveland Gold Poker Invitational to see how he was doing. First prize was half a million dollars, and each time she checked, Sam was still in. That wasn't a surprise—you don't go pro unless you're really good—but even though there was a lot of game theory involved, poker was also part luck.

And *everyone* in that tournament was a professional.

Midafternoon, Talia ate a late lunch at her desk while she watched Sam play a hand. He had bags under his eyes—strange, since he was one of those rare, annoying people who could sleep anywhere, even on a red-eye flight. Hadn't he slept on the plane?

The other players at his table looked a lot better rested. There was an older gentleman in a suit and a Rolex. A guy around Sam's age who was sporting a bushy black beard. Two other men who were forgettable in appearance. And then there was Louise Enger from the Bay Area, a stocky woman who smiled little and looked like she could be an FBI agent or a spy. Definitely not someone to take lightly.

As the dealer dealt, the live stream showed what cards each player received. (She knew it was actually on a thirty-minute delay—the live stream would show all the players' cards for the viewers, so it fed out half an hour after the fact to prevent cheating, like someone outside the tournament communicating information to the competitors.)

Talia groaned when she saw Sam's hand, especially compared to the others.

"It's okay, though," she said aloud. "He knows what to do."

He folded immediately. Talia exhaled.

The trick to being successful at poker at the professional level was to know when to fold. Amateur players thought the game was about card counting or bluffing. But the best players folded around 80 percent more often than others. And Sam was no fool.

Talia couldn't watch the next hand, though, because she had several more meetings to attend. She'd known that Omni signing the acquisition agreement was only the beginning of the process, like lowering the walls of a dam, but she hadn't known *how* much of a flood would come barreling through. Omni's massive team of lawyers now had free rein to request anything and everything for due diligence, and half of the Ideal Life team's time was suddenly spent chasing down what they needed.

A lot of it needed to be funneled through Talia, too. This startup had been her baby for years, and like Libby seeding new coral reef nurseries, Talia had had her hand in every aspect of Ideal Life. So this afternoon she first had a meeting with the developer team about getting source code and AI weights into the encrypted tech escrow, where it would be secure from outside eyes but where Omni's team could parse through what they needed.

Then she had a meeting with the contracts team to go through assignment clauses in their agreements with third-party vendors to see what could be transferred to Omni and what would need to be canceled, and if there were any penalties.

And then she had a meeting with Omni's external law firm's employment attorneys to talk about the four-year "golden handcuffs" agreement they wanted her and key Ideal Life employees to sign, which was a guarantee that they would continue working for Omni for four years once the acquisition was complete.

By late afternoon, Talia's brain had been reduced to the consistency of mushy peas. She returned to her office and slumped into her chair.

Before she dove back into more work, though, she wanted to check in on how Sam was doing. But when she opened up the tournament live stream, his name wasn't on the leaderboard anymore.

"Oh no . . ." Talia opened another tab to look at the complete standings.

Sam had been eliminated about an hour earlier, ranked at forty-eight.

She texted him immediately.

Talia: Hey, just getting caught up on the tournament. Sorry to see you're out, but you're still top 50. How did it feel?

Sam: Was off my game today. #48 means I'll take home $6,000, though, so not bad for a day's work.

Talia chewed on her lip. He was right: $6,000 wasn't bad as a general matter. It's just that the Bay Area was astronomically expensive (unless you'd bought a home in the early '80s like her parents had, before the region became the heart of tech). After taxes, Sam's winnings would only keep him afloat for a couple of months. Talia had, in the past, tried to convince him to play in more tournaments, but he'd said that wasn't how he wanted to spend his time.

Sam preferred being at his decommissioned lighthouse turned bookshop, helping tourists find the perfect beach read and locals pick the right novel for their upcoming book club. It made him happy but nowhere near break-even (last year, he'd been tens of thousands of dollars in the red). Bookstores were a razor-thin-margin business, especially here. Last year, a prominent local chain had had to declare bankruptcy. Poker was a necessary subsidy for Sam's shop.

Which was why, as Talia looked at his text and his name on the tournament rankings, she thought, *What if I rewound just a* little *bit and let him play the losing hand again?* Maybe he would make a different choice and he wouldn't get eliminated, and then he'd be able to creep up a little higher in the standings. Every place you inched up meant a jump in how much you'd take home in winnings.

But then she remembered what Sam had said—*Promise me you won't change my life on purpose.*

She sighed.

And even though she really wanted to help him, she kept her promise instead.

Talia

Jody and Jonathan Segovia, twins who were both engineers at Ideal Life, sent a poll out to the entire company about which film to watch for movie night tonight. Of course, most of the employees would still be working at 8 p.m., but that had never stopped everyone from having fierce opinions on what the film pick ought to be, even if they weren't going to watch it. In any case, a lot of the Ideal Life team would pop in for at least a few minutes to grab a slice of the free pizza that the company sprung for.

Talia herself looked forward to the monthly movie night poll. She drummed her fingers as she stared at her computer screen.

The Avengers: 35%
Hackers: 20%
La La Land: 8%
Free Guy: 18%
Ocean's Eleven: 19%

She wasn't surprised at the current voting. Either of the tech-related movies, *Hackers* and *Free Guy*, could have been a winner, but because there were two of them, they were splitting the vote. Talia could see the appeal of *Ocean's Eleven*, too, to the cerebral audience at Ideal Life. *La La Land* never had a chance (although that was definitely Jonathan's suggestion, since he loved a good musical and choreography). And *The Avengers*, well . . . that was just relaxing, pure fun, which sounded pretty great at the end of a long day.

Jody and Jonathan were making their rounds through the

floors. "Movie night in conference room A tonight—don't forget to vote!"

"Where are you ordering the pizza from?" George from marketing asked.

"Delfina?" Henry said hopefully.

Jody clutched at her heart and staggered; her brother may have been the musical theater lover, but she was the drama queen of the two. "Henry! George! I am mortally wounded. Are you suggesting that you come to movie night not for our excellent taste in films or for the companionship of your fine colleagues, b-but for . . . the *pizza*?"

George grinned and tilted his head. "I mean . . ."

Jonathan laughed. "Fine—we'll order from Delfina."

"Woot!" Henry said. "Then I'm in. Voting now." He spun in his office chair and clicked on the poll.

Next, Jody and Jonathan popped into Talia's office.

"Hey, Talia," Jody said, "movie night is tonight. Think you might come by?"

Jonathan was already shaking his head. "The day Talia Morgan isn't chained to her computer and has time to come to movie night is the day that I swear I will never add another musical to the film poll again."

But Jody snickered. "We have an opportunity here, Talia. You could single-handedly put a stop to our misery."

Talia smiled. This is what she loved about working at Ideal Life. Even though they had grown over the years to 150 employees, there was still a definite personality to the team. They were big enough to be noticed by the Omnis of the world, yet still small enough to know each other on a personal level.

Maybe *this* was an opportunity to do something social for herself. She understood that she and her employees couldn't be true friends, because there would always be some aura of "boss" around her, but still . . . That sadness she'd felt earlier when Erin asked about Sam—when Talia had realized she had no one in her life other than him, her parents, Libby, and endless work—made her think twice about skipping movie night yet again.

"Actually," Talia said, "my brain is fried, and I was just about to shut down my laptop. So, yeah, I *will* come to movie night."

Jonathan let out an involuntary gasp.

"Don't worry—you can still put musicals on the polls. In fact, I insist."

Jody sighed loudly, as if terribly disappointed.

But Jonathan stuck his tongue out at his sister, then winked at Talia. "Well, in honor of you attending movie night, I think we should scuttle the poll and have *you* choose what we watch."

"Oh, no, I couldn't—"

"Yes!" Jody said, practically vibrating. "I love that!"

She flew out of Talia's office, hopped onto a chair, and shouted to the whole floor, "Poll's over, suckers! Talia is coming tonight, and she gets to pick what we watch!"

There was a collective, amused shrug, and then everyone went back to work. They might have had strong opinions during polling, but once it was over, they didn't *really* care. As long as there was good pizza.

Conference room A was the biggest of their meeting spaces, but the turnout for movie night was twice what was expected. Luckily, Ideal Life's modular floor plan extended to the conference rooms, too, and Talia, Jody, and Jonathan just had to unsnap a couple of tabs on the moving wall between conference rooms A and B to slide the divider away, and voila! It was now room A/B.

Talia had chosen *La La Land* with the reasoning that a little bit of nontech might be a nice change of pace—not to mention balance—for her team. Despite some groans at the announcement, the forty-five or so employees who stayed for the whole film found themselves tapping their feet to the music and shimmying a little in their plastic seats during the choreographed scenes. Jonathan added to the atmosphere by jumping up to the front of the room whenever a dance number was about to begin, and he performed as decent a version of each dance as one might expect from a software engineer. He bowed each time to enthusiastic whistling and applause, Jody and Talia loudest of all.

When *La La Land* was over and all the pizza had been demolished, everyone seemed to want to linger, to hold on to the shared moment a little longer. Talia couldn't remember the last time she'd skipped out on working in the evening to simply have fun—the Omni dinner the other night didn't count, since that had definitely been work, what with the press interviews and the schmoozing with Omni execs and venture capital investors, not to mention having to do the whole day over again.

Oh! Talia thought. Tonight didn't *have* to end just because *La La Land* was over. She glanced at her watch.

She frowned at it for a second, though. She still didn't understand how it worked, and Talia briefly considered telling Jody and Jonathan about it to see if their brilliant engineering minds could figure it out. They wouldn't remember anyway, after Talia rewound.

But Jody and Jonathan would want to take the watch apart to examine its gears and guts. Engineers liked to physically tinker—even software engineers who usually worked with code—and what if they dissected the watch and it didn't work anymore when they put it back together?

Forget it, Talia thought. Besides, she didn't want to stop the momentum of *fun* she was having. It was so rare to get to relax with everyone here in a casual context rather than the usual work, work, work.

Still, Talia illogically felt like she shouldn't make them watch the same movie again, even though they wouldn't remember.

What about butterfly effects? She'd brushed them off before

when she wanted more breakfast, but now she thought of it again. Like, by picking a different film, would that somehow change something and lead to unforeseen consequences?

How can you answer a question like that definitively, though?

Time travel hypotheses were the province of theoretical physicists and science fiction writers, and neither group had figured out the answer. It was all just conjecture. Even Talia—a researcher who had *actually* experienced short-term time travel—couldn't draw decisive conclusions.

But what she could do was examine each as a mini experiment of sorts, even though they were more anecdotal evidence than scientific.

1) She'd gone back to the past to change the Tinder murder. This was certainly an alteration of the past that had measurable downstream effects—a life had been saved, and the Ideal Life AI had been improved so nothing like that would happen again. The result had seemed like a net positive. And the world had continued to function normally, even after Talia made that "edit" to the past.
2) Breakfast with her parents—Talia had rewound so she could choose different dishes, for a total of four times. Each of those times, the only thing altered was what she ate. The conversation with her parents and the behavior of the waiter had remained the same. So that experience seemed like the opposite result of the first one—no obvious butterfly effects.

There was a flaw in her tentative logic, though. Talia was assuming that the watch behaved rationally. She was treating it like a device like her phone or Omni 3Ds. But she had no idea how this watch worked. It hadn't exactly come with a user's manual when it randomly appeared on her wrist.

All the more reason to gather more data, she thought. *Maybe changing the movie pick would not only be fun, but also a good experiment.*

Besides, if there were any obvious, immediate negative effects, she could simply rewind, choose *La La Land*, and then have them all relive that version instead, right?

It made her a little uncomfortable that her experiment was so unbounded; this was not how it was done in normal research. But Talia could only work with what she had.

So when she turned the crown of her watch, she went back to the moment she announced the film pick. On the way, though, it was amusing to watch Jonathan perform all the song-and-dance scenes in *La La Land* backward. (It was less amusing to watch people un-scarf their pizza.)

At the correct point of the rewind, Talia chose a new movie, the '90s cult classic *Hackers*. It was beloved among the tech crowd, and everyone in conference room A/B cheered at her choice.

Ideal Life Queen Elizabeth: Just checking in. I've noticed again a slight increase in your body temperature and resting heart rate, as well as theta wave fluctuations.

Interesting. Those were the same physiological responses as when Talia redid breakfast with her parents.

"Go ahead and ignore those signals until further notice," she told Queen Elizabeth. The readings were consistent and not providing any new or useful data, so Talia decided she didn't need them. It would also save her some bother in the future to not have her Friend popping up to tell her what she already knew.

Talia settled in for *Hackers*.

Just as before—and thankfully—everyone had an amazing time. Jonathan didn't dance with this one, but Jody did lead everyone in reciting the most iconic quotes, which nearly everybody seemed to know by heart. When they got to "Never send a boy to do a woman's job," Talia, Jody, and all the other women in the room shouted the line in unison.

Afterward, Talia rewound and picked *The Avengers*. This, too, had an aspect of Jonathan- or Jody-led crowd participation, with Jonathan leading cheers for Team Good Guys and Jody egging on the audience for Team Mischievous Bad Guy (aka Loki).

Talia thought about doing movie night again with the other two unwatched films—*Free Guy* and *Ocean's Eleven*—but she was wiped out. For everyone else, it was only 10:30 p.m., but for Talia, she'd been watching movies for six and a half hours, so it was effectively 2:30 a.m. for her, no matter what the clocks said.

As she grabbed her purse to head home, Talia sighed happily. That had been really, really fun. Sam might even have approved, since she'd used the rewinds for good, clean fun, and he was always trying to get her to take a break and enjoy life a little.

And as an additional bonus, the small alterations to the past had again seemed totally fine.

"Thanks for that," she whispered to the watch. "We should do it again soon."

Sam

Seventeen years ago

Full Moon on the Quad was one of Stanford's many wacky traditions. At the first full moon of the school year, freshmen and seniors gathered at midnight in the middle of the university's main quad to shed their inhibitions and kiss as many other people as they could.

At least, in *theory* they shed their inhibitions. Sam had zero intention of contracting mono or any other infection from kissing some random stranger.

"We should still go," Talia said, leaning against the doorframe of his room. She had one foot in the hallway already, itching to leave, even though he was still sitting at his desk.

"I don't know, Tal. I'm really into this thought experiment I'm designing. Imagine: Two students in libraries move at relativistic speeds to each other. They exchange knowledge through light signals. How would their accumulation of knowledge differ over time?"

"Huh?"

"It's a combination of relativity concepts with epistemological questions about the nature of knowledge."

Talia smirked. "Okay, egghead. But your physics-meets-knowledge project will still be here tomorrow morning, whereas Full Moon on the Quad will not. Come on. It's a rite of passage."

"I don't understand how a student body that is so intelligent can also be so collectively idiotic about infectious disease," Sam said. "The risk of—"

"The risk," Talia interrupted, "is that you go through all four years here buried in the academic wonderland that is your mind but at the same time miss out on the rest of the college experience. Still, if you won't do it for yourself, then do it for me, please?" She stepped into his room and got down on her knees, begging melodramatically. "I don't want to go alone."

"You won't be alone," Sam said. "Like, half the dorm is going."

"Yeah, but I want to go with you."

Sam's chest sparked. It was only a small hope that Talia meant she wanted to go as more than friends, but nevertheless . . .

"Let me get my jacket," he said.

"Woo-hoo!" Talia jumped up from the floor and did an adorable victory dance.

Sam was originally from Taipei, where his parents, Jenny and Roger Chang, owned Sunshine Cakes, a popular bakery chain that specialized in Taiwanese pineapple cakes. The traditional version of pineapple "cakes" were dense bricks of dry, shortbread-like cookie filled with a glob of gummy jam, which could be bought six for two dollars at grocery stores. But in the late eighties, Jenny had revolutionized them by insisting on making her own artisanal pineapple jam and a more buttery, flaky pastry and not using preservatives. She charged a premium for her fresh, revamped pineapple cakes, and it turned out that many, many Taiwanese had been yearning for a modernized take on the classic.

After their initial success, Roger and Jenny opened Sunshine Cakes stores across the island nation, with shop fronts not just in Taipei, but in Kaohsiung, Taichung, Taoyuan, and the international airport, too. That meant they were able to afford great schooling for their brilliant little boy, Sam, including a private American tutor to make sure his English was perfect. Life in Taiwan seemed ideal.

Until 1:47 a.m. on September 21, 1999, when the 7.7-magnitude

Jiji earthquake slammed the island and shattered lives. Nearly twenty-five hundred people died. Eleven thousand were injured. And one hundred thousand were left homeless.

Somehow, three of the five Sunshine Cakes shops escaped relatively unscathed. But Jenny and Roger knew that there was no way they could keep their precious son in Taiwan anymore. He had to go abroad, somewhere safe that wasn't on the tectonic Ring of Fire where another massive earthquake could strike and take his life at any moment.

They could not go with him, because immigration laws didn't favor bakers, but Roger did have a cousin who was a professor at the University of Mississippi. They called him as soon as phone lines were back up, and he said of course he would take Sam in, even though he was a bachelor and didn't know the first thing about children.

Which is how eight-year-old Sam ended up in Mississippi. In a time when international calls were expensive, he grew up hearing from Jenny and Roger for only a few minutes each month. "Uncle" John was always at the university lab or buried in his home office, so Sam didn't speak to him much, and Sam's Taiwanese and Mandarin stalled at the second-grade level. By the time Sam was in middle school, he couldn't communicate much with his parents—let alone try to convey any subject with nuance—and so he grew up hardly knowing them.

Still, it was a good childhood. Because Sam was tall, he played basketball and was accepted by the athletes. Because he was Asian, he was allowed to be smart without teasing, since the model minority stereotype of the late '90s and early 2000s worked in his favor, with everyone assuming that intelligence was just a trait Sam was born with that he couldn't help.

When he graduated from high school, Jenny and Roger called to congratulate him.

"Stanford, good," his dad said in his limited English. "Be focus, study hard."

Sam replied in equally broken Taiwanese, "Don't worry. I will studying very diligent."

And as all mothers who love their kids said—even when their child was eighteen and had managed to survive perfectly fine all this time on the other side of the ocean plus half a continent away—"Take care, Sammy. Don't get sick."

Sam thought about this now as he and Talia walked from their dorm, along the tree-lined street with other freshmen who had started to chant, "Mo-no-nu-cle-o-sis! Mo-no-nu-cle-o-sis!" He gave Talia a wary look, but she just laughed.

The group got bigger as they got onto campus proper, with more students streaming in from their own dorms. The university looked different at this late hour, the windows dark, the professors and grad students sleeping like normal human beings and leaving the night to the shenanigans of the undergrads.

But when Sam and Talia made it into the center of the huge ring of sandstone buildings that was known as the Quad, it was like walking into another world. The night had been transformed into a party, glowing with strings of lights woven among the trees and a DJ pumping music from his station in front of Memorial Church. Hundreds of students milled around the quadrangle, some carrying neon light sticks, others dancing with friends, and a few already kissing.

Sam couldn't help but smile. Talia was right. Full Moon on the Quad as a freshman only happened once; he was glad he had come.

Near them, the Stanford Tree—the school's beloved and irreverent unofficial mascot—had an obnoxious "Kiss Counter" sign draped over her sequined redwood tree costume.

"What's that about?" Sam asked.

"Part of an eternal competition," Talia said. "Every year, the current mascot tries to break the record set by the previous

Tree for number of kisses at Full Moon on the Quad. Don't look now—she's heading your way."

Sam mocked terror and ducked behind Talia. "Quick! Hide me until she finds another target."

Talia snorted but waved the Tree past them. "Nothing to see here."

The Tree lifted a flap of her costume so that her actual human face was revealed. "Hiii, cute freshman," she called out to Sam, who really was crouched behind Talia. "I don't have mono—I swear."

"Still a hard pass, but thanks," he said.

The Tree laughed. "Then how about you?" she asked Talia.

Talia pointed to her cheek. "Right here."

She received a quick peck, and the Tree flipped the number on the kiss counter on her costume to add to the tally and moved on.

"I feel like the Tree cheated," Sam said, standing upright once the mascot had pranced away. "A peck on the cheek should've been a half kiss, not a full one."

"Well, you're the one who denied her a real kiss," Talia teased.

The stringed lights above her and Sam buzzed. Then they flickered out and cast them in shadow.

He heard Talia's breath catch in surprise. And suddenly, despite being surrounded by other students, Sam felt like they were alone in this small space of darkness.

Kissing strangers under too many lights had been unimaginable to him. But now, it seemed entirely possible that he could kiss Talia.

It would take only a small shuffle to draw close enough.

Sam moved toward her.

"Tal—"

But then a dozen naked sophomores and juniors streaked across the Quad, screaming, "We feel so left out!" while the freshmen gawked and the seniors shouted, "Boooo! Party crashers!"

The streakers were gone almost as soon as they appeared,

whooping and cackling while they sprinted out of the archway at the far end of the Quad.

At the same moment, the lights above Sam and Talia flickered back to life, even brighter than before. And the Stanford Band burst onto the Quad right next to them—where had all the musicians been hiding?—trombones blasting, snare drums rattling, and trumpets launching into "All Right Now," the song typically played at football games after a touchdown.

Delighted, Talia began clapping and bopping along to the music, oblivious to what Sam had just been about to do.

Or maybe she had known, and she'd been glad to have the excuse not to cross that line of friendship.

As she twined her fingers through his and drew him into the mass of dancing, celebrating students, Sam realized that maybe he was also glad for how it had turned out. Because he didn't ever want to lose *this*—their easy camaraderie, and Talia's hand leading his where she knew he needed to go.

So on that night, he made a pledge that he would always be there for her, too, just like she'd been there for him. And that he would never do anything to jeopardize this beautiful, precious thing between them, unless she made it clear first that she wanted more.

Erin

It was just before five in the morning, and Erin—not wanting to wake her roommate—had crept downstairs. A few of Stanford's dorms were open in the summer for students who were staying in the area for internships, and Erin and Colette had been lucky enough to snag a room in one of them. Now, Erin sat in the dorm's common area, taking deep, meditative breaths as she focused on the social media self-care coach's video.

"It's only morning," the woman (known as @HigherVibesOnly_) said, "but I know that each decision I make affects the outcome of my day."

"It's only morning," Erin repeated, "but I know that each decision I make affects the outcome of my day."

A freshly brewed cappuccino appeared on the screen. The self-care coach's hand entered the shot, picking it up from the pristine counter and taking the mug out to her balcony. There, @HigherVibesOnly_ stared off into the distance, watching the sun rise.

Erin hadn't always been into self-actualization. She hadn't even realized she needed to improve herself. When she was in high school, it had been effortless to get straight A's, and she had been on the soccer team, the choir, and the youth chapter of the Red Cross, so it had never occurred to her that she wouldn't get to continue doing all those things when she was in college.

But then she arrived at Stanford, and suddenly, she wasn't always the smartest in the room. In fact, freshman year, she was at the bottom of almost all her classes. The intramural soccer league was full of students who weren't quite Major League Soccer caliber (those players were on Stanford's actual NCAA

Division I soccer team), but nevertheless, the intramural players were echelons better than Erin, and she couldn't keep up. She auditioned for five a cappella groups and didn't get a call back from a single one. And even the volunteer organizations were intimidating, because the students there were launching international efforts rather than just teaching people how to perform basic CPR.

Impostor syndrome hovered over her, threatening. It had settled deep into some of the other freshmen's bones, and it wanted Erin, too.

Yet even though she wasn't the smartest anymore, she hadn't gotten where she was by quitting. Erin was a doer.

So she'd swallowed what little pride she had left and went to the student tutoring center, where she asked for help in every single subject on her schedule. She attended every evening session with her classes' teaching assistants. Erin pushed herself hard at the intellectual blockades in her brain, past limits that impostor syndrome told her she wouldn't be able to breach.

Midway through her sophomore year, she was pulling a B-plus average, with A's in her computer science courses.

And then she read an interview of Talia in *Palo Alto Weekly*, and Erin knew she'd found her role model—a fellow doer, who was a female tech founder to boot. She researched and read everything she could about Talia, then emailed her directly and asked for a summer internship, even though Ideal Life wasn't offering one. She professed her loyalty to Talia's philosophy of always trying to improve yourself, offering up the anecdotes of her freshman and sophomore years as evidence. Erin also included a passionate essay she wrote just for this purpose, which focused on Ideal Life's mission (including footnotes to research papers that backed up the underlying neuroscience) and her desire to be a part of Talia's vision to make the world a better place, one person at a time.

Erin got the job.

Now she watched the video on her phone as @HigherVibesOnly_ began a yoga routine under the soft pink light of the sky. Then the wellness coach sat at her desk and set a timer for ten minutes to journal. Finally, after she showered, she went through her skin-care routine, applying plumping serums and moisturizers, with a luxurious, slow lymphatic massage before she ended with sunscreen.

@HigherVibesOnly_ smiled serenely at the camera. "Now I ask you, What have you done to better your morning?"

Erin nodded. She had started the dorm lounge's coffee machine (she was always the first one up; most college students were not known for waking more than ten minutes before the class or summer job they had to get to), and she'd had a cup already. It wasn't a beautifully composed cappuccino like in the video, because they didn't have a milk foamer in the dorm, but Erin would be sure to make a nicer cup for herself later in Ideal Life's office, because they were proper adults there and *did* have a high-end coffee machine.

Erin took several more meditative breaths.

A message chimed on her Omni 3Ds, breaking the spell. It was her Ideal Life Friend, whom Erin had customized as an animated avatar of the Greek goddess Athena, because she represented wisdom, strategic thinking, personal growth, and achievement. Even the goddess's voice in the tiny speakers of the Omni 3Ds sounded regal.

> Ideal Life Athena: Erin, I've sensed that your morning coffee has hit your bloodstream and is ramping up the adrenaline in your brain and body. Now would be an optimal time for your run.

Erin stood without questioning Ideal Life Athena; in fact, she'd been waiting for that notification. Some studies showed that exercising hard on caffeine and an empty stomach burned the maximum amount of calories while also pushing your muscles harder than without caffeine, so she wanted to optimize for that.

What did people do before Ideal Life? she thought. Their lives must have been so inefficient.

Of course, Erin had experienced her high school years without Ideal Life's help, because the app had been in beta then and she hadn't known it existed. Erin sighed. If she'd had it back then, maybe she wouldn't have struggled as much on arrival at Stanford, because Ideal Life Athena would have helped her prep better, like taught her how to get into "deep work" so she could dive further into advanced online computer science courses *before* she got to college, as well as pushed her harder in her fitness regimen for soccer.

"Doesn't matter," Erin said aloud to herself, shaking off the past.

She was a better version of herself now, and tomorrow, she would be even better than today.

The sky outside was sunrise pink, nearly identical to the @HigherVibesOnly_ video that Erin had just watched. Maybe she could squeeze in some yoga, too, before her run. And afterward, she could also stop by Happy Donuts and pick up a baker's dozen to bring in to work.

How lucky she was to exist at a time when women really *could* have it all!

Talia

The chilly salt breeze rustled through Talia's hair as she walked up the gravel path to Lighthouse Books, Sam's renovated white lighthouse on the rocky coast. Even in summer, you had to wear a sweater here, but it was a peaceful, rugged kind of beauty that you fell in love with, living in the Bay Area.

Sam liked to say that the sunny, touristy volleyball-strewn beaches of Los Angeles were like paperback romances, whereas Northern California's cold cliffside beaches were like literary fiction. They were both wonderful, but most people—like readers—had a strong preference. And for Talia and Sam, it was these quiet, moody beaches, with their banks of gray fog and their slate-blue waves that sometimes whispered onto the sand and other times crashed into the rock faces with a roar.

The metal door to the lighthouse creaked as she opened it, and a little wind chime further announced her arrival.

"Welcome to Lighthouse Books," an older man hollered from inside the store. "Feel free to browse and let us know if we can help you find anything!"

Talia wove her way through the labyrinth of shelves. Unlike a normal store that could line things up at more or less right angles, the lighthouse's circular walls meant the shelves here curved and meandered, such that you were pretty much surrounded by books no matter which way you turned. They were stacked high up the walls, too, with ladders that ringed the shop. Velvet armchairs nestled into every dead end of the bookish maze.

"Hey, Kenneth," Talia said, when she finally emerged and could see him behind the register. He was in his late seventies and looked like Santa Claus, if Santa only gave books as gifts. Kenneth was a fixture at Lighthouse Books and knew where every single book was located as if they were actual extensions of him. Who needed digital inventory systems, Kenneth would say, when he could find things instantaneously in his memory?

"Oh, hello, Talia. You look lovely today. But I presume you're here for Sam and not me?" Kenneth pressed his hands to his heart melodramatically, as if it had been crushed.

"You know I keep trying to take you out to lunch, but you're awfully picky."

Kenneth wrinkled his nose. "Taco Bell is not real food. When you offer me a proper lunch date, I will accept."

Talia winked. They ran through the same joke every Sunday.

"Sam is upstairs," Kenneth said.

She thanked him and started up the spiral staircase. When Sam had bought the lighthouse, the steps had been the original metal, but he'd since had them refurbished in polished cherrywood. Combined with all the armchairs, the staircase gave the tower a softer, almost cozy feel, rather than just being a big utilitarian cylinder. It was the kind of subtle, aesthetic magic that Sam was good at, like his repurposed and restyled thrift store tuxedo jacket that he'd worn to Sugiyama the other night.

She passed the second floor, which housed the nonfiction collection as well as the bookstore's office. She unhooked the PRIVATE sign and chain that blocked the stairway to the third floor and climbed up to Sam's apartment.

It took him a minute to come to the door after she knocked.

"Hey, g'morning . . . I mean, afternoon." He stepped out onto the stairwell platform and gave her a quick hug while pulling the door shut behind him. His hair was more mussed than usual, and it looked like he'd just tossed a leather jacket on over his pajama shirt and a pair of worn jeans.

"You got something—or someone—in there you don't want me to see?" Talia teased. But although her tone was light, her chest clenched. Which was strange, because she wasn't usually possessive about Sam. Maybe the repeated breakfast rewinds of her mom exhorting her to "give Sam a chance" had leaked into Talia's subconscious.

Sam's cheeks flushed. He didn't answer Talia's question, though. "I'm starving," he said instead. "Come on—let's go blow my poker winnings on Sunday Lunch."

Sam

The most beautiful Taco Bell on the planet stood at the edge of the beach in the town of Pacifica. Unlike the cookie-cutter, plaster-and-stucco drive-throughs in most cities, this Taco Bell was a wood-shingled restaurant overlooking white-crested waves—waves so tall and majestic that surfers flocked from all over the world here, despite the chilly water. In fact, there were surfboards propped outside the Taco Bell.

Anywhere else, this would have been prime real estate for a billionaire's home. But Pacifica was still an artist's and surfer's town despite being close to the wealth of San Francisco and Silicon Valley, because the ocean wind was frigid and a salt fog blanketed this part of the coast every morning and evening, rusting bicycles and buildings alike. Tech tycoons didn't want to live where their mansions and Ferraris would be slowly corroded and eaten away by the sea.

Sam and Talia had first found this Taco Bell when they were college students. They hadn't had enough money to afford Palo Alto restaurants, but they'd still wanted to get off campus, to eat something that wasn't from the dining hall. One-dollar tacos and burritos with an ocean view seemed perfect.

Later, when Talia was in grad school and after Sam had bought Lighthouse Books just ten minutes down Highway 1 from Taco Bell, they had resumed meeting here. This Taco Bell was also where Talia had come up with the concept for Ideal Life, and where she eventually decided to drop out of her PhD program to pursue the startup.

The two of them had been coming here almost every Sunday for fifteen years now (other than a short break in time when

Sam had been working at Nowhere Cat). The "Sunday Lunch" routine would have long ago fallen by the wayside, however, if Sam hadn't insisted that it was a near-sacred tradition. It was the only way he could pry Talia from her computer, and she needed someone to make her step away from work from time to time. He was pretty sure she'd live at the office if she could. (Although he saw the irony that his apartment was literally the top floor of his bookstore. But then again, Sam wasn't the workaholic. When Lighthouse Books was closed, he didn't go into the shop.)

"Hi, can I take your order?" the cashier at Taco Bell said.

"Want to go first?" Sam asked Talia. She always got the same thing.

But she squinted through her Omni 3Ds at the illuminated menu on the wall. "Um . . . no, you go ahead."

Sam cleared his throat.

She touched the glasses. "I—"

"Tal, come on. You know the rule. No tech when we have lunch." Sam generally let Talia call the shots in their friendship, but this was one thing he was a stickler for. Devices had to be put away during Sunday Lunch.

"I just . . ." She darted another glance at the menu.

"Talia. Seriously. You can make your own decisions about what to eat." Her Ideal Life Friend, Queen Elizabeth, was probably making suggestions about what to order.

It's not that Sam disliked Ideal Life as a concept. After all, his best friend was the founder. But he didn't own Omni 3Ds, and his iPhone was a basic model from the mid-2010s. After the crash and burn of Nowhere Cat, he'd just never recovered the ability to put so much faith into software and hardware.

Sam *did* believe in Talia's dedication to ethical innovation, though. He also knew that Ideal Life could be great at helping people with certain decisions, like whether to have a second pastry or go work out instead.

Still, Talia sometimes got carried away with wanting to be the best possible version of herself, even when the details didn't matter—like what she ate from Taco Bell. Honestly, it was all terrible for you. It's not like swapping a Doritos taco for a bean burrito was going to add an extra year of health to your life.

"You're right—sorry." She folded the Omni 3Ds and tucked them into her purse. "I just want what I get every time anyway." She turned to the cashier. "One beef soft taco, a side of chips and nacho cheese, and cinnamon twists, please."

Sam ordered one of the combo meals. He didn't even know what was in it, just that it was a good amount of food, and that's what he wanted. He pulled out his wallet to pay.

The cashier furrowed her brow at the twenty-dollar bill he handed over, as if she had never seen cash before.

Talia shrugged at the cashier. "He's very dedicated to his no-tech-at-lunch rule."

After paying and getting their tray of food, Sam gathered a handful of hot sauce packets, and they sat down at one of the tables next to the huge windows looking out at the ocean.

"Crazy that the waves we're looking at could be the same ones that Libby saw, huh?"

Talia frowned. "Not the same ocean. She's in the Maldives."

"Not anymore. She and Jacob are in Japan now."

"Sheesh." Talia rolled her eyes at herself. "I really ought to keep better track of my own sister. Is she still texting you photos of her favorite snack foods in each country they visit?"

Sam grinned. He and Libby had always bonded over ultra-processed junk, going all the way back to when she'd sneak into Talia's dorm room and spend long hours there with them, powering through her high school homework while Sam and Talia did problem sets. He'd known their parents weren't great about stocking their pantry, so Sam had contributed what he could by slipping Libby vending machine snacks whenever she came over.

"She sent me a picture of a can of sweet potato drink this morning," Sam said.

"A sweet potato *what*?" Talia asked.

"It was like a soda, but potato flavored. Libby said it tasted like drinking Thanksgiving candied yams. I'd show you the photo, but it's on my phone, and you know . . . no tech at Sunday Lunch."

Talia punched his arm playfully. "You're such a jerk." She reached for her food from the tray.

Sam watched, amused, as she began her routine of reconstructing what she called the perfect Taco Bell meal. First, she unwrapped the soft taco, spreading the waxed paper flat into a smoothed-out square. Then she opened up the taco itself. She took her side of chips and crumbled them evenly across the taco filling, then drizzled nacho cheese across it all. Finally, she refolded the taco.

"Satisfactory?" Sam said.

Talia took a bite and moaned. "You know this is the optimal combination of flavor, variation of texture—soft and crunchy—and cost efficiency. Definitely more than satisfactory."

Sam laughed and examined his own meal. They'd given him a Chalupa Supreme deep-fried taco, a five-layer beef burrito, a chicken soft taco, fries with nacho cheese to dip in, and a Coke.

"You sure you can afford to pay for lunch?" Talia asked between bites of her carefully constructed taco. "I mean, forty-eighth place at the tournament . . ."

He threw a packet of hot sauce at her. "Just for that, you have to buy me lunch for the next three Sundays."

Talia grinned. "Wow, if I knew I'd be punished financially, I would have rewound time while you were still at the tournament and given you another shot at that hand. Maybe you would've made a different choice. Then I wouldn't have to worry about you buying me tacos, because you would've won a bigger prize."

Sam's smile fell off his face. He'd forgotten all about that strange watch, partly because he'd just assumed that once Talia had undone the night of the Omni party, the watch thing would be over. Like, maybe it would disappear as easily and mysteriously as it had come.

He stared at her wrist. The watch was just peeking out from under the sleeve of her sweater.

"I didn't do it, Sam."

"But you thought about it. You considered rewinding time in order to change something about my life."

"Yes, but I promised you I wouldn't. And I didn't."

Sam's eyes met Talia's. She bit her lip, but she didn't look away. "I swear, Sam."

He held her gaze for a long moment. Then he shook his head. "Okay, yeah, I know you didn't. If you *had* used the watch, you would never have left it at me losing before the final table." He tried to say it like it was a joke, because he didn't want to ruin the limited time he had with Talia. But part of him knew there was some truth to it. Talia truly wanted the best for everybody—that's why she'd invented Ideal Life—and that desire certainly extended to Sam. He was, after all, her best friend.

"But you know," he said, "even if you'd used the watch, maybe I still would have made the same choice on those cards, over and over, and you would have been stuck rewinding for eternity with nothing ever changing, yet feeling like you had to keep trying, just in case the *next* time worked."

Talia laughed awkwardly. "I guess that would serve me right."

He smiled. Not quite normal, but getting there. "Yeah."

She looked out the window toward the water, and Sam took in her profile, silhouetted against the sunlight outside. It was the same face he'd fallen in love with seventeen years ago—round cheeks and small pink mouth and long, straight eyelashes that made her crazy because they refused to take a curl (she'd vented to him and Libby many times in college).

But even when Talia was a hundred years old and covered in wrinkles, he would feel the same way about her, because it wasn't really the outside that he loved. It was her intelligence and passion and the deep empathy she felt for others. And those hazel eyes lit golden from the ever-optimistic, idealistic flame that burned within.

Most people didn't have a purpose for the greater good like Talia did, and that was okay. But it was wonderful to get to bask in the secondary glow of someone who did.

She turned back toward him. "I'm sorry I even considered using the watch."

"It's okay. We're good, Tal. I know you meant well."

"You sure?"

"I'm sure."

"Okay, then I can bug you about what—or who—was in your apartment when I showed up that made you close the door so fast behind you?" Talia smirked.

Sam groaned. "If I had known where this was going, I wouldn't have agreed that we're good."

"Was it the caterer again? Is it getting serious? You've gone out with her a few times now . . ." Talia took a big bite of her taco.

Sam rubbed his hands over his face. He didn't want to talk about Kayla. Yes, they'd gone on a few dates and she'd spent the night. But it was only because he knew Talia didn't feel that way about him, so after pining for too many years, Sam had told himself it was time to stop being pathetic and move on. It didn't mean he wanted to talk about other women with Talia, though.

"Well?"

Sam sighed. "Yes, it was Kayla from the local catering shop, but no, it's not serious. And that's all I'm going to say because gentlemen don't kiss and tell. Now, I'm going to eat some of this food that has gotten cold, okay?"

Talia laughed. "You're so old-fashioned sometimes, Sam. But I love you, you big weirdo."

He threw another hot sauce packet at her. "I love you, too."

Talia

On Monday morning, Talia gawked as she stepped foot onto Omni's campus. It would've been inaccurate to call it anything less than that, because it wasn't a single structure—it was a sprawling network of twenty different buildings across acres of manicured grounds, as if the tech behemoth had grown up like mushrooms in the middle of a lush park. There were paved paths that connected everything from the main headquarters to the engineering quad, from the biotech labs to the cafeteria, and from the outdoor amphitheater to the meditation and yoga space.

"On your left!" someone said, before zooming by Talia on a skateboard.

"On your left again," another person said, this one on a bicycle.

"And one more!" a man on roller skates said, spinning and waving to Talia with a grin as he passed by.

She blinked as the Omni employees disappeared from view. Then she tapped on her Omni 3Ds, and a digital map appeared, showing her where her meeting with the executive team would be.

It was all the way on the other side of campus! The walk would take fifteen minutes, according to the map, and her meeting began in ten. No wonder the people who worked here all had wheels.

Talia hated to be late, especially to an important meeting like this. She already knew several Omni people, including Raj Banerjee and Melanie Goldschmid, but today was going to be her first time in a room with the *big* bigwigs. Raj had told her that Jack Zimmer—the CEO!—might even stop in to say hi.

She started to compose an apology message that she was on campus but a little lost.

Queen Elizabeth buzzed into view on her glasses:

Ideal Life Queen Elizabeth: Anxiety signals are spiking, and I can see from the map and your message what the conundrum is. However, sending such a note may give off the wrong first impression of you. May I suggest an alternative? The Omni campus map shows there is a Transport Hub nearby, marked on the map with the letter *T*. The closest one is T-3. You can borrow a mode of transport there.

"Thanks, Queen Elizabeth. That *is* a better idea."

Transport Hub 3 looked like a bus stop and an REI store had had a baby. The kiosk offered five different skateboards, a row of electric scooters, bikes, a maintenance station with tire pumps and other tools, a water bottle refill station, and a vending machine full of energy bars, all free of charge. The only problem was you needed to scan an employee badge to unlock any of them.

"Crap," Talia muttered. The meeting was starting in five minutes, and she should have been there already. Walking in exactly on time wasn't a great way to introduce yourself when you were the new kid on the block. Even Erin knew that as an intern; that's why she was always the first in any conference room. And yet, Talia had not budgeted enough time for herself.

Unless . . .

She glanced at her watch.

It still made the scientist part of her uncomfortable that she didn't understand how the watch worked, but she had mostly accepted that she might never know. Plus, she'd run a number of experiments by now—each using the watch in a slightly different way—and each instance had turned out fine.

So there wasn't really anything stopping Talia from using the watch now, right? Sure, it wasn't a movie night rewind, but why did she have to limit herself to trivial things? Preventing the Tinder murder had proven that she could effectively turn back time for substantive, beneficial purposes, too. And here, Talia could have a second shot at making a first impression, which was crucial.

"Just do it," she whispered to herself.

After a few deep breaths, Talia turned the crown.

The world spun dizzyingly fast around her as she reversed in time to an hour and a half before.

"Oh god." She braced her hands on her knees as the scenery around her stopped whirring. "I've got to remember to turn that knob slower." She ought to know better by now, but the urgency and importance of this meeting had distracted her.

Once her stomach stopped roiling, Talia checked her surroundings. Yep, she was back in her apartment kitchen, the morning's news opened on her phone mid-scroll, a cup of coffee half drunk.

This was where she could shave off some time. It was amazing how you could lose yourself to the infinite feed, even when you didn't care anymore about what you were reading. Was it crucial that Talia learn about the bioluminescent moss that had been discovered in Antarctica? And that she do it right now?

No, but she recognized it for what it probably was—allowing yourself to be subsumed by the endless scroll was a way of procrastinating or avoiding something more concrete that required actual effort. Like facing your nerves about an important meeting and getting out the door to attend it.

Talia turned off the news feed, ordered a self-driving car to pick her up, and ran to the bathroom to brush the coffee breath out of her mouth before it arrived. Exactly six minutes later, she hurried downstairs and slipped into the back seat of the car. It deposited her at the entrance of Omni's campus seventeen minutes later.

She would have plenty of time to spare to get to her meeting.

All guests had to register at Omni Security. As she filled in her information (again) on a tablet at Reception, Talia asked, "I noticed the campus here is huge. And I heard there were Transport Hubs where you could borrow scooters and stuff. Are they available to visitors, too?"

"Oh, sure," the receptionist said. "I'll just need you to sign an extra liability waiver and then I can get you a temporary badge to access the hubs." Another form appeared on the tablet in front of Talia. "Basically, it says that if you get in an accident, you won't sue Omni. And if you fail to return your transport, then you'll be charged the full market value for it."

"I can't imagine I'm going to jet away on an electric scooter and try to get on the freeway with it," she joked as she signed.

The receptionist sat there, stone-faced. "You'd be surprised what people do."

With that taken care of, Talia put on the lanyard that labeled her as a visitor and took the temporary access badge back to T-3.

As she perused the offerings, a man in his early twenties rolled up almost silently on a Segway and parked it at the end of the kiosk, scanning his badge to check it back in to the hub.

"Whoa . . . I didn't know Segways still existed," Talia said as she walked over to examine it. It was goofy looking, like someone had taken a lectern or podium, encased it in metal, and stuck two enormous tires on it. She still remembered when Segways had been introduced to the world as the future of transportation. Instead, only mall cops ended up using them. Once, she'd witnessed the somewhat comical pursuit of a shoplifter at Valley Fair mall. The thief sprinted easily in and out of the crowds while the hapless police officer tried to chase him on his giant motorized podium.

Now, though, the Omni employee stroked the Segway as if it were a beloved pet. "Yeah, we have something like a hundred Segways here. You know how there are sanctuaries where racehorses or other animals go to retire? They get to live out their days roaming across pastures and woods? Well, the Omni campus is kind of like a retirement sanctuary for Segways." He laughed. "You want to give it a whirl?"

"I've always wondered what riding one would be like."

"It's all yours." He patted the Segway once more, as if saying, *Good job, buddy*, before he jogged off into the nearest building.

What an eccentric place, Talia thought. And then she realized, this would soon be *her* eccentric place, once Omni closed their acquisition of Ideal Life. That was a big part of why she was here today—to get introduced to her future bosses.

She scanned her badge on the Segway's charging station and it clicked as it unlocked. Talia climbed on to figure out how to drive the thing.

It surged backward from its parking spot—"Holy shit!"—and Talia went flying. She landed hard on her face on the cement path, hands and knees scraped and bleeding, her right cheek, too.

A couple of Omni employees started hurrying toward her. From the other direction on the walkway, another one rushed over on his skateboard.

"Are you okay?"

"I'm calling on-site medical services," a woman said.

"No, it's all right. I'm fi—" Talia started to say.

But the woman was already issuing the request via voice command on her Omni 3Ds.

Talia's own Omni 3Ds were lying a few yards away on the ground. This, at least, was a relief. She didn't want to know what Ideal Life Queen Elizabeth would say about what had just happened.

In the meantime, a campus surveillance drone had flown over and begun shooting video of Talia probably to document it for Omni Security to make sure she didn't try to sue them, despite the liability waiver.

Would this make her late to the meeting? Knowing how corporate legal departments worked, there would probably be more paperwork to fill out. And they would probably make a fuss with a medical exam to make sure there really was nothing wrong with Talia that she could later try to use against them, regardless of all the liability waivers.

Nope. I am not *going to deal with all that.* Talia reached for her watch and whirled the crown backward.

"Aw, fuck!" Talia ran over to her kitchen sink and threw up. In her haste to rewind out of that embarrassing Segway scene, she'd forgotten *again* to turn the watch knob slowly, and going backward at hyperspeed was like jolting her stomach way past zero g.

Once she rinsed out her mouth and her stomach settled, Talia checked the time. Back to where she'd last restarted. Good.

She ordered another self-driving car and brushed her teeth. On her way to the Omni campus, she watched a Segway-driving tutorial on her Omni 3Ds. By the time she arrived on campus, she understood how the damn things worked.

But ugh, did she really have to go through signing in at Reception for the third time?

Wait. What if I turn the watch crown forward? It hadn't worked on the night of the acquisition celebration, but maybe that was because Talia had already been at the future-most moment that she'd lived through up to that point. But now, she had *already* lived past this current moment, and she didn't need to change the next few minutes.

Tentatively and slowly, she turned the knob on her watch.

The world around her went a little blurry, like she was on fast-forward but not *too* fast. Talia grinned.

She kept the pressure on the crown until she reached T-3 and the Omni employee petting the Segway goodbye. She released her watch as he jogged away into the building.

"All right, let's try this again."

This time, Talia managed to ease the Segway out of its station gently. She experimented with leaning forward, then slightly to the left, then right, to test out its supposedly "intuitive" steering.

It worked.

Soon, she was whirring along the pathways toward the headquarters, which sat in the middle of the campus. The breeze rippled through her hair as she increased speed, and she almost whooped out loud as she maneuvered the Segway all over the map. It drove so smoothly, the controls incredibly responsive to a simple lean this way or that. Amazing!

Talia had been wrong—this wasn't a motorized podium. It was more like she'd suddenly grown wheels of her own and they were a part of her. What a shame Segways hadn't been more popular! She understood now why that Omni employee had petted it like a favorite horse. When she worked here in the future, she, too, would take the Segways out for a ride every day.

Alas, she did have a meeting to attend. Talia was tempted to play hooky and continue her joyride and just rewind later to undo it. But she'd never once ditched a day of school—even when she called in a sick day, she always ended up going to school anyway because she was too responsible and too afraid to fall behind in class—so she docked at Transport Hub 7 outside the main headquarters building, whispered a thank-you to her Segway, and went inside.

After the meeting, Talia did a postmortem on her performance.

She'd dopily said her name over and over as she shook hands with the two dozen people in the room—"Hi, I'm Talia Morgan. I'm Talia Morgan. I'm Talia Morgan."

She'd been too quiet during the first hour, which left her feeling more like a little girl than a CEO.

And then Jack Zimmer, Omni's founder and CEO, had come

in during the second hour, and Talia had stood up like an idiot, as if he were the king and all his subjects were expected to rise. Everyone else, of course, had remained seated. She'd bumbled then and forgotten her own name when he approached her. Which was even more stupid, given that she'd repeated "Talia Morgan" a couple thousand times not long before.

Ideal Life Queen Elizabeth: Next time, perhaps you could role-play ahead of an important meeting to be better prepared for performance under unfamiliar and stressful situations.

"Next time," Talia said, "is right now."

She rewound her watch—not too quickly—and did the meeting again.

Talia did not repeat her name each time she was introduced to another Omni executive.

She piped up with incredibly insightful comments during the first hour. (One exec said Talia was so sharp she was almost prescient.)

And when Jack Zimmer came in, she did not rise or expect heralds to start playing "God Save the King." Instead, she smiled professionally and only stood when he came over to shake her hand. She did so as an equal—one confident, self-possessed CEO to another.

Talia: Nailed it.

Sam: Congrats! I knew you would.

Talia: I admit that I gave myself a redo.

Sam: Ah.

Talia: But it still counts anyway, right?

Sam:

Talia: I mean, it's like retaking a test. It's the second better score that gets recorded for posterity.

Sam:

Talia: Hello?

Sam: Just . . .

Talia: Just what?

Sam: Don't overuse it, okay, Tal? We don't really know what the consequences of using it are, long term. I know you always want to improve yourself, but I worry.

Talia: Trust me, I'm fine, Sam. It's only a tool, and I've got it under control.

Talia

Talia overslept the next morning, which wasn't like her. She was usually up at six to do a hyperefficient dumbbell workout on an app she liked before checking email, showering, and catching up on news while drinking a smoothie (macrobalanced, of course, for the optimal combination of protein, carbohydrates, and healthy fats).

But she'd been more tired than usual lately; it was probably just because there was so much going on with acquisition due diligence and startup life in general.

Ideal Life Queen Elizabeth: Perhaps you ought to set *two* alarms for tomorrow morning.

She rolled her eyes. "Dismiss." Queen Elizabeth disappeared.

The buzz in the Ideal Life office was palpable from the moment Talia walked in. Even though the company spanned three floors, it seemed like all the employees were gathered in the common area on the fourth.

"What's going on?" she asked.

Rachel, one of the engineers, said, "BiomeLabs made a huge announcement this morning, and their stock quintupled as soon as the market opened!"

"No way." BiomeLabs occupied the offices above Ideal Life, on the fifth through eighth floors of the building. They were a tech company focused on the intersection of artificial intelligence and scientific research of the human gut microbiome. Talia and a lot of Ideal Life's employees were friends with the BiomeLabs teams, since they shared the same rooftop where everyone liked to eat lunch. (Unlike where Sam lived on the coast, Palo Alto was warm and sunny most days.)

Another engineer, Michael, said, "My buddy Ernest just turned into a millionaire overnight!"

"I think half the employees there had enough stock options that they're millionaires now," Rachel said. "It's so awesome."

Someone on the other side of the common area said, "I should've bought BiomeLabs stock when it was still cheap." Everyone, including Talia, laughed.

But then she realized she *could* buy BiomeLabs stock cheap. She could rewind to yesterday.

To be clear, Talia wasn't being greedy. Sure, on paper, she was about to sell Ideal Life to Omni for $100 million. But most of that was actually going to the venture capital firms, whose investments had been crucial for keeping the startup alive in the early days. The small percentage of Ideal Life that Talia still owned would mostly be converted into Omni stock options, and per the postmerger employment agreement, those options wouldn't vest for four years.

Put another way, Talia wasn't getting much money from the Ideal Life acquisition anytime soon, and if she didn't continue to work for Omni for four years afterward, she'd lose the Omni stock options and never be able to sell them to cash out. Those kinds of employment agreements were nicknamed "golden handcuffs" for a reason.

Erin appeared with a box of donuts. Talia took a glazed one gratefully; she hadn't eaten breakfast this morning because she'd woken up late.

"Nanobots!" Erin said. "I can hardly believe it."

"Huh?"

"BiomeLabs' announcement," Erin said. "Their new product is *nanobots*!"

Talia's eyes widened. "I thought microscopic robots were still a futuristic pipe dream."

"Apparently not. But they did a hell of a job keeping it under wraps until the big reveal, didn't they? Even *Your Gossipy Tech BFF* missed it."

The Segovia twins swept into the room. Jonathan held up his phone while Jody said, "Well, *Your Gossipy Tech BFF* might've missed the scoop, but they've still got something to say, and we're mentioned! New article just posted!"

Talia and half the room scrambled for their phones or started reading on their Omni 3Ds.

The Secret to Silicon Valley Success: High-End Sashimi?

Palo Alto, CA—Damn, what is in the sake in the Sugiyama building? Not too long ago, Ideal Life announced that Omni was buying them for a cool $100 million, and now their upstairs neighbor, BiomeLabs, has blown up the tech market with the announcement of viable nanobots.

If anyone could have kept that development mum, though, it's BiomeLabs' CEO, Eleanor Davies. We're not denying she's a brilliant scientist, but that woman's got less emotion than an AI chatbot. One of the most competitive founders in Silicon Valley, everyone knows that if Eleanor Davies sets her scope on you, you are well and truly fucked—and you won't even see the missile coming.

Now, you may be asking, did BiomeLabs violate SEC disclosure rules by not revealing their nanobot tech earlier?

Dear silly reader, how could you think that Davies could be so . . . unstrategic?

Here's the timeline and details we uncovered that kept BiomeLabs within SEC reporting requirements but still allowed them to surprise everyone:

In BiomeLabs' last quarterly earnings call—two months and twenty days ago—their head of research and development mentioned "molecular-scale engineering" without specifying applications.

This was possible because:

(1) Davies had previously created a separately funded "moonshot" division not subject to the same disclosure requirements as BiomeLabs, and

(2) regardless of corporate structure, she made sure the "molecular-scale engineering" fell under strategic intellectual property protections that limited how much BiomeLabs needed to share.

Then, just a few days after that quarterly earnings call, Davies quietly hired all the scientists from a small private research firm and licensed key technology from them. Because this wasn't an actual acquisition—it was a perfectly legal "acqui-hire" that got around government scrutiny—BiomeLabs didn't have to announce anything, while also securing the necessary brainpower and tech to compress a three- to five-year timeline on their secret nanobots to "right now."

And voila.

Perhaps Davies really is a highly tuned humanoid robot with killer business instincts.

Or maybe that Palo Alto sushi is the secret fuel for startup breakthroughs.

Let us know what you think in the comments. In the meantime, we're going to try to book ourselves a table at Sugiyama.

Jody helped herself to a donut from Erin's box. "It's wild. I hear the nanobots are ingested via a pill. Then they go into your gut and get a close-up view of the bacterial population there—both the good bacteria and the bad."

"BiomeLabs will be able to use that information to tailor nutrition to the specific needs of each person's body," Erin said. "They'd probably recommend we don't eat donuts."

"Yeah, but holy shit," Talia said. "This is going to revolutionize health care." Studies in recent years had already shown links between gut microbiome health and everything from the immune system to Alzheimer's to depression. If BiomeLabs could help change the bacterial makeup of the digestive system to maximize health . . . no wonder their stock had shot up like that.

"If you'll excuse me." Talia wove her way through the common area to her office, where she shut the door. She immediately called Sam.

"Hey, look at you, calling without prescheduling a time," he said when he answered.

"Oh, hush," Talia said. "I have something important I have to talk to you about."

"Go for it. I'm just arranging the display of new releases." Tuesdays were always the day that new books came out. The publishers sent their boxes a week or two in advance, and on Tuesdays, Sam would open them and set the books up in front of the store. Unveiling new releases was a special treat he reserved for himself, and Kenneth was happy to cede it, since it meant he got to sleep in late on those mornings.

Talia sat behind her desk. "Okay, so you know BiomeLabs?"

"The company above you that IPO-ed last year with disappointing results?"

"Yep. Well, get this—they've been in stealth R-and-D mode, but now that research and development has been revealed: They have nanobots."

"*What*?" The sound of a stack of books crashing echoed through the phone's speaker.

"Uh, you okay over there, Sam?"

"Forget what's going on here. They actually made nanobots? That *work*? Hold on—I'm looking this up."

Talia fired up her computer and did the same.

"Oh my fucking god . . ." Sam said, half to himself.

"Incredible, right?" Talia asked.

"That's an understatement. I thought this technology was still a decade or more away."

"So did everyone else. And BiomeLabs' stock has already shot up this morning. They're worth five times more today than they were yesterday. Which brings me to the reason I'm calling you."

"What does that have to do with— Oh."

"Yes. Exactly that, Sam."

"You want to rewind and buy their stock."

"It's okay, isn't it?" Talia stood up and started to pace the length of her office. "I mean, it's not insider trading, right? Because the laws only cover stock trades taken *before*, like if the CEO of BiomeLabs acted on this information *before* the announcement was public. Whereas I'm actually buying the stock *after*."

"Er, sort of after," Sam said. "Because you're in the after *now*, but you're going to rewind to the *before*."

"Yeah, but the law wasn't made to cover that scenario, because it's impossible."

Sam made a noncommittal noise.

"Also," Talia said, "I'm not an officer of BiomeLabs, so it can't be insider trading if I'm not an insider."

"I don't know, Tal. Just because it's possible doesn't mean it's ethical."

But it wasn't like she was taking today's winning lotto numbers and then going back to buy a ticket. There was something icky about that, something closer to the line of cheating. Buying BiomeLabs stock, though, didn't seem bad. It wasn't hundreds of millions of dollars. It was only bending the rules a little.

Talia frowned as she flopped onto the purple couch in her office. "I'm not hurting anyone. Think of it this way—what if yesterday I had just happened to buy BiomeLabs stock without knowing anything. It would've just been a normal stock market transaction."

Sam sighed. She could hear the sound of books being stacked

on top of one another, the quiet thump of hardcover on hardcover.

"You could buy some stock, too?" Talia said. "I could go back and tell you to invest your recent poker winnings."

"No, thanks."

"Why not? Six thousand dollars—minus the few bucks you spent at Taco Bell—would turn into thirty grand today. You could relax a little about the bookstore's bills."

"I don't know . . ."

"How about this? I'll rewind and talk to Past Sam about it. And if Past You is also unsure, then I'll leave you out of it."

He laughed at that. "Why do you think that the me from twenty-four hours ago is going to think any differently? Besides, aren't you supposed to be on Omni's campus yesterday?"

Crap. Talia had forgotten about that. As much fun as she'd had on the Segway and with impressing the Omni execs, she didn't really feel like redoing that all again, just so she could put in a stock trade in the middle of it.

She couldn't just rewind to yesterday afternoon when the meeting was over, either, because the stock market would already be closed.

Was having to go through the long Omni meeting worth it?

Talia thought of her student loans. College hadn't been cheap, and she'd scraped her way through grad school on teaching assistant stipends.

So yes, it was worth it.

"Happy book-release day, Sam. I'll talk to you yesterday."

She called Sam from the Segway, on the way to the Omni meeting.

But Future Him had been right; Past Sam was still wary of buying BiomeLabs stock. He couldn't put his finger on why he didn't want to do it, but it just didn't sit right with him.

Talia had come this far, though, so she wasn't going to miss the opportunity.

She hung up with him, then invested all $5,000 in her savings account in BiomeLabs.

Maybe she could have fast-forwarded through the Omni meeting and it would have stayed the same. But she was nervous about it—this wasn't just fast-tracking check-in at the reception desk—and she decided not to risk it.

So Talia went to the meeting and nailed it again. In fact, this time she was even wittier, and their CEO, Jack Zimmer, and the rest of their executive team liked her even more than the previous yesterday. "I'm very impressed with your business acumen," Jack had said. "It's uncanny—some of the ideas you suggested matched mine before I could even voice them!"

The rest of yesterday had been inconsequential enough that Talia felt it was okay to forward through it. It took a while, since she had learned not to turn the watch crown too fast.

But that also meant that Talia felt like she had spent a lot of time patiently rewinding twenty-four hours to buy BiomeLabs stock, then getting herself back where she belonged twenty-four hours later.

What a disconcerting sensation, to be exhausted by time passing personally for *you*, while no time at all had passed for anyone else.

This seemed like a physics problem for Sam: How do you keep track of the time you spend *moving* through time?

If time is known as the fourth dimension, would the time inside of time be a fifth dimension? Or something else even more inexplicable?

Regardless, here Talia was again, back on the purple couch in her office, worn out before her new day began.

She stumbled over to her computer; she was dizzy, an after-effect of going backward and forward in such a short span, even though she'd done it slowly.

Talia logged into her investment account, and there it was—BiomeLabs stock, worth five times as much as she'd bought it for yesterday.

$25,000.

Her smile was so bright satellites probably picked up on it from outer space.

Sam

In the early afternoon, Sam sat at the computer in his "office" on the second floor of the lighthouse, a small area separated from the nonfiction bookshelves by a simple folding screen with a painted scene of the nearby Fitzgerald Marine Reserve tide pools.

A video call rang, but he'd been expecting it, of course. His monthly calls with his parents were always scheduled, because the time difference and the fact that Sam didn't like to carry around his phone would otherwise make it impossible to reach each other predictably.

Jenny and Roger called in the wee hours of the morning in Taiwan, in that sliver of time between the first batch of pineapple cakes coming out of the oven and the bakeries opening. Even though they had franchisees running the individual shops now, Jenny and Roger still made sure to be physically in one of the bakeries every single day; with fourteen stores across the island, that meant they maintained a two-week circuit of daily travel. It was tiring, but it was their way to ensure that the quality of their pastries and their stores met the high bar they'd set for Sunshine Cakes.

"Good morning, Sammy!" Jenny's radiance carried even through a computer screen, her energy so potent that it wasn't diluted at all by having to traverse through fiber-optic cables across the Pacific Ocean. While Roger was the quiet financial brains behind the bakery chain, it had been Jenny's recipe and her personality that inspired the loyalty of the patrons of Sunshine Cakes. (This was also the origin of their logo—two cartoon pineapples holding hands, one wearing a chef's hat, the other wearing glasses, both of them smiling.)

"Good morning, Mom. Good morning, Dad," Sam said self-consciously. His Taiwanese was stiff and too formal, always reflecting the fact that he only knew how to speak the language from the perspective of an eight-year-old talking to his parents. He was sure that Jenny and Roger didn't care, but Sam always felt awkward nonetheless. It was such an unsettling feeling to be a fully grown, intelligent adult but unable to communicate properly.

When he was younger, he'd wondered how his parents could have sent him away. If you loved your son, how could you willingly part with him? Even sending him to boarding school in the same country would have seemed a cruelty, let alone across the ocean to live with a distant relative, rarely to see your child again.

But when Sam went to college and studied East Asian philosophy, he started to understand a little better. There was a fierce self-sacrificing element in filial relationships in Taiwanese culture; parents would give literally everything to their kids to make better lives for them, even if it meant having to give up their only child to another country to be raised by someone else, to never hold him in their own arms. As Sam met other Taiwanese American students at Stanford, he realized he was far from the only one who'd been sent to foreign shores alone.

"How are you? How is bookstore?" Jenny asked. She liked practicing her English on Sam. He suspected it was also her gentle way of making sure he could understand her; she would never embarrass him by subjecting him to a conversation that exposed his linguistic insufficiencies.

"The bookstore is good," Sam said, returning the favor in Taiwanese but wishing his vocabulary encompassed more than basic adjectives.

"No big earthquakes?" His parents had been worried when he chose Stanford years ago, having sent him away from Taiwan to Mississippi for fear of earthquakes, only to have him end up back in an earthquake zone. It had been nearly two decades, however, and their fears had slowly been allayed. She still asked, though.

"No big earthquakes," Sam said. "How are the bakeries? What city are you in today?"

"We are in south, in Kaohsiung," Roger said, also in English like Jenny. "Very hot today."

She laughed. "So hot, inside bakery and outside on street. We think both *too* hot. We going to retire!"

Sam smiled. "You like to work. You will not retire."

"No joking," Roger said. "Mom is serious. We retire. We sell bakeries." He shrugged, like there was nothing he could do once his wife made a decision, which, to be honest, was probably true.

"No way," Sam said in English, before catching himself and switching back to Taiwanese. Except he didn't know how to express that sentiment, so he just said, "You are selling Sunshine Cakes?"

Jenny grinned and patted Roger's shoulder. "Dad is smart businessman. He find very good deal. We sell to 85°C Bakery."

"Wow." Even Sam knew 85°C. They were so popular they'd expanded overseas, including to the Bay Area. "That is very good. I am very happy for you!"

Internally, he sighed at how completely inadequate of a congratulations this was, but they were the best words his brain could find. He knew there must be other phrases in there somewhere, but they were buried deep, in the way that children didn't remember much of what happened to them when they were very young, even if the memories were happy.

"Okay," Roger said. "We sell Sunshine Cakes today. Then we come visit you next week."

"Wait, what?" Sam blinked at the computer. "You're literally signing the papers and selling the bakeries today? And then you're coming to the Bay Area *next week*?" The surprise made all this come out in English. "Where are you going to stay?"

(Taiwanese parents usually expected to be put up in their kids' homes, but Sam lived in a tiny studio apartment atop a lighthouse.)

But Jenny smiled, apparently having caught most of it despite their language barrier. "You no worry. We stay very nice hotel near you. I see it on YouTube. And we okay use Uber. Taiwanese very good using phones."

That was true. The country seemed to run on QR codes and apps. Even senior citizens had no problems doing bank transactions via mobile or organizing dinners with their friends on group chats. Sam's parents were probably more adept with their phones than he was.

"Okay, um, I . . . vacation from bookstore," he fumbled as he switched languages again.

"No, no," Roger said. "We only stay one week. We want see your normal life."

"Then we go travel, whole world!" Jenny said, her excitement again beaming through the screen. "We work whole life, no leave Taiwan. Now we sell bakeries, we going to enjoy retire."

"Your mom have big plans. She watch so many YouTube."

Sam laughed. "Okay, then. I will see you soon."

"Okay, bye-bye!" Jenny said, while Roger waved.

This was the longest stretch that Sam would spend with his parents since he visited Taiwan five years ago. Short monthly phone calls were one thing, but an entire week was another. As family, they loved each other by default. But in reality, they didn't know each other beyond surface-level details.

Sometimes, he wondered what his life would have been like if he had stayed in Taiwan and never moved to the States. Would he be stepping up to take over Sunshine Cakes now? Certainly he would know Jenny and Roger better, be closer. What would it have been like to grow up with an actual family?

But then he took in the lighthouse around him, the nonfiction shelves in view beyond his folding screen, and the jovial sound of Kenneth's voice echoing up the curved stairwell as he greeted a new customer to the store.

Sam smiled. He really liked the life he had. It wasn't perfect, but it was one he had carved out for himself.

He just had to figure out how to show his parents—how to really communicate to them—that their decision to send him to the United States had worked out, and that they had done right.

Sam hoped that they would be proud.

Libby

It had been a week since Libby found out she was pregnant, and she and Jacob hadn't been able to resolve what they were going to do with their lives. It's not that she was hard-and-fast on *not* having their baby in their content. It was that she didn't know what would happen if she *didn't* think about the possibility that their baby would grow up and be upset that her entire life had been put on display, that her parents had made that choice for her without knowing what kind of person she would end up being and how the adult version of her might care.

Libby knew, too, that Jacob would never use their baby as a prop. She wished she'd never said that out loud, because it had wounded him, the idea that she would ever think him capable of using their child as a strategic way to "level up" their careers. He was already so in love with their little bean and sang to Libby's belly every morning when they woke up and every night before they fell asleep.

Being a mother was hard, and Libby hadn't really even gotten started yet! It actually helped her see her own parents in a new light. Maybe Vera and Dave had partied so hard with their high school friends not only because they needed to let off steam, but also because clinging to that fragment of the past was a way to hold on to a time in their lives when things were simpler, not complicated by the massive responsibility of raising children.

Still, Libby needed to figure out what to do next. There had been an uncomfortable tension between her and Jacob all week, even as they wrapped up work in the Maldives and flew to Japan to begin their next gig for a food tour company. It hadn't helped that the first shoot they'd had to do in Tokyo was a sushi-making class, and since Libby didn't want anyone to know that she was pregnant, she'd needed to fake-eat the raw fish for the video and then lie to their hosts that she wasn't hungry. Jacob had had to consume both their portions of sushi so they didn't insult their chefs' hospitality.

So while Jacob was out shooting a promo for "The Ultimate Sumo Experience" tour, which included a wrestling lesson followed by *chanko nabe*, the heavy stew eaten by sumo wrestlers for weight gain, Libby called Talia. Maybe her sister, being in tech, would have another perspective on kids' online privacy that could help Libby decide what to do.

"Libby! Hi, wow, what a surprise!" The video camera was on, and Talia was in her apartment, hopping around in a silk blouse and skirt while trying to pull on sheer tights. "Where in the world are you right now?"

"Tokyo," Libby said. "But what the hell is going on over there? Is that really you? I don't know that I've seen you dressed up since, what, your high school graduation?"

Talia stuck out her tongue. "Ha ha, very funny."

"Okay, but seriously. You're in a skirt. And tights. Where are you goi— Oh my god, do you have a date? Please, please tell me the answer is yes. I won't believe it, because you're always too busy working and you don't have time to date, but I *want* to believe it."

Talia made a face at the tights she was still struggling with, then yanked them off and threw them over her shoulder onto her bed. "Whose idea was it to make tights trendy again?" She laughed. "But yes, I really do have a date tonight. Well, I'm going to one of those singles mixers, where we all mill around and possibly meet our soulmate but mostly just make the owners of the bar rich from all the overpriced drinks we buy."

Libby smiled. "I'm happy you're putting yourself out there, Sis."

"Thank you! But that's not why you called."

"No . . . I wanted to pick your brain about something."

"Of course!"

But as Libby watched Talia running around her apartment, looking for shoes and her purse and earrings, she knew this wasn't the right moment for the conversation. She wanted to enjoy telling her sister she was going to be an aunt. She wanted to have enough time to debate the problem of balancing her child's privacy with the business that she and Jacob had built. And she didn't want to weigh down Talia's excitement at finally going out.

"You know what? Let's schedule a time to chat," Libby said.

"Oh, no, I'm sorry," Talia said, stopping her nonstop movement to stand right in front of the camera. "Please, I'm all ears."

"No, honestly, don't worry about it. You go have fun! We'll catch up another day—soon."

"Are you sure?" Talia asked.

Libby gave her sister her best smile, the kind she'd practiced and perfected over years of photo shoots.

Was it disingenuous if you were genuinely faking for the other person's best interests?

Talia

Silicon Valley had a thing for naming places after trees—even "Palo Alto" meant "tall tree"—and the Manzanita & Oak was no exception.

On its face, it was an upscale hotel, but everyone knew the sleek glass-and-wood building was really a watering hole for the engineers, software programmers, and AI enthusiasts of the Valley looking to network.

Tonight, though, it was home to the Techie Singles Mixer, a dating event for people just like Talia who didn't want to go to Madera. (Madera—which meant wood—was a restaurant and bar inside another tree-named hotel, Rosewood Sand Hill, and it had a reputation for women on the hunt for wealthy, divorced venture capitalists looking to acquire trophy wife number three or four. That was definitely not Talia's scene.)

Pushing her Omni 3Ds back up her nose, she walked into the Manzanita & Oak's interior courtyard, a green, leafy sanctuary with teak chaise longues for relaxing in and a small, burbling waterfall surrounded by orchids growing out of the stone. A jazz quartet played in the far corner under a canopy of palm trees, and servers flitted in and out of the mingling crowd, carrying trays of hors d'oeuvres—mini cones filled with beet tartare, duck spring rolls, and bite-size crab cakes topped with a dollop of crème fraiche and a snip of chive.

A perky woman at a table at the entry greeted Talia. "Are you here for the Techie Singles Mixer?"

"Yes. Talia Morgan."

The woman checked for her name on her laptop, nodded, and handed over an electronic name tag with Talia's name preprogrammed onto it. The background changed colors every two seconds.

"You can customize it if you want. Just scan that QR code for instructions." She pointed to another table just a few feet away, where a cluster of new arrivals were paying no attention to each other and were instead intently focused on tailoring their name tags just so. Talia laughed. It was so typical of her industry that even at an event designed to meet other people, their priority was still the technology.

But hey, Talia was one of them, too, so she shuffled over to the name tag programming table and took a few minutes to get hers the way she wanted it. First impressions mattered, and in a crowd like this, it didn't say great things about you if you let your name tag remain on the generic default. (Erin had been right that people really, really loved the ability to personalize their accessories.)

After changing her name tag from the obnoxious two-second color cascade to her favorite color, Ideal Life's particular shade of purple, Talia took a deep breath and plunged into the crowd.

As predicted, the ratio in the Manzanita & Oak's courtyard was heavily gender-skewed in Talia's favor. In Silicon Valley, it was estimated that there were 40 percent more single heterosexual men than single women. Before she could even grab a crab cake for herself, Talia was approached by a red-haired man with what could only be described as a very earnest, open face.

"Hey, Talia," he said, reading her name tag. "I'm Colin. I'm thirty-seven years old, I work in sales for Future Rapidity Software, I have three young boys who are sweet, chaotic hellions, and I'm looking for a career woman who is smart and wants a family but maybe doesn't have time to start her own and therefore would be interested in my children as a 'quick start.'" He chortled at his joke.

Yes, chortled.

"Oh, um, wow," Talia said. "That's . . . a lot of information."

Colin shrugged and chortled again. "Well, I find that the introduction part of these events is the most awkward, so why not tear it off like a Band-Aid and get it out of the way?"

Talia chewed on her lip. Even though she already knew Colin wasn't going to be a match—his kids were probably lovely, but she was not looking to dive straight into the deep end of the pool when it came to having a family—he did have a point about not wasting time at a mixer like this.

Finding the right person was a numbers game, Talia figured. In theory, what you needed to do was go on as many first dates as possible and then cut them off and never do a second date if the first one wasn't promising. In the past, though, she hadn't had the luxury of time to run this experiment properly.

But now, with the watch on her wrist, she did. That's why she'd chosen the mixer—there was a high density of single men in one location, and if she didn't like one of them, she wouldn't have to waste time. She could cut it short and rewind and use those minutes on someone else.

"It was really nice to meet you, Colin," she said.

He wrinkled his brow, confused by the abrupt end of their conversation.

Okay, she could have been smoother, but it was fine. She was about to rewind, and he wouldn't remember any of this anyway. It will have never happened.

"Good luck with finding a brilliant stepmom for your boys," she said, and she really did mean it. Then Talia turned the crown on her watch.

In reverse, Colin's face went from confused to awkward to optimistic, and then he was walking backward away from her, she was un-reaching for the crab cake she never got, and then Talia was again at the edge of the name tag table.

She gave herself a few seconds to find her bearings.

One—the room stopped wobbling as her vision readjusted.

Two—she dismissed Ideal Life Queen Elizabeth, who was tutting over Talia's brief disorientation and corresponding cortisol spike.

Three—memories of the Tinder murder came back, and Talia decided to take off the glasses for the night. Maybe it was better if she interacted with these dates on her own. Not that there was anything wrong with Ideal Life, but . . . She stuffed her Omni 3Ds into her purse.

Then she stepped once more into the crowd.

But this time, as Colin approached, Talia turned left and power walked directly to the nearest server.

"Crab cake?" he offered.

"Why, yes, thank you." She actually took two, just in case she got sidelined again before she could acquire more.

And indeed, just as she polished off the second delicious bite, a man in the typical Silicon Valley "dressed up" outfit of a blazer over a T-shirt and jeans came up to her.

Except he had a huge food stain on the front of his shirt, and it wasn't like he'd accidentally dropped an hors d'oeuvre on himself. More like he'd spilled a strawberry milkshake on it several days ago but hadn't bothered to change yet.

Talia braced herself, but a slim, compact man in a clean button-down and khakis swooped in, linked his arm through hers, and steered her away.

"Thought I'd save you the trouble," he said in a slight German accent once they were a safe distance away from Milkshake Stain Guy.

"Thanks, Oskar," she said, reading his name tag. It alternated between his name and a quote that streamed across the electronic surface: "Eternity resembles a wheel that has neither beginning nor end"—Hildegard von Bingen.

"Interesting quote," Talia said.

"Ah, yes," Oskar said. "'Die Ewigkeit gleicht einem Rad, das weder Anfang noch Ende hat.' One of my favorite lines from a German abbess in the twelfth century. It encapsulates the profound philosophical concept of the nature of eternity in such a concise and poetic manner, do you not agree?"

"Hmm," Talia said. Whether she agreed or not wasn't the right question. A better one was, Could you imagine spending the rest of your life with a man so pretentious he opened conversations like this?

"It was nice to meet you, Oskar. Thanks for sparing me from Milkshake Stain Guy."

Like too-earnest Colin, Oskar furrowed his brow at Talia's sudden end to their conversation. She wiggled her fingers in farewell, then turned the watch knob.

Okay, back at the side table. Name tag set. Talia stepped into the breach once more, avoided Colin of the sweet hellion sons, snagged a couple of crab cakes—still delicious—dodged Milkshake Guy, thereby avoiding Oskar coming to rescue her, and found herself at the bar next to a tall, broad-shouldered man in a fitted white T-shirt (very bright and clean) and pressed, dark jeans. She tried not to stare at his impressive biceps and pecs—"eyes up here" applied equally to men as to women!—and focused on his face. Which was also impressively chiseled.

Talia swallowed hard and tried to find words.

He flashed incredibly straight teeth.

Too straight. Veneers?

"Hey," he said, extending his hand. "I'm Thaddeus."

Talia shook his hand, still not sure what to say to someone this beautiful.

But also, he seemed a little young. Not that there was an age minimum to attend this mixer. But Talia was thirty-five, and Thaddeus was . . . ?

"So, Talia," he said, leaning against the bar. "Tell me something fascinating about yourself or that you've recently learned."

She startled a little. Not in a bad way, but she had expected some small talk first. Although, she supposed, it was a nice change to have someone ask about her, rather than blurt out everything about themselves—or a pretentious quote—first.

"Something fascinating, huh?" It was difficult to come up with a good one on the spot. "How about something a little odd but interesting? I was listening to a podcast the other day about how it's possible that a very intelligent life form lived on Earth long, long before us, but we wouldn't know, because if their technology was sufficiently advanced, it's possible that no trace exists anymore, or if it did, we don't yet have the means to detect it. And I have to admit I buy it, even though the podcast went on to posit that the life form could have been a kind of cephalopod—like, superintelligent octopuses."

Thaddeus arched a brow. "That *is* odd but interesting. I like it."

Talia smiled. "Now your turn. Tell me something about yourself."

"I believe that Atlantis exists. And I'm going to find it."

She blinked. "Oh. Um . . . okay. Tell me more."

He tilted his head to the left, cracked his neck, tilted it to the right and cracked his neck again. Then he shook out his shoulders like he was gearing up for a big workout.

A little strange, but Talia would see where it went. She knew plenty of people who had small, quirky procedures they had to run through before getting down to business. A novelist friend of hers had to light a candle and open two fortune cookies before she could start writing each morning. One of the engineers at Ideal Life sang "Scotland the Brave" before he fired up his computer. And Sam had his no-distractions, total-immersion routine before poker tournaments.

"So, I've always loved the water," Thaddeus began. "See, I'm a competitive swimmer—I'm on the team at Stanford—and I'm also majoring in earth systems there with a focus on oceanography."

"Wait, did you say you're *majoring* in earth systems?" Talia took a step backward from the bar. "As in, you're an undergrad?"

Thaddeus's eyes widened. "Yeah, but don't worry! I'm twenty-one, totally legal for everything! I've always been told I had an old soul, and I'm really into mature women."

Talia almost gagged on *mature women*. "I just . . . no, sorry, I can't do this," she said. "You seem smart and nice, Thaddeus, but this isn't going to work."

"But—"

She turned the watch crown back again.

This time, she spent half an hour with an age-appropriate chief technology officer who seemed great until he mentioned that he still lived with his mom.

On the next rewind, Talia chatted with a carpenter who liked talking too much about wood, a crypto bro, and a guy who had come straight from a forty-mile bike ride and smelled like it.

No, no, and no.

And yet, she didn't know if she had it in her to reset the clock again. She'd been turning the watch dial slowly, but even so, the scenery around her still spun every time, and a baseline level of nausea was settling into the bottom of her stomach. A faint fog of fatigue was beginning to float around her head as well. A pattern was establishing itself clearly—moving through time was not without physical toll.

Maybe she should just call it a night. After all, even with a numbers game, there was no guarantee that you'd win on the first try.

Talia wondered what Sam was up to right now. She briefly considered calling him to find out but then decided she didn't want to bother him. He was probably doing something cozy yet so very typically Sam, like curling up in his armchair and reading Dostoyevsky or . . . What was the name of that philosopher he'd mentioned recently? Alain de Button? Botton?

She snagged a few of the petit fours that were being circulated on dessert trays and wrapped them in a napkin, then headed to the front of the hotel. As she waited for her car to be pulled up—

the Manzanita & Oak did free valet for those who'd participated in the Techie Singles Mixer—she unwrapped the napkin and nibbled on a small chocolate tart.

"That's probably the best part of the night, huh?" a woman said as she handed her ticket to the valet and unfolded her own napkin, revealing a selection of petit fours.

Talia laughed.

"I'm Evangeline," she said. "I'd offer you my hand to shake, but it's occupied right now." Evangeline raised a small square of lemon cake as a kind of toast instead.

"Totally get it," Talia said, raising her own half-eaten chocolate tart.

"Did you meet anyone promising in there?" Evangeline asked.

Talia shook her head. "Proud of myself that I made an effort, though. I'm usually too busy for it."

"Same."

"Where do you work?" Talia said. "I'm at a startup, and the hours are relentless. I love it, though."

"I'm actually not in tech. I'm an independent journalist."

"Oh yeah? What outlet?"

Evangeline gave Talia a sly smile but didn't say anything.

Talia's eyes widened. Could she mean *Your Gossipy Tech BFF*?

Of course, no one knew the identity of the writer behind *Your Gossipy Tech BFF*, but besides scoops on dramatic boardroom power struggles, scrapped IPO plans, and big product disasters before they went public, there was also plenty of dish about who was dating whom.

"I love your work," Talia said.

"I'm sure I have no idea what you're talking about," Evangeline said. "But women in tech are still too few and far between, and we have to stick together, so let me know if you ever want to connect and grab coffee." She fished a business card out of her purse and gave it to Talia.

Evangeline Gray
Journalist

"Wow, this is old-school," Talia said, turning the heavy card stock in her hand. "I don't think I've seen a physical business card in the last decade."

Evangeline laughed. "Everything we do is digital these days. It just seems nice to have something real to hold on to. But of course, Silicon Valley being what it is, there's a QR code on the back to my LinkedIn profile."

The valet pulled up with Talia's car, a beat-up purple Honda Accord she'd had since her grad school days.

"Well, it was great to meet you, Evangeline."

"Likewise. And good luck with Ideal Life."

It wasn't until Talia was driving away that she realized she'd never mentioned the name of her startup to Evangeline.

Talia laughed out loud.

The mystery writer of *Your Gossipy Tech BFF* really did know everything and everyone.

Erin

Don't worry—your date's going to be amazing. And you look great," Erin's roommate, Colette, said. She was flopped on her bed on the other side of their tiny dorm room.

"Easy for you to say. You're French and everything you put on automatically gets translated into 'effortlessly chic.'" Erin waved at Colette's gray T-shirt and sweatpants and blond hair in a messy bun.

Colette laughed. "It's not my fault Americans have some weird cultural filter that does that to French people. I'm a slob, but it just so happens that I'm a Parisian one."

"I hate you," Erin said.

"You love me."

Erin turned back to the mirror and tugged at the hem of her top. It was a green bias-cut satin tank that Ideal Life Athena said Erin liked, since her dopamine levels had spiked when she tried it on. Erin had paired it with a black midi skirt and thought it looked very put-together.

Fifteen minutes before her date, though, she wasn't so sure. She put on her Omni 3Ds, which she'd taken off just a few minutes ago so she could pull the tank top over her head.

"Athena, how do I feel about this outfit?"

Colette threw a pillow at her. "Why do you need to ask an app how you feel? *You* feel, not the code."

Erin shook her head and ignored the comment. Colette was a "fuzzy"—that's what the liberal arts students were nicknamed, the opposite of "techies" who studied STEM fields—and that meant Colette had a stronger, built-up resistance to technology. But Erin knew Ideal Life and its brethren were the future. She saw it every day she interned at the company, and she envisioned herself like Talia someday, hopefully not too long from now.

Talia was always pushing herself to be the best. Erin wanted that for herself, too.

Ideal Life Athena marched into the field of vision of the Omni 3Ds and reported to Erin how Erin felt about the outfit.

> Ideal Life Athena: Based on current chemical levels and activity in your anterior cingulate cortex, you are currently experiencing emotions of uncertainty. However, remember your tendency to assign causation where there may only be correlation. Ask yourself, Is it possible that my feelings are *not* the result of my outfit but that they come from elsewhere?

Erin sighed. "Good point; thanks for the reminder."

"That's what roommates are for," Colette said. Even though their room was small, she was still far enough away that she hadn't been able to hear that Ideal Life Athena had responded on the Omni 3Ds. So she thought Erin was still talking to her. Erin let it go.

Ideal Life Athena had been extraordinarily helpful in planning the date with Georgia Tan, a girl in Erin's computational logic class. Ideal Life Athena had homed in on the best way for Erin to ask Georgia out, examining what had caused Erin anxiety in the past and minimizing for that (the conclusion had been to write down *Hey, Georgia, can I take you out to dinner sometime?* on a piece of paper and show it to her; if Georgia said no, Erin could tear the paper up or burn it to purge the feelings of rejection, plus rest assured that there was no digital record of the failed attempt—other than her conversations with Ideal Life Athena, of course, but those were private).

Ideal Life Athena had also assisted in choosing a place to eat, taking into account what cuisines Erin tended to pig out on (unattractive!) and what gave her heartburn or gas (super embarrassing and uncomfortable!) as well as considering cost (it analyzed Erin's past brain activity for clues on the kind of spending that stressed her out).

Erin looked at her outfit in the mirror once more, took a deep breath, and grabbed her purse. "Okay, I'm heading out. Wish me luck!"

She was in the hallway when Colette came running out after her. "Wait—I wanted to give you a good-luck hug."

"Aww." Erin opened her arms.

But instead of coming in for the hug, Colette yanked the Omni 3Ds off Erin's face.

"Hey! Give those back!"

Jackson, a football player who lived a couple doors down, poked his head out of his room. He was an Italian literature major and also a wide receiver on the Stanford team, here for the summer to help the new recruits acclimate. "What's going on out here?"

"Think fast," Colette said, throwing the Omni 3Ds at him. Jackson caught them and dangled them up high.

Erin let out a huff. She was supposed to pick up Georgia at her dorm on the other side of campus. She didn't have time for this!

"Jackson, come on. I'm running behind schedule."

"Do *not* give those to her," Colette said. "She's going on a date, and she needs to do it on her own, not with that thing telling her what to do."

"It's not *telling* me, it just makes suggestions. And I can turn it off."

Jackson was a huge guy compared to Erin and Colette, and also a huge sweetheart. He frowned and looked back and forth between them, genuinely torn.

After what seemed like eternity (Erin was definitely going to be late picking up Georgia now—what a great first impression),

Jackson shook his head. "Sorry, Erin. I'm with Colette on this one. But have fun on the date, okay?"

Erin rolled her eyes. "Fine. It's not like I *need* them to function. But if this date doesn't go well, I'm blaming you two fuzzies."

Erin and Georgia found a parking space in downtown Mountain View relatively easily, which was lucky, because it could get crowded here on this long street of restaurants that were cheaper than the ones in Palo Alto but equally delicious.

Delicious, too, was how Georgia looked tonight. Her long black hair fell in soft waves over her bare shoulders, the red of her halter top a contrast to her tanned skin. Georgia also wore oversize sunglasses, giving her an air of Singapore glamour—she had attended one of the most prestigious academies there, an international feeder school for Stanford—and it seemed to Erin that she'd somehow scored a date with one of the characters in *Crazy Rich Asians*. She'd had a hard time not stealing glances at Georgia as they drove here. (Erin had almost missed their freeway exit because of one such instance; if she'd had her Omni 3Ds, though, that never would have happened.)

Georgia's eyes darted everywhere as they walked into the courtyard of Taste the World. It was a hidden alcove off the main road, hosting ten shop fronts of different international street food. Colorful flags had been stitched together and draped overhead, making the whole place feel like a joyful, gastronomic circus tent. The air smelled like garlicky grilled seafood, buttery Scottish pie pastry, and the sharp tang of lime and chili peppers from the nearby taqueria. "I've never heard of this place, but I think I already love it," she gushed.

"I thought we could just buy a bunch of little plates from different vendors and try them," Erin said.

"Oh my god!" Georgia's hands flew to her chest. "They have a Singaporean stand!"

Erin smiled. Ideal Life Athena had done a fan-freaking-tastic job of finding Taste the World.

They split up, and Georgia took it upon herself to get a variety of Singaporean dishes from Lah Lah Express, while Erin went around and bought a hodgepodge of European bites—French cheese puffs, Polish pierogi dumplings, and Italian fried risotto balls.

"Everything looks amazing," Erin said, when they reunited at a plastic table in the center of the courtyard. "What did you get?"

"My childhood favorites." Georgia beamed at the steaming paper plates and bowls in front of them. "Chili crab, *nasi lemak*, which is coconut rice, and *laksa*, a spicy noodle soup. Oh, and they had sugarcane juice and Milo Dinosaur, my favorite chocolate malt drink that I used to get after school!"

"I can't wait to try them," Erin said. Her own haul looked so bland next to Georgia's; everything was beige or brown. Ideal Life Athena could have helped her choose a more impressive spread.

Still, the only thing she could do now was commit to what she'd bought on her own.

No—wouldn't it be better to eat what Georgia had gotten first? That would be the smart move on a date, right?

Eep. Erin didn't know. Because on the other hand, if you went to a restaurant and people said they were going to share but then everyone ordered their own entrées, it was assumed that the "sharing" was only a small bite. The entrée actually belonged to the orderer. So was that the case here?

Georgia moaned as she ate some of the chili crab. "Sooo good."

The sound of that moan shot straight through Erin, and she forgot all about thinking. Her id was leading now.

"With a reaction like that, how could I resist?" Erin took the fork from Georgia, letting her fingers graze hers. Another warm shiver vibrated through her.

Then the chili crab lit up her taste buds. "Oh, wow," Erin said.

"Right?"

After Georgia ate more crab, she grabbed a spoon and scooped up some of the laksa. "You *have* to try this next. My grandma used to make this soup for me any time I was feeling low, and it always made life ten times better. Not that we're feeling low right now. But if you want to know my soul, laksa is the key."

With a flirtatious glint in her eye, she held the spoon out to Erin but didn't relinquish it, instead offering to feed her.

Erin's pulse sped up as she leaned in. She tried to make her mouth as sexy as possible as she wrapped her lips around the spoon, although she suspected she looked more like a fish than a very kissable girl.

"Oh god! Hot!" she spluttered as she failingly slurped and spilled soup all over the table.

Georgia floundered for a napkin, but she was laughing as she mopped up the mess.

"Sorry!" she said. "That didn't work as well as I'd hoped. Was it too hot spicy, or too hot temperature-wise?"

"Just temperature," Erin said.

"Okay then, here—let's try it again." Georgia filled the spoon with soup but blew on it this time to cool it down.

Erin sat mesmerized. Georgia, at least, knew how to make her mouth look incredibly sexy around food.

"I think it's edible now," she said, holding the spoon out.

Erin leaned in and sipped it. The coconut soup was sweet but also rich with all sorts of spices she wasn't familiar with. "Mm, that's incredible. If that's the window to your soul, I need more."

"I'm so happy you like it." Georgia put some noodles into the spoon this time, along with more soup, and fed Erin again.

Within minutes, they'd polished off the bowl together.

Georgia pointed to the dishes Erin had gotten. "Should we have some of those, too?"

"Sure, I—"

But Erin couldn't finish. Her throat started closing up. She gasped.

"Are you okay?" Georgia's eyes went wide.

Erin winced. "I'll . . . be . . . fine. Just—" She rubbed at her neck.

"Here." Georgia thrust the cup of sugarcane juice at her. "Maybe some liquid will help?"

Now Erin's pulse was really racing, but not because of the date. She frowned at the empty bowl of laksa.

"Nuts?" she managed to say, pointing.

"No, just noodles and coconut—oh no, coconut!"

But Erin shook her head. In terms of allergies, coconut was a fruit, not a tree nut, despite the name. It shouldn't have been a problem.

Georgia was furiously typing on her phone.

Meanwhile, Erin's eyes started to itch and her nose was running. She could also feel little red hives beginning to rise on her cheeks and around her mouth. She fumbled for her purse to get her EpiPen, but the bag tumbled off the chair and onto the food court floor, spilling its contents everywhere.

"Shit," Georgia said. "There's a little bit of candlenut ground up into a paste in the laksa. Are you allergic to them?"

Erin had no idea what candlenuts were, but it didn't matter now, because it was pretty clear what was happening.

She fell to her knees and scrambled after the EpiPen, which had skidded a couple of feet away. But even when she had it, her hands shook with panic because her throat was closing up more, and Erin couldn't get the safety cap off. Involuntary tears spilled from her swollen eyes.

"Somebody call an ambulance!" Georgia shouted, before dropping down to the ground next to her and taking off the EpiPen's cap. "Let me help. Show me where to inject it."

The thigh was the best place because it was a large muscle with good blood supply and would rapidly absorb the medicine. Erin yanked up her skirt, inadvertently exposing her seamless but ugly nude-colored panties that she'd chosen for smoothness, not sexiness. Georgia jabbed the EpiPen in while snot ran down Erin's hive-ridden face.

A few minutes later, the swelling in her throat began to ease, and the ambulance arrived. The EMTs insisted on taking her into the hospital, just in case.

Mortified, Erin told Georgia not to accompany her. Could there have been a worse date?

By the time Erin was released, Georgia had driven her car back to campus for her and left the keys at the dorm with Colette. She'd left only a short note:

I'm sorry how that turned out. Hope you feel better soon.
See you in class.
—G

This is what happened when Erin had to go on a date on her own.

If she'd had Ideal Life Athena with her, she would have *known* not to eat the laksa. She would have known it contained some form of nut.

She might have gone home *with* Georgia. Instead, she'd spent the evening at the hospital, hideously red-faced and mortified.

And alone.

Sam

Some bookstores were event hubs, frequently hosting authors on book tours and signings. The events were usually free to the public, and the benefit was that you got foot traffic into the shop. Some people would buy the featured author's book, and others would pick up a copy of something they hadn't known they'd wanted.

Lighthouse Books wasn't an event-focused shop, since there were plenty of other bookstores between San Francisco and Silicon Valley that were in more population-dense cities. Sam's lighthouse was the kind of place visitors stopped by on a whim while driving along the Pacific Coast Highway. It didn't make sense to host a robust events calendar with that kind of clientele.

In fact, Sam had never intended to do *any* events at Lighthouse Books. But it was Talia who had nudged him to venture out of his comfort zone of burrowing in his tower of tomes. She'd encouraged him to actively invite more readers into his store, another one of her ways of reminding him to engage with the world.

The first event he'd hosted was a local writers' group. That had been a good way to start because it'd been relatively low effort—the group of four women and one older gentleman had just wanted a place to meet once a month where they could exchange critiques of each other's manuscripts while drinking in inspiration, and the lighthouse's round rooms did just that by surrounding them on all sides with books. Now they came every first Wednesday of the month at 3 p.m. on the dot, and Sam and Kenneth looked forward to them brightening the store with their literary enthusiasm.

As for book tours, an author's name would occasionally pop out to Sam from The Grid. The Grid was an online database that the major publishers used to let stores know which authors they were sending on tour. Bookstores could then "bid" to have authors visit their shop by submitting detailed proposals about how big an audience they could rally, what kind of marketing they would do to advertise the event, and an estimated number of the author's books they thought they could sell that night.

So when Chloe Hanako Quinn's name appeared on The Grid, Sam jumped. Chloe Quinn had unintentionally created a global phenomenon a couple of years ago by writing uplifting messages inside yellow origami roses. She had begun the project just wanting to spread some kindness around New York City, but it had turned out that the entire world was hungry for inspiration and connection, so the paper flowers had gone viral, with millions of people on every continent making their own and spreading joy. Now she'd written a book called *Tiny Kindnesses: How Your Small Actions Can Change Everything*.

Sam had devoured an early copy sent by the publisher, then read it three more times since. In a culture focused on big stunts that could bring fame and fortune, Chloe Quinn's message of finding purpose in the small, quieter things in life had really resonated with him.

He didn't think he had a shot at being picked for the book tour. But he and Talia had brainstormed for weeks to put together the best proposal possible, including hiring a local origami artist to lead a workshop as part of the event and bringing Kayla in to cater book-themed food. He also pledged to donate a portion of the bookstore's profits that day to a kids' art program here on the coast. Sam had hoped that would appeal to the publisher, since Chloe Quinn herself had publicly announced that 100 percent of her own royalties would go to her nonprofit, the Paper Roses Foundation.

Yet, when Sam got the email that Lighthouse Books had been

chosen as a stop on Chloe Quinn's book tour, he'd had to read the message five times before he believed it, because he'd been in competition with all the other more well-known stores in the Bay Area. Jack Kerouac and Allen Ginsberg had made City Lights in San Francisco their bookstore home base. Kepler's Books in Menlo Park was renowned for their gorgeous, black wood stage built specifically for author events. And Fireside Books was a beloved Redwood City shop that hosted more book tours per month than Lighthouse Books had in five years.

But the publisher had said that Chloe Quinn handpicked where she wanted to go, and she'd loved Sam's generosity in offering to support his local children's art program. Plus, she was tickled by the idea of visiting a lighthouse that had been converted into a bookstore.

Now, with only one day before the event, Sam couldn't stop running around the store and up and down the stairs, trying to arrange all the little details. Tomorrow, a party rentals company would bring folding tables and chairs for the origami workshop and Chloe Quinn's talk and book signing. But today, he had to make room for all that.

In stores more accustomed to holding events, many of their bookshelves would be on wheels, allowing the employees to move them aside temporarily and create a large, open space. But the most common events at Lighthouse Books were local author signings, where the guest list was only a dozen or so, and a small card table next to the new-releases display would do.

That's why the store was closed today, and Kenneth was emptying books from the shelves into boxes, and Sam was schlepping them one by one upstairs to the nonfiction level. The wheelless shelves were too heavy to move when fully loaded.

After hours of this, Sam declared a break. Kenneth went out back to smoke a joint while watching the waves roll in. (There was a weather-worn picnic bench on the cliff, just outside the boundaries of the lighthouse property and therefore not subject to any rules about drug use that the chamber of commerce might have for businesses.) Sam used the time to run upstairs to his apartment and wash off the sweat he'd worked up.

When he got out of the shower, there was a text from Talia.

Talia: How's set-up going for your big event tomorrow? You ready?

Sam stretched out his back, which was already sore. When he was younger, he'd thought that aches and pains like this didn't come on until you were in your sixties. What a rude awakening that thirty-five was the reality.

Sam: Kenneth and I just finished clearing the shelves in the middle of the floor. Now we have to move them against the walls, then decorate them so we don't look like the worst bookstore ever with nothing but empty bookcases.

Talia: Can you imagine being an author and walking into your next tour stop, and there are NO books anywhere? haha

Sam: Also imagine being an author and there is no one in the audience.

Talia: Mortifying.

Sam: It happens, sadly. But not tomorrow, right??

Talia: Don't worry, I invited basically all of Silicon Valley, and Erin confirmed the RSVPs a couple days ago. You know everyone in the Valley is on an eternal quest to become a better person.

Sam: I think they're just addicted to self-help books.

Talia: haha . . . But also true.

Sam: I do believe that YOU want to be a better person. It's why Ideal Life exists. Everyone else, though . . . They just want self-improvement to make more money.

Talia: So cynical.

Sam: I am the refreshing balance to your unfettered idealism.

Talia texted back a laugh-crying face. (They were millennials, which meant that unlike Gen Z, they were not too cool for emojis.)

Talia: Anyway, Mr. Cynic, I think your event is going to have great turnout. People love the idea that they can do something small and make a difference. If they didn't, then Chloe Quinn's story wouldn't have been as impactful as it was.

Even though Talia couldn't see him, he nodded, because she did have a good point.

Sam: Thanks, Tal. I couldn't do this without you.
Talia: Sure you could. But I'm always here for you.

He wanted to ask her how everything else was going. But he also didn't want to know about last night, because she'd told him about signing up for a singles mixer and that she planned to use her watch to maximize what she could get out of it.

He had hated the idea. Not just because she'd be flirting with men that weren't him and maybe taking one home. Sam had accepted that Talia didn't see him that way and probably never would.

But it was the *way* she was using the watch. While Talia had always been into life hacks in college and grad school and had her "Relentless pursuit of constructive criticism" motto, Ideal Life had kicked her desire to optimize the future into a whole new gear.

And now, the watch gave her the ability to apply that same aspiration to the *past*.

She thought it was making her life better, but Sam wasn't so sure.

Is it really a perfect life if you have to obsess over every detail to make it so?

Talia

The next afternoon, Talia arrived at Lighthouse Books half an hour before the event was supposed to begin, only to find the seats already filled. She was a bit surprised, not because she didn't believe in Sam's ability to draw a crowd to the store, but because it was one of those rare sunny *and* warm days at the beach, and usually that meant people wanted to be outside picnicking and building sandcastles while watching the surfers on the waves.

But there was palpable buzz about this author, and Sam had designed an event that stood out from normal book signings. First, there was the workshop with the local origami artist, and afterward, the author would arrive and give a talk and then autograph books. There would also be some light bites inspired by the author's work—charcuterie and fruit cut and shaped like roses, a nonalcoholic cocktail called "Tiny Kindnesses," and mini chocolate ice cream sundaes with mulberry syrup, because there had been a news article somewhere that mentioned that this was the author's favorite flavor combination.

Talia gasped as she took in what Sam and Kenneth had done with the store. All the bookcases had been pushed to the sides—she knew what a gargantuan effort that had been—and then draped in cascading fabric that matched the yellows and blues of Chloe Quinn's book cover.

In the center of each bookcase, a couple of shelves had been left visible, and Sam had filled them with displays of *Tiny Kindnesses: How Your Small Actions Can Change Everything*. Instead of the lighthouse looking like a store that sold lots of different books, he had transformed the space into a lighthouse that shone its spotlight on one book, and *only* one. Talia was sure the author would feel Sam's tremendous admiration of her work as soon as she stepped foot inside the shop.

A momentary pang of something flared in Talia's chest.

Ideal Life Queen Elizabeth: There seems to be increased activity in your basal ganglia and ventromedial prefrontal cortex, perhaps indicating jealousy.

Talia frowned at herself. *What? Because of Sam and the author?*

"Hey, you're here!" Sam jogged down the staircase and hopped over the rope with the sign UPSTAIRS AREA CLOSED. WE'RE SORRY FOR THE INCONVENIENCE that cordoned off the steps. He'd blocked off the second-story nonfiction section, since that's where he and Kenneth had stashed all the extra books from the main floor.

"Wouldn't miss it," she said, giving him a hug. She held him a little tighter than usual; that irrational echo of jealousy still lingered.

Ideal Life Queen Elizabeth: You are experiencing continued spikes of activity in your basal ganglia and ventromedial prefrontal cortex. Would you like some suggestions to alleviate your current emotions?

Talia ignored Queen Elizabeth. "Looks like you've got great turnout," she said to Sam.

"I know. I'm thrilled. And this isn't even everyone. Kenneth is up to his eyeballs at the register with preorders ready to be picked up."

"Is the author here yet?" Talia asked with as much nonchalance as she could feign.

"Not yet, but she and her fiancé got in last night. They're staying down in Half Moon Bay, and her publicist confirmed they'd be on time."

Talia didn't hear anything other than "her fiancé." She let

out a long exhale, relief following as the jealousy left her lungs, while at the same time thinking, *Since when do I care who Sam likes?* Only last week, Talia had badgered him about Kayla the caterer, and Talia hadn't felt anything about it then.

Well, mostly not.

But maybe that was because she knew Sam wasn't serious about Kayla. They just went out every now and then. Whereas he had been so excited when Chloe Quinn's name appeared on The Grid. Talia hadn't seen Sam want something—the book tour stop—so badly since he'd bought Lighthouse Books.

Ideal Life Queen Elizabeth: I am again detecting a slight increase in the activity in your—

Talia whipped off her Omni 3Ds and crammed them into her purse.

"Everything okay?" Sam asked, eyeing her purse.

"Totally. I just realized I don't need them right now. It's Sunday, and you always say no tech for Sunday Lunch."

He smiled. "Yeah, sorry we're missing that today. But thanks for being here even though there aren't any tacos."

Talia laughed. "I'll order double next weekend."

"Fine by me. Next weekend is your turn to pay anyway."

She socked him lightly in the arm, and they were their old selves again.

The origami-folding workshop was a success, with the artist teaching everyone three kinds of origami—a rowboat made out of a dollar bill, a classic Japanese crane, and of course, a paper rose.

Chloe Quinn arrived on time, as promised, along with her fiancé, Oliver, who acted as both Biggest Fan and assistant, writing down reader names on Post-its while they waited in the signing line so that Chloe wouldn't have to ask them how to spell their names. He and Chloe shot each other quick, adoring looks throughout the entire event, and Talia's jealous flash did not have reason to return.

Mostly, though, she noticed how alive Sam seemed, happy to be the generous but almost invisible hand behind the scenes orchestrating the event.

In Talia's friendship with him, she'd always been the one leading. Not that he was a mindless follower. It's just that it could be hard for two CEO types to have such a long and close relationship. But Sam was smart yet not an alpha personality, so it worked really well. Neither Talia nor Sam stepped on the other's ambitions.

Still, she had always defined success as something external—valedictorian, fancy university degree, selling your startup to a company like Google or Omni. But watching Sam be himself and thriving in his cozy, not-famous business made her think that maybe success could look different for different people. He didn't need to be popular on social media or in the news headlines. He was happiest when he could just do the things he loved.

When the last book was signed and Sam had sent Chloe and Oliver off to a local restaurant with an ocean view, Kenneth closed out the register and flipped the sign on the door to CLOSED.

"Need me for anything else?" he asked.

"No," Sam said. "You've done more than enough for a weekend, Kenneth. Thanks so much."

Kenneth saluted and pulled out a joint as he left. He lived just a ten-minute walk from the lighthouse and would presumably unwind with a smoke on the way.

Kayla was cleaning up the long table where she'd had her snacks and cocktails on display.

Sam crossed to the other side of the floor where Talia waited.

"Congrats," she said. "That was such a cool event!"

"Even better than I could have hoped."

His face glowed, still on the high of how well it had gone. The corners of his eyes crinkled as he smiled. And the way he looked at her, all soft and warm, suddenly made her joints go loose and tingly at the same time.

She hadn't felt this way about anyone at the singles mixer Thursday night. She'd played the numbers game, and she'd come up empty.

But maybe that's because she'd already won a long time ago?

Was *Sam* the one she was meant to be with?

Talia's breath caught in her throat.

He'd been there all this time. On the other end of every text. At every important event in her life. And without fail, at Taco Bell with her every Sunday.

How had she failed to recognize it? Ideal Life Queen Elizabeth had even pointed out Talia's spikes of happiness whenever she was about to see Sam, but Talia had chalked it up to being excited to spend time with her best friend.

He was still looking at her, although now he raised a brow in question. She'd been staring at him, mouth hung open.

Talia rushed across the space between them and kissed him.

Sam froze.

And he didn't kiss her back.

"Oh god," Talia said. "Oh god, oh god, I'm sorry, shit, what the hell was I thinking!"

He rubbed his hand over his mouth, speechless as he stared at her.

Had she ruined their friendship? All those years spent building this incredible thing they had, gone in one impulsive, indulgent moment?

"Pretend it never happened," Talia said. "You know how trucks make that beeping noise when they reverse? Let's beep beep beep . . . Oh my god, I sound like an idiot."

Her eyes shot to her watch.

"Talia, no—"

But Sam was too late. Talia wound the watch crown backward. Just a couple of minutes, but it was enough.

★

Kayla was cleaning up the long table where she'd had her snacks and cocktails on display.

Sam crossed to the other side of the floor where Talia waited.

"Congrats," she said. "That was such a cool event!"

"Even better than I could have hoped."

His face glowed, still on the high of how well it had gone. The corners of his eyes crinkled as he smiled.

Talia averted her gaze so she wouldn't see the way he looked at her, all soft and warm. She held her arms and legs straight so her joints wouldn't go loose and tingly.

Instead, she caught Kayla watching them, probably trying to gauge whether Sam and Talia were going upstairs together tonight, or if Talia was truly just a friend, as Sam had told her before.

"Um, well, I'm really happy for you," Talia said a little louder than necessary. "I should probably head out now. Lots of work to do."

"Do you really have to go so soon?" Sam asked.

Talia knew it wasn't like her to cut and run like this, especially not after he'd pulled off something big that mattered a lot to him, but she couldn't stay. Not only because the mortification of Sam's lips unmoving on hers still reverberated through her. But also because she'd promised him she wouldn't rewind and change his life without his permission.

And that unreciprocated kiss was not something she could confess.

She gave him a quick hug with plenty of distance between them, arms barely touching, and whispered, "Have fun with Kayla."

Then she fled the lighthouse, taking the book she'd bought and all her conflicted feelings with her.

Libby

Libby wore a strapless silver gown, and Jacob was in a tuxedo in the glass tunnel of the Umeda Sky Building, forty floors above the city of Osaka. It was daytime in Japan right now, but that was irrelevant; special-effects tools had gotten so good in the last couple of years that it would be easy to transform the backdrop from 7 a.m. to midnight. The sun could be obliterated with the mere touch of a finger.

The Umeda Sky Building was closed at the moment, which was why Libby and Jacob were here shooting the ad for the Japan National Tourism Organization. Sure, software could edit people out of backgrounds, but it was still easier to ask the creators to come in early when there was no one around to gawk. Libby had been up since four thirty to ensure her hair and makeup would be up to the task of the shoot.

Their job was to give the tower an aspirational feeling of the romantic and the awe-inspiring. The Umeda Sky Building boasted a 360-degree bird's-eye view of the city below, but even though it was already a known tourist stop, Osaka wanted to do more to put themselves on the map. They didn't want to be merely a day trip from Kyoto; they wanted people to stay overnight and spend money in the city, visiting Osaka Castle for its deep history (of particular interest to fans of the TV series or book *Shōgun*), sampling snacks like *takoyaki* and *torikara* at the Dotonbori food stalls, even visiting the Cup Noodles museum. And of course, going to the top of the Umeda Sky Building.

"We're going to shoot videos and stills at the same time," the director, Mark Yamamoto, said. "The idea is for you two to waltz around this glass tunnel, luxuriating in the view and in each other, while we capture it all in one fluid take." He gestured at the half dozen cameras on robotic arms with motorized wheels, which would follow Libby and Jacob while recording and taking photos from all different angles. "Ready?" Mark asked, looking at Jacob.

Libby bit the inside of her cheek. Mark was no misogynist; he'd treated both Libby and Jacob with extreme Japanese courtesy since they arrived an hour ago to check lighting and other technical details. Still, little moments of bias like this still slipped out no matter where they were in the world, where people assumed Jacob was in charge because he was the man. There had been a lot of progress made in terms of gender equality since Libby and Jacob had begun working as creators when they were just out of college, but there was definitely still a ways to go.

Jacob, though, didn't confirm their readiness to the director. Instead, Jacob turned to Libby, smiled with his deep dimples, and asked, "Are we ready?"

Libby smiled back at him—god, she loved this man—then turned to Mark and said, "We're ready."

Two and a half hours later, they finally wrapped shooting, just as the ticket booths downstairs opened the Umeda Sky Building for the day. Libby sank into one of the chairs in the café on the fortieth floor and groaned as she kicked off her heels. She was early in her pregnancy and not at the point yet where her feet would swell, but *anyone* would ache after waltzing for 150 minutes straight.

"You doing all right?" Jacob asked, as he brought her a cup of green tea and a *furutsu sando*, a sandwich made of super fluffy white bread stuffed with sliced strawberries, kiwis, bananas, and lots of whipped cream. Libby had fallen in love with the unique dessert-in-sandwich earlier in the week in Tokyo, and the baby must have, too, because Libby now craved furutsu sando every morning, even though it wasn't considered by the Japanese to be a breakfast food.

She took a bite and swore the baby moved in her belly, even though there was no way Libby would actually be able to detect such a thing yet. Maybe if she used Talia's Ideal Life app, it would identify changes in her brain chemistry that were tied to the baby being happy?

But no, it would probably just register the hit of sugar to her bloodstream, which was obvious even just by looking at the whipped cream sandwich.

Libby was lucky that morning sickness hadn't hit her yet. It would have made doing their job a lot harder, especially since she wasn't ready to let people know she was pregnant. Once the news got out, it might affect the jobs offered to her and Jacob. That is, unless they decided to include their little bean and document the progress of growing their family. Brands liked being associated with wholesome families.

She and Jacob had talked about it a lot recently, but they still hadn't reached a conclusion. What they knew, though, was that there was no pausing in a creator career. It had always been true—the internet wanted only relevance, and if you weren't in front of their eyeballs with fresh content *constantly*, you were negligible.

But that reality was even harsher now. The proliferation of photo- and video-realistic AI models with perfectly symmetrical faces and flawless bodies had already pushed the mid-level human creators out of business. Only the top ones who had had massive audiences before the AI revolution (like Libby and Jacob) had managed to survive. Still, they had to work harder than ever to hold on to that status and to fight off obsolescence, because it was costly for companies to fly real live people around the world and feed and house them, whereas digital models didn't need any of that.

The main thing Libby and Jacob had going for them was "authenticity," which basically meant letting the cameras into their private lives so that followers could feel connected to them. What had started out as two twentysomethings backpacking around the world had grown into a couple in their early thirties inadvertently starring in their own reality show.

Libby took another bite of her sandwich. The whipped cream squirted out and got all over her face. Before she had a chance to wipe it off, though, the elevators opened and two groups of tourists spilled onto the fortieth floor, and one woman, eyes wide, shouted in a German accent, "Is that Libby and Jacob?"

They raised their phones and started recording immediately as they rushed over to the table where Libby sat with whipped cream smeared on her cheek, her shoeless feet propped up on a chair. Jacob put on his camera smile and quickly stood in front of her, giving her a spare second to wipe her face clean.

A moment later, they were surrounded by not only the Germans but also the others who had just arrived on the fortieth floor, giggling and jostling for selfies with the YouTube and Instagram personalities. Libby was pretty sure half of them didn't actually know who she and Jacob were but wanted to capture themselves with them just in case.

"Say 'sushi'!" one of the tourists said as they snapped a photo.

They immediately posted the photo to socials, tagging Umeda Sky Building as their location.

The Japan National Tourism Organization would be happy.

And Libby and Jacob remained relevant for at least one day more.

Talia

Talia needed to talk to someone about the kiss, but then she'd have to explain the watch. She also realized again that there was no one she was close enough to these days anyway. Whenever her old friends from grad school had wanted to grab drinks after work, she hadn't been able to, because the end of the workday for them was only two-thirds through a regular workday for her. If they wanted to get together on the weekends for a hike or a day trip to Napa for wine tasting, that was out, too. Talia's weekends were spent at Ideal Life, other than Sunday Lunch with Sam.

She knew she owed Libby a call back, but it was morning here in California, which meant the middle of the night in Japan. So Talia reached out to the only other person she could talk to about this—her mom.

This was suboptimal because (a) Vera was going to be over the moon about the kiss, and her hopes and dreams would probably run off in the complete opposite direction of where Talia needed things to go, and (b) Vera had an aqua aerobics class at the senior center this morning.

Which is how Talia found herself in the shallow end of an indoor pool with a bunch of sixty-to-eighty-year-olds.

"Ladies! So great to see you bright and early!" the perky blond coach, Didi, said from the pool deck. "And it looks like Vera has brought a special guest to Aquarobics today."

Vera beamed. "This is my oldest, Talia. She's the CEO of a very successful startup that's about to be bought by Omni."

"Ooh!"

"My goodness!"

"What is an Omni?" the oldest of the women asked.

"It's a very big technology company, dear," Vera said. "Ask your grandkids. I'm sure they know all about it. Talia is going to be famous soon."

"Oh god, *Mom*." Talia considered sinking down into the bottom of the pool and not coming back up until Aquarobics was over.

"What?" Vera said. "You're such a smart and accomplished person—you should be proud. Men brag all the time and think nothing of it. Women should shout their achievements, too. Right, everyone?"

"Your mother is right, sweetheart."

"We are so proud of you, and we just met you!"

"Are you single?" the oldest woman asked. "My grandson is a very nice boy, and—"

"Okay, ladies," Didi said from the pool deck. "I know we all love to chitchat, but we're here to do some aquarobics, right?"

Talia had never been more grateful for a phys ed instructor in her life.

"Let's begin with some gentle water stretches to wake up our muscles."

The group fell into what must have been their standard formation, with three women in each row. Talia and Vera were in the back.

"Arms up, ladies. Let's salute the sun."

There was a lot of splashing as everyone raised their arms. Didi turned on a portable speaker, and slow instrumental music began to play. The women all swayed from left to right, not in unison, but they tried. Talia had been worried about keeping up because she'd never done a pool calisthenics class before, but it was apparent now that wouldn't be a problem.

"So, what did you want to talk about?" Vera asked, as Didi led them through some arm rotations.

"Er . . ." Talia didn't want to shout, so she lowered her arms into the water and inched closer to her mom.

"Talia, keep those arms up," Didi said. "You're not going to quit on us so early, are you?"

The women in the two rows in front turned to look at Talia.

"You can do it, dear."

"If you get tired, just think about something else to distract your mind."

"Embrace the burn," the oldest of the women growled with an intensity that made Talia yank her arms up from the water and straight out to her sides again.

"Wow, zealous crowd," Talia said under her breath.

Vera snorted. "You have no idea."

After the warm-up, Didi told them to march in place. "Lift your knees up if you can!" The water in the pool sloshed against the sides.

Talia took the opportunity to march over to Vera, keeping her knees high so Didi couldn't find any fault to call her out again.

"Something happened yesterday," Talia said.

Vera arched a brow. "Something good or something bad?"

Talia rubbed her face with her hands, forgetting that they were wet. She flinched as chlorine got in her eyes.

"Something bad . . . I kissed Sam."

"Hallelujah!" Vera yelled, practically leaping out of the water.

All of the women turned again to look at them.

"Focus, ladies," Didi said. She gave Talia the side-eye, no longer as welcoming about the miscreant addition to her class.

Sorry, sorry, Talia mouthed.

Vera continued marching in place but couldn't wipe the grin off her face. "It's finally happening! I always *knew* you two were perfect for each other. Tell me everything—where did it happen, how did it happen, and when am I getting beautiful grandbabies?"

"Ugh, Mom, no grandbabies because it was a mistake and I undid it all."

"What?"

Talia looked around. The other women were clearly trying to eavesdrop, although she was pretty sure they couldn't hear her over the churning of the water.

But then she remembered, *So what*? She might not have the watch right now (she hadn't known if it was waterproof), but the instant class was over, Talia could go to the locker room and rewind all this. None of the women would remember anything Talia said.

"All right, it's Aqua Zumba time!" Didi declared as she switched to a new playlist, this one like salsa music at 0.25x speed. "Let's move those hips, ladies, and get sultry!"

The women whooped as they started to dance very slowly in the pool. The movements were languid in real time but felt fast and sexy to them, which put a smile on Talia's face despite the conversation she was smack in the middle of. Making people's lives better was what drove her, and she had a heightened appreciation now for what Didi did with aquarobics.

Vera sashayed with the class, but her attention was all on Talia. "What do you mean you undid it all? And how could kissing Sam be a mistake? You're destined for each other."

Talia took a deep breath. "Okay, what I'm about to tell you is going to sound a little nutty, but bear with me. I have a watch that can rewind time."

Her mom blinked. "I don't understand what that means. Is this a new Ideal Life product?"

"No, it's not new technology . . . I'm not sure it's tech at all. I have no idea how it works. It just does."

She explained everything—when the watch had first appeared after an 11:11 p.m. wish, how it allowed her to go back up to twenty-four hours to redo things, and how she'd used it to improve her meeting at Omni and to buy stock before it quintupled.

"But then yesterday, I kissed Sam at his bookstore. He didn't kiss me back, and I panicked and spun the knob on my watch to undo it, so he doesn't know, but I can't forget it. So . . . what do I do?"

"Oh, baby." Vera stopped water dancing and hugged Talia. "I don't understand about the watch, but as for Sam, I'm sure you just caught him off guard. He loves you."

"He doesn't, Mom. Not like that. I threw myself at him, and he just went rigid. It was humiliating. And the other thing is, Sam knows about the watch, but he'd made me promise that I would never change his life with it. But now I have. I broke that promise, and I can't tell him."

"Are you sure about that? I think Sam would understand."

Talia shook her head. Maybe he would. But maybe he wouldn't.

She didn't want to risk their friendship, and telling him would expose her on two fronts: breaking the promise *and* making a move on him that he had no interest in reciprocating. Any scientist worth her salt would see that the results of the kissing experiment were negative.

Didi shot both Talia and Vera an *I don't see you Aqua Zumbaing* look. Vera immediately started sashaying again. Talia did so with a lot less enthusiasm.

"I guess it is what it is," Talia said of the whole kissing failure. "Thanks for listening, though. And for believing me about the bizarre watch. It did feel better to think through the situation out loud."

"Of course, sweetie," Vera said. "But, um . . ."

"Yeah?"

Vera puffed out her lips in the kind of frowny smile that moms give their kids when they're in tough positions and the moms want to—but can't—help. "I know you're usually private and keep your feelings close to your chest. So it's okay with me if you rewind this conversation once we're out of the pool. I'm aware that means I'll forget about it, and I'll also lose this really lovely time I got to spend with you. But you don't have to feel bad on my account for erasing this, okay?"

Talia thought of the watch in the locker room. "Rewind this? Are you sure?"

"Positive."

Talia power-water-walked over and hugged her.

From the pool deck, Didi shook her head; she'd given up on Talia as an unteachable student.

Vera squeezed Talia back. "Just one favor, honey."

"Anything."

"The next time you decide to rewind, do you mind buying some good stock for your dad and me?"

Sam

Jenny and Roger Chang arrived at SFO on Monday morning. Sam picked them up and brought them to the lighthouse, since they wouldn't be able to check in to the Ritz-Carlton in Half Moon Bay until the afternoon. (How much had they sold Sunshine Cakes for?? But regardless, Sam was happy for them. They'd worked literally every day of their adult lives without a break. They deserved the Ritz and more.)

"Hmm," Roger said, as Sam showed them inside Lighthouse Books. His dad browsed the shelves and kept repeating "Hmm" every so often.

"Hmm?" Sam asked.

"All books in English."

Sam shrugged apologetically. "Sorry." He didn't know how to say in Taiwanese that there wasn't much demand here for works in foreign languages.

"No café, Sammy?" Jenny asked. "In Taiwan, many bookstores have café."

"No space for café," Sam said. Again, he didn't mean to be terse, but he didn't have the vocabulary to explain that he would've loved to have had a little coffee shop, but it was a complicated and separate permitting process to get a license to cook and sell food on the premises. Besides the fact that there really was no space for a café.

"Let's go upstairs?" he said, pointing. "My office. My apartment."

He gave them a brief tour of the second floor of the lighthouse, which took all of five minutes, and then they all crammed into his tiny studio at the top. Thankfully, they'd left

Jenny and Roger's luggage behind the counter with Kenneth, although Roger had been a little wary of the employee who was clearly half-stoned. But Jenny had smiled and held up two fingers in a peace sign and said to Kenneth, "Groovy, dude." Kenneth had grinned and placed both hands over his heart. "Peace and love to all," he'd said, and then Jenny had whispered something in Taiwanese to Roger that Sam didn't catch, but apparently it had made it okay to leave the suitcases with the groovy dude.

Now he pulled out chairs at his tiny kitchenette table for his parents and bustled around to make them some green tea. He'd even baked a batch of pineapple cakes last night, using Jenny's recipe—technically, it was a trade secret, but the recipe was also Jenny's most prized possession, and like hell she wasn't going to give it to her own son. Or, at least, that was the gist that Sam had gotten, because she'd said all that years ago in Taiwanese when she had gifted him with the recipe as his college graduation present.

"Here, eat a snack," Sam said, setting the plate of pineapple shortbread onto the table with a teapot and two mugs. "I know they're not as good as the way you bake them . . ."

Jenny took a big bite and patted him on the arm. "Very good, Sammy. You are my son, good baker. You are your dad's son, good math, good . . ." She turned to Roger and asked how to say a word in English.

Roger shook his head but pulled out his phone and typed in the query. The translation popped up. "Phi-lo-so-phy," he said.

Sam frowned. "Philosophy?" He knew his dad was a numbers guy—he'd run all the financials for Sunshine Cakes for decades—but where did philosophy come in?

"Hmm . . ." Roger typed something else into his phone, then held it up for Sam and Jenny to read: I majored in philosophy at the university. Fascinating topic, but there aren't jobs for philosophers. That's how I became a baker's husband.

Jenny laughed and whacked Roger lightly on his shoulder. "Ah, you! Always joke!"

Sam was stunned, though. He himself had majored in philosophy—well, double-majored with physics, but that was irrelevant right now—so how come this had never come up before?

But of course he knew. It was because he never really had long conversations with his parents. The barriers of language and culture had kept them at arm's length, and to be honest, Sam had been a typical kid who hadn't really thought of his mom and dad as full-fledged people with robust histories. To him, they'd just been parents.

"How Talia doing?" Roger asked. "She make good deal, too. Omni *big* company."

"You know about Talia's deal?"

"Of course," Jenny said. "She your friend. We use Google Alert. Very easy, Talia Morgan not popular name. Too many Sam Chang, no news about you. But lots news about Talia."

"It's kind of bizarre that you probably know more about my friend than about me," Sam mumbled in English.

"What you say?" Roger asked.

"Nothing," Sam said. But he was feeling a little stung over it, even if it was silly to be jealous over something like a Google alert. They weren't wrong; there *were* too many Sam Changs, and anyway, he didn't do anything particularly newsworthy, other than occasional top-ten finishes in poker tournaments. Still, he changed the subject. "Tell me about your big travel plans."

In her excitement, Jenny quickly swallowed the bite of pineapple cake she'd been eating and whipped out her phone, swiping open YouTube with an easy flick. She really was more dexterous on the phone than Sam was on his.

"I love this channel, Libby and Jacob."

Sam's jaw dropped. "You follow Libby?" he said in English, and then in Taiwanese, "Libby is Talia's sister."

Jenny rolled her eyes. "I know that! They look same, both so pretty. You and Talia, beautiful children together."

"Mom!"

"What? I dream be grandma."

"Oh my god." Sam crammed a pineapple shortbread into his mouth so he wouldn't have to talk for a minute.

"Anyway," Jenny said, scrolling through Libby and Jacob's YouTube channel, "I study many, many videos. I pick best ones for me and Dad. Libby recommend, we go."

No wonder hotel chains and tour operators loved sponsoring Libby and Jacob. Even sixty-year-old Taiwanese women hung on their every word.

Soon, though, Jenny's energy ran out as jet lag caught up with them, and she and Roger napped for a few hours on Sam's bed while he went back downstairs to help Kenneth in the store.

The illogical sadness of his parents knowing more about Talia and Libby, though, followed Sam as he shelved books. Not that they knew Talia and Libby on a deep level, because the sources were all public. But it was still more access than they had to Sam and his life. And yet, he couldn't change that; it's not as if he was going to start a YouTube channel, and he certainly didn't have a high-flying startup to make headlines with. Very few people wanted to write articles about a man who eccentrically bought a lighthouse and filled it with books.

Sam thought about how his dad had majored in philosophy, and how he'd never known this, and he felt hollow over all the conversations they'd missed out on having over the years because they just couldn't talk properly. He knew his parents were smart—they'd built a hugely successful business from scratch—and they knew that *he* was smart, but all that intelligence was locked up behind second-grade-level language that trapped them eternally in childish chatter—

Unless . . .

His dad had used his phone to translate. That was a relatively basic technology, too clunky for one-off sentences here and there.

But Talia had mentioned that she used her Omni 3Ds for simultaneous interpretation with her attorneys in France! It took their voices and translated what they were saying in real time, then played it through the speakers in her glasses in English, still in the speaker's voice.

Sam didn't have or want Omni 3Ds, but surely this technology was also available elsewhere?

A quick search found that yes, indeed, if he bought certain earbuds, they'd be able to do the same thing.

And if he got earbuds for his parents, too . . .

Maybe they could actually, truly communicate for the first time. With depth and nuance. Without human barriers of vocabulary and poor syntax.

With trembling hands, he placed an order on his phone for three sets of earbuds. And then Sam tried to smother the fizzing in the center of his chest, not wanting to hope too hard that there could be a solution to the yearning he'd buried deep inside himself for so long.

Talia

In an effort to bring more green spaces downtown (and acknowledgment of startup culture's love for shared community spaces where people and ideas could freely mingle), the landlord of the building that housed Ideal Life had built a rooftop garden. There were potted citrus trees from which you could pick fresh oranges and kumquats in the winter, and now, in summer, there was plenty of shade from the delicate green leaves of Japanese maples. Sprinkled around the rooftop were groupings of tables and chairs for when teams from Ideal Life or BiomeLabs wanted to work outside, as well as benches for taking lunch breaks (or dinner breaks, as the case may be, since the employees of both companies worked long hours).

It was here that Talia went after Aquarobics to screw her head on straight again. You didn't become CEO of a startup worth $100 million by being the type of woman easily felled by an errant kiss.

The other thing about being CEO was that you could hold your meetings outside whenever you pleased.

"Morning, boss," Erin chirped, plopping down across the table with her laptop.

"Good morning. Thanks for agreeing to do your midsummer performance review up here."

"It's a nice change of pace. Oh, I haven't seen Sam around. Not that he would come to the office, but, um, how is he? Have you two been hanging out more?"

Talia could feel the blood drain from her face. It took a second to remember that Erin didn't know about the doomed kiss.

But it still felt like Erin had poured salt water into the open wound of Talia's mortification, and Talia snapped. "Sam and I are not getting together, so I don't want to hear about it again. Let's focus on work when we're at the office, huh?"

Erin flushed all the way from her neck to the tips of her ears. "Um, of course. Sorry. I was just trying to speak up like you told me to, a-and I'm so sorry. I crossed a line; I won't do it again." She flipped open her computer, hands poised on the keyboard, and swallowed hard, not looking at Talia. "I'm ready. Tell me what I can improve."

"Okay then," Talia said, still simmering but trying to get back into CEO mode. "As before, I'm glad you're open to improvement. I have several suggestions for you, all of which lead to raising your profile and garnering more respect.

"First, it's nice that you think of the team and bring donuts and such to the office, but stop. It paints you as a submissive girl. You are very intelligent and want people to respect you, rather than treat you as the kid who is here only for the summer. So even though you're still in college, start acting like you deserve to be treated as an equal, because you do.

"Second, you ought to invest in a more professional wardrobe. I know it's a bit unfair to say that because most of us wear T-shirts and jeans to work, but since you're young and you *look* even younger than your age, it would be helpful to your career if you dressed up a little more than we do. Again, it's a subtle way of demanding respect.

"And third, I'm happy to be your mentor. But maybe make it a little less obvious to others, so it doesn't come off as sycophantic or idolizing. I'm not saying stop learning from me. I think it's great that you're absorbing everything like a sponge. Women should support other women, of course, and I—"

Talia stopped talking, because Erin had stopped typing. Her face was bright red again, and she was holding herself very rigid.

Oh shit. Talia had taken her shame of kissing Sam out on Erin, and she'd been too harsh.

Erin was amazing, and Talia should have just said so. Who cares if Erin expressed her generous personality by bringing donuts? And as for what she wore, some of the clothes Talia had worn when she first started working had been pretty questionable, and she'd turned out fine.

"Erin, I'm sorry. I didn't—"

"No, no, it's okay," she said, although it was apparent she was having to do some serious internal peptalking to hold herself together. It wasn't easy to hear so many criticisms from a person you admire, especially when the meeting had begun with a dressing down.

Talia bit her lip, then touched her watch. "I really am sorry. Let me try that again."

She turned the dial slowly backward, watching the scene in reverse as Erin's face went from stiff and red to animated and normal-toned again, as she picked up her laptop and stood and walked backward to the elevator, until the doors opened and swallowed her inside.

"Do better," Talia said under her breath.

The elevator chimed as the doors opened. Erin stepped out.

"Morning, boss!"

"Good morning," Talia said quickly to head off any inquiries about Sam. "Thanks for agreeing to do your midsummer performance review up here. I'm on a tight schedule, so let's dive right in."

"Of course." Erin sat down, flipped open her computer, and poised her hands on the keyboard. "Okay, I'm ready. Tell me what I can improve."

Talia smiled, perhaps too hard. "You continue to impress me with your desire to push yourself. In the five weeks that you've been with us, you've already integrated so well with the team."

Erin blushed. Her skin really did not hide how she was feeling.

"I appreciated your contributions at the recent marketing

meeting," Talia continued. "It's smart to expand our audience to your generation, and I'd like to task you with brainstorming more ideas we could explore."

"Oh my gosh, I would love to do that!" She blushed harder but then reined in her outward enthusiasm. "I mean, thank you, of course, I'd be happy to."

"Okay then, great."

Erin frowned. "That's it?"

Talia smiled again. "Yes, you're doing a wonderful job."

"But what about improvements?"

"Don't worry about it. Everyone enjoys having you around."

"Oh, um, all right . . ." She closed her laptop and stood, hovering for a few more seconds before the awkward silence got her, and she walked back toward the elevator.

She stepped inside, but before the doors closed, she called out, "Talia, I'm really sorry if I did anything to disappoint you or to make you think that I couldn't handle feedback. I want you to know I will study this morning and figure out how I can improve so that next time, I'll be more prepared. Thank you for your time."

The elevator doors shut.

Ah, dammit. Talia had gone too far on the other side of the spectrum and babied Erin, which is not what she needed—or wanted—at all. Erin deserved better from Talia.

"Let's try this once more." She rewound the watch crown, until Erin was back where she'd started, emerging from the elevator for the first time.

"Morning, boss!"

Talia's stomach lurched, even though she'd turned the clock back slowly. The external world around her had stopped spinning, but her internal one still seemed to be going.

She thought she'd outwitted the nausea recently after getting better with the watch, but the vague motion sickness seemed to be creeping back. That and the fatigue that was always just under the surface nowadays, no matter how many hours she slept.

"Um, good morning." Talia held the table with both hands to steady herself. "I'm . . . on a tight . . . schedule . . . Let's get started."

Erin didn't sit like she had in the previous two iterations. "Talia? Are you okay?"

"Yes, fine. I got weirdly light-headed." She forced a smile. "Anyway, thanks for agreeing to do your midsummer performance review up here."

"Of course. It's a nice change of pace. But I don't want to make you run late on your next meeting, so I'm ready." She sat down across from Talia and flipped open her computer, hands poised on the keyboard. "Tell me what I can improve."

"Well, first I want to say that you continue to impress me. But maybe that's egotistical, because you remind me of myself at that age. All brainpower and ambition, wanting to change the world."

Erin's cheeks pinked. "Wow, thank you—what a compliment."

"But I know that you want constructive criticism, and if I were in your position, I would ask for it as well. So I just have one suggestion for now, and that's to pull back on bringing in treats to the office. It's kind of you and endears you to the rest of the team, but you'll want to do it sparingly—that way they view you as a future equal who *occasionally* buys donuts for her colleagues, rather than, if you do it all the time, then it starts to cast you into a certain old-fashioned female stereotype and could be read as subservient. I *hate* that, believe me, but it is something that can happen. And take this with a grain of salt, because it's just my very subjective opinion."

"Noted," Erin said, typing everything Talia said word for word. "And I can see what you're saying. There is the world the way it should be, and there is the world the way it is. You're trying to help me succeed in the way the world currently is, even though we both hope for more change and equality in the future."

Talia nodded, even though that made the rooftop around her look wobbly, and her stomach flipped. *Damn watch.*

She paused for a second, then said, "Exactly. And your ability to consider both logic and emotion while keeping them separate when necessary will take you far. So that's it. Just keep working on that brainstorming project. I look forward to what you come up with."

Erin tilted her head. "Brainstorming project?"

"The one we just talked about."

She started typing furiously and squinted at her computer, looking for something.

"I'm sorry, Talia, but . . . maybe I misfiled the email. I don't see anything about a brainstorming project."

Dammit again! Talia had mentioned it the first time—no, the second time?—they'd done this midsummer performance review, but she hadn't explained it this third time, had she?

"No, Erin, it's my fault—sorry. I'm feeling a little off this morning. I must've thought about the project but not said it out loud. I appreciated your ideas at the recent marketing meeting. It's smart to expand Ideal Life into your generation, and I'd like you to come up with more ideas we could explore."

"Oh my gosh, I would love to do that! I mean, thank you, of course, I'd be happy to."

"Wonderful. Well, that's all from me. Keep up the great work."

Erin grinned as she picked up her laptop. "Would you like me to get you a Tylenol—no, wait . . . Scratch that. Too submissive?" She looked to Talia for guidance. "Or is it good to be nice?"

Talia wondered if she'd given the wrong piece of advice. She didn't want to break the part of Erin that made her a fundamentally good person. Maybe she ought to rewind again.

But she didn't think she could do it so soon without feeling more ill. Using the watch at Aquarobics and twice in such quick succession here on the roof (plus the cumulative rewinds overall) seemed to be taking a toll.

"I'll be okay, Erin. But I appreciate you offering."

Staying put in the present for the rest of the day grounded Talia again. By midafternoon, she felt steady enough to check the stock markets, which had closed in New York, to see if there was anything she could invest in for her parents.

Last year, as part of their "graduation" from the Ideal Life app and becoming more responsible adults, Vera and Dave had hired an attorney to help them write a will. During that process, they'd also given Talia power of attorney to handle their money. She had opened a brokerage account for them and helped them invest their savings, which wasn't a lot, but they were only in their early sixties and still had time.

Today, there were no big surprises like when BiomeLabs' share price quintupled overnight, but there were some mid-cap nontech companies that had done well. Talia noted the exact time of each one's lowest price earlier in the day, then rewound very, very slowly to before those moments. She bought each stock at the dip for her parents.

If they continued to rise tomorrow, great. If not, she could come back and sell them for a small profit, then take the proceeds and invest in something else.

Talia felt a twinge of guilt.

But it was for a good cause—her parents! And every little bit would help.

If Sam were here, he wouldn't let Talia accept the rationalization so easily. But he wasn't here, and she'd already done it. And really, if Sam had his way all the time, Talia never would've dove so deep into the tech world because of his post–Nowhere Cat reticence, and she wouldn't have Ideal Life, and so maybe he *wasn't* the best with advice!

Ideal Life Queen Elizabeth: I'm sensing agitation, reflected by higher beta activity and diminished alpha rhythms in your brain activity—

"Dismiss!" Talia shouted, aware that this probably made her alpha and beta bands even more irregular, but sometimes Queen Elizabeth was such a pest.

When Talia got back to present time, a wall of exhaustion hit her. She could hardly think; it was like her brain was lost in a thick, pea soup fog.

The sun dappled through the trees, and a warm breeze made their leaves' shadows dance hypnotically. *Maybe I'll just close my eyes for a few minutes*. There was no one on the roof right now, since lunch had been a while ago.

But then the elevator dinged and the doors opened, and Ideal Life's chief privacy officer, Sara Trankjaer, stepped out. "Hey, Talia, I heard you were up here. Do you have a few minutes?"

For a moment, Talia's breath hitched as she thought Sara had figured out that Talia had gone into the back-end system and deactivated the account of Rebecca Lawrence—the would-be Tinder murderer. Talia wouldn't be able to explain that she was preventing a death, so how would she explain what she'd done? In the grand scheme of things, it wasn't a big deal, but it *was* still a breach of privacy protocols and something that should have been logged . . .

"I wanted to go over some of the due diligence requests from Omni," Sara said.

Oh. That's a lot easier. Thank goodness.

"Of course," Talia said, gesturing at the chair across from her to invite Sara to sit. "What's up?"

"Well, I'm not sure if this is concerning, but I wanted to flag it for you. Omni is asking for detailed information about the medical and behavioral health histories that our customers have provided and how they granted those permissions."

"Okay, that should be fine," Talia said. "We only collect information our users self-reported voluntarily. They're not official medical records, so our lawyers said there shouldn't be any HIPAA issues."

"Agreed," Sara said. "But the curious thing is that Omni's legal team is doing an analysis of the assignability of that user data. Put another way, it seems like they're poking around to see if they'll be able to use Ideal Life's customer information for something broader than what we use it for, which is only to let the app make suggestions to the user themself."

Talia shook her head. "They didn't say anything about that when I was on their campus the other day. It's not in any of the road maps. And our privacy policy is clear; the information our customers volunteer can *only* be used to help them."

Sara chewed on the inside of her cheek. "Okay, well . . . I just wanted to bring it up."

"I'm glad you did. Ideal Life's integrity is important to me. Our customers trust us, and that's not negotiable."

As Sara returned back downstairs, though, Talia's stomach turned, and this time it wasn't because of the watch.

Because what if Sara was onto something? What if this was one of those acquisitions where a Big Tech company buys a startup, guts it for code or data, and then tosses the rest aside?

Or something even less scrupulous?

Talia stood and walked to the edge of the roof. From here, she could see over the top of Palo Alto. Out of view but to the south was Omni's campus. She replayed in her mind that last version of the meeting she'd had there, and what everyone, including their CEO, Jack Zimmer, had said. Nothing jumped out at her.

"Innocent till proven guilty," Talia said in Omni headquarters' direction.

She lived and worked in Silicon Valley, so she knew Big Tech were not the pure villains that some media liked to portray them as. That was too reductive. Some companies certainly wielded too much power. But others did good things, like investing in research that had no guarantee of profits but that might change the world, like when a Google team won the Nobel Prize for their work in genetics. A smaller company never could have spent that much money on research unrelated to their core business.

But being in Silicon Valley also meant Talia was not naive. Idealistic, yes, in that she wanted to improve lives. But not naive.

She'd been keeping one eye on Omni before, but now she'd watch them with both.

Libby

Libby sat in front of one of those vanity mirrors with all the bulbs around it like you saw in old films when movie stars were putting on makeup, but instead of being in Hollywood, she was in Seoul, Korea, doing a live stream to promote personal color-analysis services for Myeongdong Color Experts. Jacob sat in a chair to her left, not caught by the mirror's reflection. He would get his own color-matching session later, but Libby was going first since the portion of their audience who would care most about this was women.

The idea of color analysis itself wasn't new—back in the '80s, color wheels had been all the rage—but new technology and interest on social media had revived the art and "science" of using your skin tone and eye and hair color to find the best—most flattering—colors for you to wear. And Korea was an international hot spot for the consultations, which could cost close to $1,000 in New York but only $150 in Seoul.

The room they were in was bland and floor-to-ceiling white on purpose. Myeongdong Color Experts had chosen the precise shade of paint to ensure it would not interfere with their work with their clients—cream walls would have imbued the room with subtle hints of yellow and pink; a colder white would have cast undertones of blue. Libby and Jacob had been impressed when they explained this at the start of their session. It was hard to imagine being able to perceive such slight differences in whites, let alone how it might impact people and other things around them.

Eunice Park, the aesthetician and color expert, approached

Libby with a gray handheld device that looked like a giant high-tech inhaler turned upside down.

"This spectrophotometer will analyze how your skin reflects or absorbs light, okay? You won't feel anything."

Libby smiled as she looked at her reflection in the mirror, aware that her webcam was also capturing everything on their live stream. She had purposely come in without makeup so that the color matching could be accurate, and she felt a little washed-out, all blond hair and light skin that never really tanned, just freckled. And yet, there were little emojis of clapping hands popping up on her laptop screen, along with message bubbles like *You're so authentic!* and *I'm so excited to watch this!*, her and Jacob's followers living vicariously through them and already invested in the color-makeover outcome.

The spectrophotometer pressed against the right apple of Libby's cheek, then beeped. Eunice noted the data into her own computer.

"I am going to take several more measurements because the sun hits your face at different angles, so some places will be lighter, and others, more pigmented by melanin," she explained, as much for Libby's and Jacob's benefit as for their live audience's. After all, this was a sponsored event by Myeongdong Color Experts. "However, do not worry. We will make sure to find colors for you that match, whether it is winter and you are more pale, or summer and you are more golden." She lined up the spectrophotometer to Libby's forehead, the bridge of her nose, her jawline, neck, and décolletage, inputting each reading into her computer.

"Ah, good, as I suspected," Eunice said as she put the spectrophotometer away. "Our advanced, personalized program has a prediction for your color palette. Nevertheless, we will try several so that you can see for yourself and we can decide together. Technology is not always right, you know, and we need to include a human touch. That is why we recommend in-person consultations at Myeongdong Color Experts, instead of trying to do this at home by yourself with an app."

Off camera, Jacob tried to hide an amused smile, but Libby knew what the sudden appearance of his dimples and the covering of his mouth with his hand meant. Eunice's sales pitch had actually been well timed, but Libby and Jacob did these kinds of things for a living, and it was always obvious to them when companies were trying to use small psychological tricks on their target clients' subconscious. The *You wouldn't want to use an inferior product, would you?* technique was a classic. Because who wanted to feel like they deserved less?

Eunice brought over a stack of fabric swatches that were connected by a metal ring in the corner. She placed them across Libby's left shoulder and the left half of her décolletage; the color on top was a pale yellow. "What do you think about this one? We are looking for colors that make you glow, as if you have inner light radiating out from you."

Libby studied it in the reflection. "The color is very pretty."

"Hmm," Eunice said, bringing over another stack of fabric swatches. These she laid across Libby's right shoulder and right half of her chest. Now Libby had two different fabric swatches on her, next to each other and easily contrasted.

Eunice revealed a lemon yellow, which Libby would have thought too bright on its own. But next to her skin, it was unexpectedly lovely.

"Whoa," Jacob said. "That's crazy what a difference it makes."

Libby nodded at her image in the mirror. The lemon yellow lit up the features of her face and even made the slightly dark circles beneath her eyes disappear. "How did you do that with just color and not makeup?"

Eunice beamed. "Surprising, isn't it? Now, how about this?" She flipped both color swatches to a shade of pink—on the left, a very pale rose, and on the right, a strong fuchsia.

"I had no idea I could wear colors so strong. Wow. I've always chosen what I wear based on how it looks on the model online, or whether I liked the color itself. I hadn't realized there could be such a huge difference when the color was *matched* to me." These lines had, of course, been scripted ahead of time to make sure that the company got what it paid for with Libby and Jacob; that's how their industry was run.

However, she and Jacob had a core principle that they would only take on jobs where they were interested in or curious about the product or experience. They didn't want to become shills who hawked infomercial-quality junk that no one needed. And while they couldn't control whether the end result of their gigs would be things they loved (for example, they had done a partnership with a sweater company where they got to try their hand at shearing sheep—it had sounded fun but ended up smellier than expected because damp wool on live animals could be, uh, pungent), they at least knew they weren't compromising their own values for money.

Right now, Libby was legitimately surprised and pleased with the results of the color matching.

Eunice flipped through other colors in both swatches—oranges, greens, blues, and purples. The fabric on the right won every time.

"Now let us compare to a third color profile." She removed the pale fabrics on the left and replaced them with a new stack, these more saturated than their predecessors but not as vivid as the ones still on Libby's right. "These colors on the left are actually the ones that the computer assigned to you. What do you think?"

Eunice flipped through both sides simultaneously, comparing the rich blue on the left to the bright blue on the right.

"Huh," Libby said. "I actually think the new blue is better."

"Me, too," Jacob said.

"How about this?" Eunice flipped to the reds. The one on the left was like a deep-red wine held up to the light. The one on the right was a purer, bolder cardinal red.

Libby looked back and forth between the two.

"Remember," Eunice said, "it's not about which color you think is prettier on its own. Look at your skin. What does each shade do for you?"

"Ah, right." Libby looked at her reflection. On her laptop screen, her audience's vote was also coming in rapidly in floating comment bubbles.

"I think this time, the one on the right is the winner," Libby said. "It makes my skin all glowy like I've put on a nice blush. On the other hand, the new one on the left makes my face look fine, but more neutral, you know?"

Jacob leaned over so his face appeared in the camera, and he addressed their audience. "Looks like most of you agree with Libby's assessment."

Immediately, thumbs-up and heart emojis popped up on the screen.

Eunice smiled. The indicator on the top of the live stream feed indicated that there were currently twenty-three million viewers tuned in. And many more would watch the recording of this event later.

Libby and Eunice went through the remaining colors together, and it was an interesting split between the left and right.

"This is why we do not automatically trust the computer result," Eunice said. "When we see the colors in person, we find that you will sometimes have matches in different palettes. *And*, sometimes you have colors that no matter *what* the palette is, they are never right for you."

She held up a dark tobacco brown to Libby's face, as well as a rich chestnut one. Both made her skin look flat. Libby wrinkled her nose. "Okay, good to know. Not a brown person!"

Eunice then went on to recommend makeup colors for Libby, with specific foundation, eyeshadow, and lipstick. They were again not products Libby ever would have picked up on her own, but they really enhanced the natural glow of her skin.

When they were finished, Libby stood up so that Jacob could

take a seat. As they were switching places, though, Jacob put his hands around Libby's waist and joked to Eunice, "Can you do *predictive* color matching so we know the best color clothes to buy for our baby?"

Libby's jaw dropped. Her face wasn't on camera, because she was standing and the webcam had been trained on the chair, but her stomach was on display smack-dab in the center of the screen.

Comment bubbles started flurrying in the live stream feed faster than she could read them all.

OMG OMG OMG Libby ur preggers?

Please tell me ur gonna do a livestream baby shower!

im so happy 4 u Jacob and Libby i feel like i know u so it's like im gonna b ur baby's auntie omg

Eunice clapped her hands. "Congratulations! I did not know you were going to be parents!"

Shit, I'm sorry, Jacob mouthed to Libby, eyes wide.

She knew he hadn't meant to let it slip. She was lucky that she had a husband who was so genuinely excited about being a daddy.

But fuck. Not only had they not figured out what to do about their business with a baby on the way, but now twenty-three million strangers knew.

And Libby hadn't even told her parents or Talia yet.

Erin

Do you have to run with those things on?" Colette pointed at Erin's Omni 3Ds. They were warming up on the Oval, the iconic expanse of lawn in front of Stanford's sandstone buildings. During the school year, the Oval was full of students playing volleyball or studying. Now that it was summer, though, it was emptier, with only one group of high school summer camp kids at the far end playing Frisbee before going back to their dorms for the evening.

Erin stroked her Omni 3Ds melodramatically. "I am never taking these off—at least not until I have to return them at the end of my internship." (The glasses were on loan from Ideal Life, along with a laptop and smartwatch. The Temple Dots, of course, were meant to be replaced after two weeks of use, so Erin wouldn't have to return those. But she loyally had them on all the time, too.) "My date with Georgia was a disaster because you and Jackson stole my glasses, and therefore, I didn't know what to do!"

"I'm really sorry that you ended up in anaphylactic shock," Colette said.

Erin sighed. "I know. And I also know it's not really your and Jackson's fault. Stuff happens."

"Welcome to dating like a normal person."

"Ugh, it's overrated. Why would anyone want to do that, when Ideal Life Athena knows exactly when I'm getting nervous or about to start spouting nonsensical verbal diarrhea, or when it knows that I'm going to eat something I'm allergic to and could have stopped me?"

"There are some of us who still manage to live with allergies *without* an app," Colette said gently. She had a hard time digesting eggs and managed just fine on her own.

"It's possible that I've outsourced part of my intelligence," Erin said.

Colette snickered. "You are a hopeless human being."

Erin tapped her glasses. "Exactly. So it's actually a good thing I've got these to augment my mind. Okay, you ready to run?" She glanced down Palm Drive (lined with palm trees, no surprise) toward Campus Drive. It was a 4.3-mile loop all the way around the university and along the foothills. "If I warm up anymore, I'll be dripping sweat before we even get going."

"Almost—just let me get in my fence drills real quick."

While Colette did the last of her stretches, a new notification popped up in Erin's glasses. It wasn't from Ideal Life, though. This one was from YouTube about one of the accounts she subscribed to.

Erin squealed. "Oh my god!"

"What?" Colette sprinted over.

"Libby and Jacob are pregnant!"

Talia

Ideal Life Queen Elizabeth: It has been four days since you have seen or communicated with Sam, even though he has texted you. I have analyzed your prior messages and his recent ones, and there does not seem to be any conflict between the two of you. However, your mood markers have been a bit lower recently. May I suggest that you reach out to him? I think it would be good for you.

Talia sighed and leaned back in her office chair as she dismissed the notification. But Ideal Life Queen Elizabeth was right; she usually was. After all, Talia and her team had worked tirelessly to improve the accuracy of Ideal Life's brain-activity correlations with external indicators, as well as ongoing analysis of each user's individual history. In Talia's case, Ideal Life Queen Elizabeth knew that she and Sam were close and texted all the time, even if they only saw each other once a week for Sunday Lunch.

The current barrier, of course, was her own doing. In the last few days, she'd been able to move past replaying the kiss again and again in her head. But she hadn't gotten over the guilt of erasing it, which is why she hadn't responded to Sam's texts, even though Sam himself had no memory of her horribly awkward mistake.

"Oh, fine." She opened up her messaging app on her desktop.

Talia: Hey . . . sorry, been super busy at work. I know it's only Thursday, but are you free tonight? I could come out to the coast. Miss you.

She hit Send and held her breath.

There was no reason Sam would think anything strange of it. Still, her pulse trembled as she waited.

The thing was, she might be waiting for hours if Sam was busy unpacking boxes of books or chatting with customers or even just reading. He often left his phone in the little office on the second floor of the lighthouse, and he didn't wear a smartwatch or Omni 3Ds or any of the other tech that Talia found useful. Which made him maddeningly difficult to reach when she wanted to hear from him.

Sam: Who is this? I don't think I've heard from this number in a while. I don't rendezvous with strangers. It's dangerous, you know.

She laughed, relief filling her chest.

Talia: I know it's not Sunday, but can we do Taco Bell?
Sam: Are you trying to get out of paying by changing the day?

She sent him an animated emoji of herself arching a brow and wrote "See you soon." Then she shut off her computer and grabbed her purse, leaving the building before she could change her mind. It was only 5 p.m., which meant it was five hours earlier than she usually left the office.

But this was important. Ideal Life Queen Elizabeth had said so. And the queen always knew best.

Sam

Sam's parents were sightseeing in San Francisco today, so it worked out that Talia wanted to hang out. But when she walked into Lighthouse Books, he blinked twice and had to make an effort to keep his face neutral.

She was a sickly shade of pale and the bags under her eyes were more pronounced than usual, and it wasn't just because of the fluorescent lights overhead.

Kenneth, though, wasn't trained in subtlety. "Damn, Talia," he said from behind the register. "You burning the candle on both ends? You look like shit, no offense."

She paused in the middle of the floor, before she plastered on her CEO smile and said, "Don't be a dick, Kenneth. This is what a powerful woman looks like, and you're just intimidated."

Kenneth hooted and slapped his knee. "Touché, Talia. Touché."

On the way to Taco Bell, Sam watched Talia as she drove. This close, he could see how her collarbones stuck out too sharply beneath her skin. Her normally shiny hair was dull, and she slouched in her seat, her shoulders slumped forward.

He'd suspected something was wrong this week when she didn't respond to his daily texts. But he also knew not to push her, that Talia would clam up more if you asked directly about how she was feeling. Sure, you could get away with a "How are you?" But if you tried to make her open up deeper when she didn't want to, she'd just clamp shut even tighter. Sam had to draw her out on her own terms.

When they arrived at the Taco Bell in Pacifica, Talia left all her devices in the glove compartment, honoring Sunday Lunch rules even though it wasn't Sunday.

Then they went inside, and she ordered the same thing as always—a beef soft taco, a side of chips and nacho cheese, and cinnamon twists. Sam, on the other hand, studied the menu for a good minute.

Talia tapped her finger on her watch, pretending to be impatient even though he knew she was actually curious about what he would order. And because helping her relax was step one in getting Talia to share what was really going on, he erred on the side of ridiculous.

"Today's theme is 'supreme superlative'—I will only eat items that have the word 'supreme' in them."

Talia snickered.

The Taco Bell cashier was a lot less impressed by a thirty-five-year-old acting like he was eighteen.

But Sam didn't care whether the cashier was amused, only if Talia was. Back when they were in college, he used to make up themes all the time for their Taco Bell runs. It had been years, though, since he'd done it, and now Sam was committing to it. He ordered a Crunchwrap Supreme, a Double Decker Taco Supreme, and a Chalupa Supreme.

"For here or to go?" the cashier asked, bored and monotone.

"For—" Talia began.

"To go," Sam said. "Let's go to the beach to eat."

The chilly wind whipped Talia's hair everywhere as they walked along the cliffside beach. It had been a little warmer earlier in the day, but now the temperature had already begun to dip, even though sunset was still a couple of hours away.

"Samuel Jason Chang, this was a terrible idea," she said, although there was an undercurrent of laughter in her tone.

"Just wait and see."

Sam took off his coat and wrapped it around her. Hearing her soft sigh as she sank into the warm shearling was more than worth it to him to brave the cold.

They traipsed across the sand, Talia clutching his coat and their precious bag of bad tacos close, before he steered her toward a crevice in the side of the cliff. She cocked her head, confused. It didn't look like much from the beach, just a narrow opening barely big enough for an adult to wedge into sideways.

"Do you trust me?" Sam asked.

"No," Talia said.

Sam smirked and led the way in anyhow.

A couple of meters in, the crevice turned right and opened into a small cave. Fissures led straight up to the top of the cliff, letting in streams of soft evening light. In the distance, they could still hear the sounds of the waves as they rolled onto the shore, but otherwise, it was secluded and perfectly quiet.

"Wow . . ." Talia spun around. It was fifteen degrees warmer in here, sheltered from the cold but still with a nice breeze that blew through and kept the air fresh. It was comfortable enough for her to shed Sam's coat. "Have you been keeping this place from me all these years?"

"I found out about it from Kayla the other day."

"Ahhh, Kayla." Talia was facing away from Sam, but he could hear the teasing in her voice.

"It's not like that," he said.

"She didn't seem to think so at the Chloe Quinn event last weekend."

"Yeah, well, we actually talked after you left. I thought that if we were going to keep seeing each other, then maybe we *should* be more serious, like you suggested. But Kayla wasn't interested. She said she just wanted to have fun, didn't want to be tied down."

Talia turned to him now. "I'm sorry, Sam."

He shook his head. "I wasn't in love with her or anything. I mean, I thought that maybe if we were in a relationship, I could see where it led . . . Really, it's not a big deal. We're friends now, and when I told her that you and I had a tradition of coming to Pacifica once a week, she told me about this secret cave."

"Well, tell Kayla thank you for saving me from the cold the next time you see her."

They set up a picnic area, and Talia went through her routine of unwrapping her soft taco, crumbling and evenly distributing tortilla chips over it, then drizzling the entire operation with nacho cheese. She asked about his parents, and he told them about how happy they were to be visiting, and how they were living it up at the Ritz-Carlton in Half Moon Bay, eating lobster rolls with a beachfront view and ending their evenings by making s'mores in their personal firepit on their hotel room patio.

Then she asked if there were any new Kenneth stories (because there was always something going on with him that made Sam's life more, well, lively), and he told her about some drama that had happened when Kenneth had opened a box of Stephen King's next novel—highly anticipated books were *clearly* marked by publishers with a neon sticker on the box that warned NOT FOR SALE UNTIL whatever the official release day was—and Kenneth had completely ignored the warning sticker and set the books out anyway. (Another reason new releases were supposed to be Sam's job.)

When a tourist noticed the book out before it was supposed to be available, she had immediately posted about it online. Sam had received an angry call from the publisher soon after and had to run down onto the showroom floor and pack away all the books himself.

"What did Kenneth say when you confronted him?" Talia asked.

"He said, 'Oh, oops, I didn't see the sticker on the box—sorry.' Then he went out back and smoked a joint."

Talia laughed. "Sometimes, I wonder if we'd all be better off if we were Kenneth. We'd be a lot less stressed, anyway."

Sam laughed, too. "Yeah, but if you had the same attitude as Kenneth, you wouldn't be able to change the world. And then you wouldn't be happy."

She got quiet then, and Sam didn't push it. He just let her methodically clean up their taco wrappers—folding them all into neat, compact squares, then stacking them inside the paper bag and folding *that* until it took the minimum amount of space possible—before she decided to speak again.

"The watch makes me tired," she said.

To anyone else, it would've seemed like a non sequitur. But Sam knew they'd been building toward this the whole time. Talia volunteered her emotions on her own schedule. He'd just made sure to give her the space and lack of pressure to do it.

"I didn't know the watch could do that," he said. "Are you using it a lot?"

"Um." She looked at it on her wrist. It was the one piece of technology she hadn't left in the glove compartment, but maybe it didn't really count as technology. Sam wasn't sure *what* it was, and given that she'd had it now for a couple of weeks and they still didn't know where it had come from or how it worked, they would probably never know.

"I don't use it *too* much." Talia didn't elaborate after that.

Sam didn't say anything, either. He'd already cautioned her not to overdo it that day when she rewound her meetings on the Omni campus and ended up attending them three times.

She was a grown woman and didn't need him micromanaging her. Besides, between the two of them, Talia was the one running a successful startup. He was the one who'd bought a bookshop that couldn't turn a profit.

Speaking of which . . .

"Hey, I signed up for an open poker tournament in San Jose this weekend. It's called Summer Million, and first prize is . . . Guess."

Talia grinned. "A million dollars? Sam! I'm so excited for you!"

He waved it off. "There are over two thousand other players. I still have to play well."

"I'm sure you will."

Sam thought she glanced at her watch.

But no, he must've been mistaken. She'd promised she wouldn't use it on him.

Talia drove them back to the lighthouse. As she pulled into the parking lot, she asked Sam to hand her her phone from the glove compartment.

They said their goodbyes, and he was halfway out the door when she started checking her messages.

Talia gasped. "What?"

Sam slid back into the car. "What happened? Are you okay?"

She gaped at her phone. Then she passed it to him so he could read the message.

Erin: Oh my gosh, I just saw on YouTube that Libby and Jacob are pregnant! Congrats on becoming an aunt soon!!

"Libby didn't tell you?" Sam asked. The sisters weren't as close as they used to be, ever since Libby got married and started jet-setting around the world, but they still loved each other fiercely, and he knew Talia would be very hurt that she hadn't found out before the entire internet.

Talia sank into the driver's seat. "I think she tried to. But I was too busy."

The Ideal Life app dinged as a suggestion popped up on her phone. Sam was still holding it.

Ideal Life Queen Elizabeth: I am detecting increased activity in your bilateral limbic and paralimbic structures, which may signal transient sadness. I see you have also just read the message from Erin Berg about your sister. Assuming a correlation between the two, perhaps your feelings are related to Libby, with whom you had a truncated conversation last week and have not reconnected with since.

To alleviate your distress, may I suggest that you reach out to her, as I suggested you do with Sam?

His heart sank.

It hadn't even been Talia herself who'd wanted to see him. It had been an AI bumblebee that had reminded her that he was her friend.

Disappointment was too weak a word to describe how he felt.

Sadness? Dismay?

But it didn't really matter if he could define it, because the knot in his chest was tight enough that it was hard to speak.

Sam shook his head as he put the phone down on her console. "Call your sister, Tal," he said quietly. "I'll . . . see you later."

Then he got out of her car and walked away, not sure whether this friendship only went in one direction anymore.

Talia

Talia watched Sam walk across the parking lot to his bookstore. She waited for him to turn around again and wave, but he didn't. Was he upset about something?

She thought about rewinding for a few minutes to double-check, but she couldn't do that, not after she'd just undid her kiss earlier this week.

Then she picked up her phone and saw Ideal Life Queen Elizabeth's note.

"Oh no. Sam!"

Talia opened the car door to go after him, but then her phone rang.

It was Libby.

As Talia answered the video call, she realized with a pang that she didn't know where on the planet Libby was. She'd been even worse than usual lately with keeping up on Libby and Jacob's posts; time had gotten tangled up in her head, thanks to the watch.

"Oh god, Talia," Libby sobbed, her eyes red and face puffy. She was on a bed in a hotel room, no obvious decorations to indicate what country she was in.

"Libby, what's wrong?" Talia sat straight up in the driver's seat. "Is the baby okay?" She had expected this to be a regular conversation, besides her own apology for being so unavailable, and that she and Libby would then squeal over the baby.

"Jacob didn't mean to . . . I-I don't . . . I don't know what to do!"

"What the fuck? I will kill him. Did he hurt you? The baby?"

"No, I—" Libby devolved into tears again.

Jacob appeared, wrapping his arms around her and stroking her hair.

"Hi, Talia," he said. "I'm sorry you found out over YouTube. Libby wanted to tell you first, but I slipped—"

"And now the whole world knows!" Libby cried. "Our baby is doomed and she never even got a choice!"

"Hey, hey, shh." Talia leaned in toward her screen. "It's going to be okay, whatever's going on. Just tell me what happened."

Libby spilled everything the best she could, and when she got caught up in tears, Jacob filled in. They talked about their qualms about including the child in their public life, from documenting the pregnancy to turning their Libby & Jacob accounts into a family affair. In a world of AI models that could easily be edited into any place and any situation, there was a certain cache to still being real humans. But while Libby and Jacob had made the decision to sell parts of their lives as a business, their future child had not, and she wouldn't be able to consent—or even understand the magnitude of what she was giving up—for more than eighteen years.

On the other hand, there *were* examples of loving families who had made the transition well, like the Globetrotter Quartet. Jacob and Libby sometimes crossed paths with them and therefore knew that they were genuinely good people. Plus, they were giving their kids a global upbringing and education.

"So what do we do?" Libby asked when they had finished.

It was an echo of when she and Talia were kids, their parents out at another party, having left them without anything to eat for dinner. "What do we do?" Libby had asked all the time back then, looking up at her big sister for help while also knowing that Talia would have an idea, Talia would figure something out, Talia would keep them fed and bathed and cared for.

"Well," Talia said now, "it sounds to me like if you could do things entirely your way, you would *not* put your baby online in any of your content. But because of the momentum of 'Libby & Jacob' and the pressures of the creator industry, you feel like you have to consider it. Is that an accurate summary?"

Libby nodded. She'd always found it comforting when Talia broke down a big emotional problem into logical chunks. It made things seem more manageable.

"Okay," Talia said. "Then you have three paths: One, quit the business and do something else—maybe not as profitable, but you'd be able to find work in a marketing agency or something similar, given your background and experience in the field. Two, continue your existing business with the baby, or three, find a way to continue the business without the baby."

Jacob squeezed his eyes shut. When he opened them, a sheen of tears covered them. "We've worked so hard to build a business and a life that didn't confine us to an office. If I hadn't fucked up and accidentally announced to the whole world that Libby was pregnant, maybe we could have salvaged this. We could have found a way to avoid filming her stomach in the next months, and then we could have made sure that contracts we signed for the future were just us, not the baby. But now everyone will want our baby as part of the deals, too."

Libby's lip trembled. "So I guess that means we're out of options. Our fans already know about the pregnancy and want more. So . . . we have to quit."

"Unless . . ." Talia touched the watch on her wrist. According to them, it had only been a couple of hours since Jacob had revealed their secret on their live stream.

"Unless what?" Libby looked at her through the screen with those same hopeful eyes from their childhood.

Talia told them everything about how she could rewind time. She didn't include *all* the details, because the most important thing right now was to make Libby feel better and to make things okay for her as soon as possible.

"Do it," Libby said as soon as Talia was finished.

But Jacob frowned. "This can't be real, can it?"

"It's real—I swear," Talia said. "But you're going to forget all this, and I'll explain it to you again after I rewind."

Libby turned to Jacob. "Please, honey. Who cares how it works? If Talia says she's going to do something, she will. And she can make all of this go away. She'll call us and tell us about what happened this time, and then you won't say anything about the baby during the live stream and it will buy us more runway to figure out how to adapt our business."

Jacob pulled her into his arms. "Of course. Whatever you want." He turned to Talia on the screen. "Just help me fix this for Libby, okay?"

Talia turned the crown on her watch back.

She hunched over the trash can in her office. It was early afternoon and several hours before she would meet Sam on the coast and eat at Taco Bell, but she swore the ground beef and nacho cheese were previewing a rebellion in her stomach.

After half an hour, the walls around her finally stopped spinning, and the light of a screen didn't make her want to throw up anymore. She dialed Libby.

"Hi, Tal!" Libby chirped. "We were about to head out to do a live stream for a color-analysis service. Can I call you later?"

"Actually, no—this is important," Talia said.

Libby stopped short. "Oh, okay." She turned off-screen and said, "Jacob, honey, I need to talk to Talia real quick." She ducked into the hotel bedroom and shut the door. "Um, what's up? Is everything all right?"

Talia nodded. "I just wanted to check in. You called me a week ago, and I'm sorry I ran off to that silly singles mixer that didn't even work out. I should have stayed home and talked to you about whatever it was you called for. But here I am now. You'd said you wanted to pick my brain?"

"Yeah. I think we'll need more than the five minutes or so that I have to spare right now, but I do have something huge I want to tell you." Libby's face glowed even though she wasn't wearing any makeup. "Jacob and I are having a baby!"

"Oh my god!" Talia clapped her hand over her mouth. "I can't believe it. Wow wow wow . . . Congratulations!"

"Thank you. I'm just so happy, Tal."

"I know. You always wanted a family."

Libby nodded. "And you get to be her auntie, and I won't even get mad if you spoil her rotten."

Talia laughed. "It's a plan. But hey . . . will this change what you and Jacob do? I'm sorry if I'm overstepping, but my protective-auntie instincts are already kicking in about my baby niece or nephew being broadcast to three hundred million strangers."

Her sister let out a long, pained exhale. "You read my mind. That's exactly what I'd wanted to pick your brain about."

"Don't worry—I can help you think it through."

Jacob knocked on the bedroom door. His voice came in from off the screen. "Hey, sweetie, we need to head out now. You ready?"

"Tell Jacob to come over here," Talia said.

His face popped on the screen as he sat next to Libby on the bed. "Hey, Talia!"

"Libby just told me the wonderful news. Congratulations, Future Daddy."

He grinned, his world-famous dimples showing. "Thank you, Future Auntie."

"All right, well, I know you two have to get going to that color-analysis thing, but just remember, Jacob—no jokes about color matching for the baby, okay?"

Jacob looked confused. "Why would I make a joke like that?"

"Exactly," Talia said.

She decided in that moment not to tell them about the watch. Let Jacob move forward without feeling any guilt about his previous mistake. Talia was happy to be able to help them without taking credit for it.

She turned her attention back to her sister. "Call me when you're done, and we'll brainstorm, all right?"

"Definitely. Thank you, Tal!" Libby blew her a kiss, and they hung up.

Talia flopped forward, head on her desk. Disaster averted.

A notification popped up, chiming at the same time on her Omni 3Ds, her computer monitor, and her phone.

> Ideal Life Queen Elizabeth: It has been four days since you have seen or communicated with Sam, even though he has texted you. I have analyzed your prior messages and his recent ones, and there does not seem to be any conflict between the two of you. However, your mood markers have been a bit lower recently. May I suggest that you reach out to him? I think it would be good for you.

Her heart did a little pirouette at the thought of getting to spend the next few hours with him again in the hidden cave off the beach.

At the end of the evening, when she drove him back to Lighthouse Books, a flashback of the last time they'd been in the parking lot flickered through her memory.

But Talia had taken care of all that. She'd done it again, better. So hopefully, this next part would be fine.

As she pulled into the parking lot, she asked Sam to hand her her phone from the glove compartment.

He passed it over without looking at the screen.

There was no message from Erin, gushing over Libby and Jacob being pregnant.

Whew.

"I'm glad we got to hang out, Tal," Sam said, opening the passenger door. "I missed you."

"Same. Good luck at the Summer Million tournament."

He crossed the parking lot toward the lighthouse, but before he got there, he turned back and waved again. Not mad.

All right, maybe she'd broken her promise to him again, changed things a tiny bit.

But it's innocuous, she thought, *so it's fine*.

Sam

The mail had arrived while Sam was out. Kenneth had already taken what was addressed to the bookstore and had left Sam's personal letters and packages in his office.

Sam settled into his desk and flipped through the stack of mail, tossing most of it—ads for junk he didn't need—into the recycling bin. But when he got to a slim brown paper package, he tore into it eagerly.

Three sets of wireless earbuds tumbled out onto his desk. They'd been a pricey investment, but he hoped they'd be worth it. They were the ones that could provide real-time translation.

Hands shaky, he ripped open the packaging on one set and popped them into his ears, at the same time pulling up YouTube on his computer. After pairing the earbuds with the laptop and following the instructions to set up automatic, real-time translation, Sam hit Play on a Spanish-language video about book binding. (He had auto-dubbing turned off).

On-screen, the woman's mouth was making the shapes of Spanish, but the words streaming into Sam's earbuds—in *her* voice—were flawless English.

"Whoa," he said.

But Spanish was a very popular language and relatively easy to translate. What about something harder, like . . . Finnish?

He searched for a video about a random topic—"best books in Finnish"—and watched as the same thing happened. On-screen, the very blond man's mouth moved in shapes that were clearly not English, and yet, his voice came in through the earbuds in clear and perfect English.

Sam tried a video on Libby and Jacob's channel, where they

visited a Moroccan souk. They spoke in English while in the background, the market vendors spoke Moroccan Arabic, a couple of Berber languages, and French. The earbuds translated all of them seamlessly in English with only a fraction of a second of lag, and all in the speakers' original voices. Sam watched the video again, at times without the earbuds and at times with, just to double-check that the video hadn't actually all been in English already.

He found a video in Taiwanese and confirmed that the earbuds could handle that, too.

Then he flipped the settings and watched a video in English, while having the earbuds translate the speech into Taiwanese.

It worked.

By the time Jenny and Roger walked in the door of Lighthouse Books after a day of touring Fisherman's Wharf, Sam was practically ricocheting off the shelves, waiting to try the earbuds with them.

And yet, when his mom asked how his day had been, he hesitated. What if the earbuds worked well with videos but not as smoothly with real people?

Or . . . what if they worked as well as Sam hoped?

For his entire life, his relationship with his parents had been one of respect and love, but in a distant, polite way. What happened when this tech suddenly tore down those walls, those well-worn, learned paths for interacting?

How did a person handle having the ability to be close to someone if they'd always been most comfortable being far?

But then Sam thought about how close Talia and Libby were, and how he'd always envied it. And how Talia had also reconnected with her parents in the last couple of years, after decades of their negligence. Even with that tension in their history, she'd been happy with this new, stronger version of her family. And Sam's parents were nothing like Talia and Libby's; it had only been language and an ocean that had kept them apart.

"Here—I bought something." Sam led his mom and dad up to his apartment, then handed each a set of earbuds.

"We already have," Roger said. "Not same. But already have."

"These newer," Sam said in choppy Taiwanese. "Better. You use now and . . . uh, listen."

They put them into their ears. Sam had already set theirs up to translate into Taiwanese as the default language.

"Okay, this is a test," he said in English. "I'd love to hear about your adventures today in San Francisco. You went to the Ferry Building and then walked along the piers to Fisherman's Wharf, right? What was the most beautiful thing, the most surprising thing, and the most delicious?"

Jenny's mouth fell open. Because—if this was working correctly—she'd just "heard" Sam speak flawless Taiwanese, with more fluidity and vocabulary than he'd ever uttered before. Sam himself certainly didn't know the Taiwanese words for "ferry" or "pier."

"How you do that?" she said in English.

"These earbuds use a new technology to provide real-time interpretation of any language into another," Sam said. "So I'm speaking in English, but it's turning it into Taiwanese for you."

"It sounds just like you," Jenny said, this time in Taiwanese, but the response piped into Sam's ears in English. "When you hear my voice, is it me?"

He grinned and nodded. "Yeah, wow. It's exactly you. Dad, do you want to try?"

Roger touched the earbuds delicately, but he shook his head and waved Jenny on. Between the two of them, she was the talker 95 percent of the time. But Sam had never known whether it was because he preferred listening, or if he just didn't have much to say.

"What were your questions about San Francisco?" Jenny asked.

"Most beautiful thing, most surprising thing, and most delicious," Sam said.

"Oh yes, the most beautiful," Jenny said, "was a tiny garden we found tucked between buildings near the Embarcadero. It had these amazing flower sculptures and a little waterfall. A perfect hidden gem in the middle of the city.

"The most surprising was the microclimates. We started in fog at the Ferry Building, walked into sunshine at Pier 23, hit a wall of wind at Fort Mason, then back to warm sun at Ghirardelli Square. All within a couple of miles!

"And the most delicious thing was oysters at the Ferry Building Marketplace. I'd heard about them in one of Libby and Jacob's videos from a few years ago. The oysters were coming in fresh from Tomales Bay, and we just stood there at the counter slurping them down with a little mignonette sauce. Absolute heaven!"

Sam's eyes prickled. He'd never been able to understand his mom like this. Just the insight into what piqued her interest was like opening a door into who she truly was, a personality that he'd only ever been able to observe from the outside—Jenny Chang, cheerful proprietor of a bakery chain.

"God, I'm so sorry we missed out on so many years," he said, wiping away a tear that had escaped. "I should have worked harder to not lose my Taiwanese or Mandarin. I should've visited home more often, or I don't know . . . been a good son and taken over your business."

"No, Sammy, we never expected you to come back to Taiwan," Jenny said. "We were the ones who sent you here."

"I feel like I did a terrible job, though, of keeping my Taiwanese side alive. I mean, there was no one else like me in Mississippi, but even in college here in California, where there were a lot more Asian immigrants, I didn't exactly gravitate toward them. I'm not Asian enough, I guess."

Roger made a small sound, then, and laid his hand on Sam's shoulder. "Do you know how much courage it takes to thrive as you did? You were so little when you were sent off to foreign shores alone, and you forged a whole new life in this unfamiliar place.

"I feel nothing but awe for you, Sam. And you shouldn't cling to binary ideas of 'Taiwanese' or 'American.' You and those in your generation who were latchkey kids sent without their parents, or the children of immigrants, made a *new* culture here, all your own. It is the best of both worlds. You don't need to belong to 'Taiwanese' or 'American.' You're simply a new version, a new iteration. It's wonderful."

Sam hadn't ever heard his dad talk for even a third that long at once. Maybe Roger left small talk to Jenny, and he only spoke up when necessary. Or maybe it was just that there was finally a way to convey everything he'd wanted to say but hadn't been able to in the past.

The disingenuous ghosts of Nowhere Cat still prowled in Sam's memory, but it was time to move on from the technological skepticism that Nowhere Cat had left in him. He probably should have listened to Talia more often about trying out new gadgets. Because these earbuds were *life*-changing.

Talia

On Friday, Ideal Life converted conference room A/B into Due Diligence Headquarters to manage everything that Omni's bankers and lawyers needed to review for the acquisition. While there was a digital database online that housed all the contracts, it was still helpful to have a central location where the Ideal Life employees could stop in if they were working on acquisition-related matters. Sometimes it was to ask questions; sometimes it was just the camaraderie of being together on a project. After all, collaboration had been a core philosophy for Ideal Life since its earliest days when it was just Talia and a handful of engineers in a single room, building on an idea and a dream of a better future for humanity. Even though the company had grown a lot since then, that innate desire to work together still laced its way through the startup.

Talia had put Erin on the acquisition team for the rest of her summer, figuring it was the best way for her to be exposed to a little bit of everything. Here at Due Diligence HQ, there was talk of financial records for the investment bankers, API source code for Omni's developers, real estate leases and licensing agreements and even office supply contracts. A tech business wasn't only technology; there were so many underlying components that made a company run, and it was good for Erin to see all that.

"Happy Friday, everyone," Talia said as she entered the conference room just after 10:30. There were a dozen people here, including Erin, and the long table was covered in stacks of paper, highlighters, and sticky notes.

There were greetings all around, but everyone's faces also showed the drag of even longer hours than normal, because work on the acquisition was on top of each department's other responsibilities. Sleep-heavy eyes were a little more pronounced, yawns were begun and not stifled, and the room was populated with three empty coffee cups per person.

Jody and Jonathan waved her over. "Hey, Talia, you feeling okay?"

"Um, yeah. Why?"

"Nothing," Jonathan said.

But Jody, ever the blunter of the twins, said, "You've looked like a zombie lately."

Talia tried to shrug it off. She knew the rewinds were starting to cost her, but she'd thought her concealer was hiding it. Then again, she'd never been any good at makeup. "Well, everyone here's working extra hard. I couldn't let you have all the fun, right? Anyway, it'll all be worth it once this deal closes."

Jody eyed her skeptically, but she and Jonathan nodded and got back to work. Talia settled into a chair on the far end of the table. She didn't have anything she *had* to do here, but after reconnecting with Sam and Libby last night, she'd been reminded how disconnected from people she'd become in general. Being the boss could be inadvertently isolating, so Talia ditched her private office to work communally for a bit.

Like others, she had a small routine she went through before she could really give in to work, which involved clicking through the major tech news sites to see if anything had happened since the last time she checked. Talia didn't necessarily have to have up-to-the-minute knowledge of the goings-on of Silicon Valley. It was more like cleaning the slate (like how some people needed to clear the notifications on their social media before they could settle), which then allowed her to get started on her own tasks.

At first, Ideal Life Queen Elizabeth had suggested that this was a mild addiction and that Talia could rewrite her neural pathways to avoid it if she put in the effort to retrain her brain.

But it was one of those annoying little habits in life that didn't inhibit her too much—it only took a few minutes to click through the news sites, as long as there weren't any big developments to read up on—so Talia had overridden Ideal Life Queen Elizabeth's suggestion. Sometimes it was easier to give in to a small nuisance and get it over with than to put in a ton of effort to rewire yourself.

Yes, she knew it was an ironic opinion for the creator of a program made precisely to help people rewire themselves for the better.

Still, Talia let herself go through the motions of checking her news sources—*TechCrunch*, *The Information*, and several Substacks by excellent technology journalists who had left mainstream media to write for themselves.

She had almost gotten through all of them without anything noteworthy when *Your Gossipy Tech BFF* refreshed on her screen, and a new article popped up:

Breaking News: Sugar Daddy Omni Plans to Buy CerebraLink for $1 Billion

Palo Alto, CA—According to multiple sources within OmnisZcience, the company is getting ready to flash its wallet again to buy another startup.

CerebraLink's IQ5001 chips have been successfully implanted in human clinical trials and not only helped paralyzed soldiers regain control of their legs, but also are making serious headway (sorry, couldn't help the pun) into sending other kinds of communication into the brain.

What is Omni going to do with this? Who knows, but whatever their plans, I'm sure it'll bring in boatloads more cash than the $1 billion they're paying CerebraLink's happy shareholders. Who needs an IPO these days when Sugar Daddy Omni's here to make all your wildest dreams come true?

Talia scrolled for more, but that was it. A short piece, not unusual for breaking news when details were still scant. She'd have to check back again later for an update.

CerebraLink wasn't a company she could rewind to buy stock in, since they were still privately owned. But as Talia looked around Due Diligence HQ, something else occurred to her, and it wasn't that CerebraLink's offices would soon look like this, too.

What if it wasn't coincidental that Omni was going on a buying spree of brain-tech companies like Ideal Life and CerebraLink? Talia had idealistically thought that Omni wanted Ideal Life for the good they could do—that's how Raj Banerjee and Melanie Goldschmid had pitched it to her.

But what if Omni wanted to use Ideal Life in ways that Talia never intended—combining it with CerebraLink's ability to communicate *to* the brain?

She thought about the concern that Sara, her chief privacy officer, had mentioned over some of Omni's recent due diligence questions.

Once Omni owned both Ideal Life and CerebraLink, they could use Ideal Life customers' weaknesses for all sorts of things, like persuading them to buy products or services that didn't make their lives better, only made Omni richer. What if Talia was selling Ideal Life to create a monstrous advertising AI that would get its talons *directly* into the people's heads, invading their subconsciouses so they weren't even aware of the marketing?

Brain waves indicate that you're feeling down. Why not buy this chamomile-scented candle to lift your spirits?

Looks like you're wanting to treat yourself after a hard day. This chocolate cake can be delivered to your door in thirty minutes!

In the opposite of what Ideal Life intended, they wouldn't even be able to fight against the suggestions made directly into the depths of their brains.

"Oh my fucking god," she said out loud.

All the typing in the room stopped, and everyone swiveled to look at her.

But she couldn't tell them about this. Not yet. Not until she was sure.

Ideal Life Queen Elizabeth popped up, about to say something. Talia ripped her glasses off.

Maybe I'm overreacting, she thought, trying to calm herself.

Hopefully she was overreacting.

Talia tried to smile at everyone in the room who was still staring at her and waved away their concern. "Sorry; it's nothing—just some silly celebrity news. I'll, uh, go somewhere else so I don't interrupt you again."

She grabbed her laptop and fled.

Upstairs in the rooftop garden, she staggered to the wall overlooking downtown and took deep, gulping breaths.

This couldn't be happening.

Surely she was wrong.

But if she wasn't . . .

Talia couldn't rewind to before she signed the acquisition documents, because the watch only went back as far as twenty-four hours. And she couldn't just walk away from the deal. The termination clause imposed a $1 million termination penalty if it was Ideal Life's fault that the deal didn't go through.

> Section 8.3 (B) In the event this agreement is terminated by Ideal Life (by choice or through material breach), then Ideal Life shall pay OmnisZcience a termination fee of One Million US Dollars ($1,000,000) ("Ideal Life Termination Fee") by wire transfer of immediately available funds within two (2) business days after such termination.

That was $1 million they didn't have to spare; they had only six months of operating funds left in their bank account. And Talia herself had meager savings, even counting the small amount of BiomeLabs stock she'd recently bought. The Omni acquisition was supposed to swoop Ideal Life up just before they ran out of money.

Ironically, the original, unchanged version of the past—when the French document had been late, the merger signing had been delayed, and Omni had canceled the deal—would have gotten Talia out of the acquisition *without* a million-dollar penalty.

But then she would have had the Tinder murder on her conscience.

Was it ever possible to use the watch to make changes that would guarantee a better outcome?

The elevator doors dinged, and Eleanor Davies, CEO of BiomeLabs, stepped onto the roof.

"You look like you could use one of these," she said in her crisp British accent as she held out a box of cigarettes.

Talia almost said yes out of the habit of listening to Ideal Life Queen Elizabeth; apparently, she had subconsciously accepted that British accents came with authority.

"Is it that obvious I'm stressed?" she asked while declining Eleanor's offer.

"A CEO knows what it looks like when another one is having a meltdown." Eleanor tapped out a cigarette for herself. "Sorry, I know this is a nasty habit, but it's my one vice I can't shake." She lit it and took a long drag. Then she looked around the roof as if making sure there was no one else near them. Only a couple of BiomeLabs employees sat on the other side of the garden, working together on their computers.

"So," she said, "you want to tell me what's going on?"

Talia hesitated. She hadn't had enough time to decide whether

her worst-case Omni-CerebraLink scenario was plausible. Even though, in her gut, she was pretty sure she knew.

"Can I ask you a question instead?" Talia said.

Eleanor waved her cigarette in the air, its smoke leaving a zigzagging trail behind. "Sure."

"Why did you hold out for an IPO? BiomeLabs didn't go public until last year, and there were multiple offers from bigger companies to buy you before that. From what I've heard, your company nearly went bankrupt *three* times in the last decade. So how come you didn't accept any of those earlier offers to save you?"

Eleanor took another long drag from her cigarette, then let out a long plume of smoke over the view of downtown Palo Alto. "For better or for worse, I have an enormous ego. Women generally aren't allowed to say things like that, let alone act on it. But I wanted to run BiomeLabs *my* way, or no way. If I had let someone else acquire us—especially when we were financially on our knees—I would have had to accept whatever terms they offered.

"It wasn't about money; they offered plenty of that. It was about vision. This is *my* company. My dream. I couldn't stomach the idea that someone else would scoop it up and digest all my hard work into something different from what I wanted, or worse, dismantle BiomeLabs for parts and then junk the rest.

"Which meant I had only one option each time my company came to the cliff's edge—*I* had to be the one to save it."

Talia leaned against the railing. "And you did. All three times."

"I did. Not without cost. I mean, look at me—I'm a chain-smoking forty-year-old who looks like she's in her sixties, but I'm still here. At the helm of the company I started with five hundred dollars in a garage off Page Mill Road, now worth bloody well more than if I'd sold it years ago." She smirked. "Like I said, enormous ego."

She turned to look at Talia. "But there isn't only one path, you know. What was right for BiomeLabs might not be what's right for Ideal Life. Are you getting cold feet about Omni?"

Talia looked down at her shoes, as if they'd actually tell her the temperature of how she was feeling. "I don't know."

"*Your Gossipy Tech BFF*?" Eleanor asked.

"You read it, too?" Talia forgot her feet and looked at Eleanor now.

"They somehow scoop the other outlets fifty percent of the time," Eleanor said. "I have a notification set to alert me whenever a new piece is published. Anyway, yes, I saw the article that Omni is in serious talks to acquire CerebraLink. And yes, if I were you, I would also be rethinking what they meant to do with Ideal Life's technology, in light of this new information."

"Then I'm not crazy."

"Not in my opinion. But then again, some wouldn't say that the way I run things is entirely sane, either, so perhaps you shouldn't listen to me. Whatever you decide, though, I don't envy you, because I know how difficult it is." Eleanor took one last puff of her cigarette before stubbing it out. "Good luck, Talia."

"Thanks, Eleanor."

Talia wasn't sure she felt any better than when she came out here.

Later, she consulted Ideal Life Queen Elizabeth, but the bumblebee didn't have any solutions to her very specific problem, only suggestions to help her alleviate her "heightened levels of cortisol, indicating stress."

She thought about asking Sam but then remembered that he was out with his parents today in Monterey, visiting the aquarium and taking them out in kayaks to see the otters.

Nevertheless, Talia somehow got through the workday, probably because she'd learned during childhood how to compartmentalize huge, looming problems. But that didn't make the potential Omni-CerebraLink–Ideal Life issue disappear. It just lay in wait until she could think about it again.

At 10:30 p.m., she finally left the office and went home.

Ideal Life Queen Elizabeth: I continue to detect elevated readings of cortisol. Perhaps a bath, soothing music, and hot cup of tea?

“Not a terrible idea,” Talia said. “But maybe not tea.”

She ran a bath with lavender salts, put on a slow jazz album, and sank into the tub with a mug of hot milk, sugar, and vanilla.

But it didn’t help. In fact, it made things worse because as Talia soaked, she thought about how, in the future, Omni would be able to tell that someone was stressed and then pipe advertisements for lavender bath salts and a recipe for warm vanilla milk straight into their brain. Or if it noticed that she was feeling impulsive, it could push offers for expensive handbags or luxury vacations.

From there, she began to think about more nightmare scenarios. Ads were only the start of a slippery slope. What if Omni used Ideal Life and CerebraLink’s technology to artificially shape user moods, tweaking content on social media to spark amusement, anger, or anxiety, since studies had shown that those emotions kept people on social media longer?

They could also associate certain neural activity with rewards, and condition users to spend more money or watch more content. Or develop addictive algorithms that would make it neurologically repulsive or painful to sign off.

Omni could sell the brain data not only to advertisers, but also to political campaigns, corporations, governments. Or they could build products that allowed companies to monitor their employees—to check their focus, to measure their loyalty, to monitor any dissent. Same with governments, which could also tailor certain kinds of beliefs to trigger positive associations, thereby reshaping society without anyone realizing they had lost their free will.

Ideal Life Queen Elizabeth: Multiple regions of your brain are showing signs of fight-or-flight, and your heart rate is very high. Are you in danger? Please indicate if I should dial 911. If you do not respond, I will immediately summon emergency services.

"No, do not call emergency services," Talia said, even though she could feel her pulse pounding against her chest. "I'm just thinking; I'm not in danger."

Ideal Life Queen Elizabeth: Confirmed. Would you like suggestions to calm your mind? How about exercise?

She dismissed the app.

"Stop it," Talia told herself. "You're spiraling. This is not a dystopian sci-fi novel."

And yet, even if only 10 percent of her imaginary scenarios came true—like using or selling brain data for the benefit of advertisers—it would still be a nightmare. Talia couldn't be a part of that happening to humanity. She'd invented Ideal Life to give people more awareness and agency, not the other way around.

But how could she prevent the acquisition from going through?

It was close to midnight now, but she was too jittery to go to bed. Ideal Life Queen Elizabeth had suggested exercise, and it might actually help burn off some of this excess energy. Talia changed into workout clothes and put on her sneakers.

She wasn't much of a runner. But she didn't feel like being cooped up inside the gym, so Talia decided to go for a jog. She could run up toward Stanford and then around campus for a bit before looping back home.

Talia started down Alma Street at a decent pace and soon veered onto a bike path parallel to the train tracks. The air was cool and refreshing at this time of night, and there were hardly any cars downtown. Palo Alto was a tame kind of city; if anyone was out late, they were more likely working than not. If she hadn't had her earbuds in, she probably could have heard crickets chirping.

At Embarcadero Road, Talia turned left.

Suddenly, a wave of vertigo hit her, and she wobbled on the sidewalk.

"Whoa whoa whoa," she said, bracing herself on a tree trunk. It was the same feeling that accompanied her rewinds, except she hadn't touched her watch. A familiar ebb of exhaustion lapped against the edges of the vertigo.

You've got to be kidding me, Talia thought. She knew she was out of shape from spending too many hours sitting at her desk, but she'd barely even run half a mile.

Or was this the result of too many rewinds catching up to her? There did seem to be a cumulative effect building up.

A moment later, the spinning sensation passed. Talia stood upright slowly, so as not to tempt its return.

Should I turn back home?

But pride kicked in. She wasn't a quitter in any aspect of her life, and she certainly wasn't going to give up after a pathetic half-mile jog.

Talia wasn't stupid, though, so she took it easy for a bit, passing Town & Country Village, the shopping center where her Trader Joe's was located. The parking lot was usually packed, but of course it was empty now.

She jogged slowly until she felt solid again. Then she increased her pace and crossed El Camino onto Stanford's campus.

Erin

Erin was the last person to leave the Ideal Life offices, right around midnight. She'd been working hard on the Gen Z social media campaign, revising the plan based on the marketing team's feedback and putting together the list of creators they ought to target. Her eyelids drooped as she walked over to her car.

Should I call an Uber?

But no, her dorm was only seven minutes away. She could make it that far. Besides, if Erin left her car here overnight, she'd have to walk back to get it tomorrow, and that would be a pain. It made way more sense to just drive back now.

She yawned as she started her car, forgetting to turn on her headlights because it was well lit downtown. She cruised onto University Avenue, which soon crossed El Camino and into the palm tree–lined entrance to Stanford. It was peaceful out (any parties going on this Friday night would be on the other side of campus on the Row), and Erin let her mind settle into autopilot.

At Campus Drive, she made a left. Her eyelids felt like they had anchors on them. Her head nodded, and she fell asleep for a split second, before jerking awake.

"Come on, Erin." She slapped herself lightly on the cheek. "It's just a few minutes now."

Up ahead was the roundabout at Galvez Street. Erin yawned as she eased into the traffic circle.

Bam!

She'd hit something—*someone*!

Erin screamed and slammed on the brakes.

Talia

The car didn't have its headlights on.

It hit Talia just as she was darting across the Galvez Street roundabout.

She rolled over the hood and slammed into the asphalt on the other side.

Brakes squealed. A car door flung open.

"Fuck, oh fuck!" a woman shouted as she ran to Talia's side.

"Are you okay?" she asked. "Can you hear me? I'm so sorry, oh my god, I didn't see you, it's my fault, shit, please be okay—"

Talia, face down on the street, groaned. There was a sharp, throbbing pain in her hip where she'd been hit, and her skin stung, burning where she'd slid on the road.

"Oh, thank god, you're alive. I-I'll call the ambulance right now, I should've right away, I'm sorry, I'm so sorry."

Talia pushed herself up to sitting.

"Ma'am, don't move. You might hurt yourself more—" The driver gasped. "Talia?"

Talia blinked. "*Erin*? What're you doing here?" Her brain, in shock, hadn't pieced the situation together yet. Irrationally, she decided it was important then to try to stand up. She glanced at her legs, which seemed to be intact other than the pain in her hip. Her leggings were torn at the knees and she was scraped and bleeding, but nothing felt broken. The car hadn't been going that fast.

She started to stand.

"Talia, please! Don't move. I am literally dialing 911 right now."

Erin turned away to talk to the emergency operator. "Yes, hi, there's been a car accident. We're on Stanford campus at Galvez just across from the track . . ."

Meanwhile, Talia continued to get up. She winced as she put pressure on her right hip and ankle.

And she *would* be all right. She could undo the last few minutes.

"Hang up," Talia said, even as a fresh bolt of pain shot up from her ankle to her calf to her torso. "It's going to be fine."

Erin turned back around to look at her. The usual pink in her cheeks had drained away, washing her out even more than the streetlamp. She was crying, staring at Talia, her boss from her dream job whom she'd hit with her car. "Please, Talia, please sit, I'm so sorry, I'm so, so sorry, I was working late, and I shouldn't have gotten behind the wheel, and it's all my fault, oh god, oh fuck—"

"Shh, it'll be okay," Talia said. "I'll make it okay."

"How? I almost *killed* you!" Erin was sobbing now.

Talia shook her head. "But you didn't."

She reached for her watch and turned the crown.

Back in her apartment.

Workout clothes and sneakers on.

Nausea and fatigue—now familiar companions of her rewinds—came in fast like high tide.

Talia untied her laces and shucked off her shoes. Her joints creaked and her ankle popped as she laid herself down slowly into bed, avoiding sudden movements because it would make the vertigo worse.

Horizontal, she tested her ankle. It wasn't broken or even strained. Her knees weren't scraped or bleeding. Of course they weren't. The accident had never happened.

Yet she still felt wrecked, not quite like being in a car accident, but like being in the emotional phantom of one.

Talia curled up on her bed and clung to her pillow as the waves of nausea washed over her.

It was my *fault that Erin hit me*. *Mine.* Talia wasn't wearing any reflective gear, and she hadn't checked for traffic when she'd crossed the road; she'd assumed no one was driving at that hour.

Logically, Erin was also at fault. But Talia didn't see that clearly in the moment, because all her life, Talia had operated under the principle that she was imperfect and she could do better. Therefore, if something had gone wrong, the blame *must've* been hers.

She also decided it was her fault that Erin had been working so late and had to drive home after midnight. The poor, impressionable girl was following in the footsteps of her mentor, drinking up everything Talia did or had ever said.

But what kind of example was Talia setting? What kind of life was she leading Erin to, if every waking minute was work? And by rewinding the accident, was Talia preventing Erin from learning from bad decisions?

No . . . That was one of those awful things that anyone would undo if they could. Erin didn't need to learn from *that* lesson. Maybe Talia shouldn't have rewound all of her performance reviews . . . Or maybe in the future, there would be a different lesson she would choose not to rewind for Erin—a smaller lesson, but still valuable.

But why the hell was she thinking about something like that now?

The apartment was still spinning around her. Even when she squeezed her eyes shut, the visual memory of her bedroom walls continued to whirl round and round and round.

Meanwhile, one of Sam's texts from a while ago—about the watch—resurrected itself in her thoughts:

Sam: Don't overuse it, okay, Tal? . . . I know you always want to improve yourself, but I worry.

Talia: Trust me, I'm fine, Sam. It's only a tool, and I've got it under control.

If there was ever a time to use it, though, undoing the accident was it. Nothing else could have been more important than saving Erin from something like that that would have traumatized her and affected her future.

Still, Talia was uncomfortably aware of her other frivolous rewinds and how addictive they'd become.

She took the watch off and shoved it to the back of her nightstand drawer.

I won't use it anymore, she told herself. *True emergencies only*.

Talia

When she woke up, it was already early afternoon. Exhaustion and sleeping in seemed to be her default state these days because of the watch, and being a sloth was *not* how Talia liked to picture herself. In a disgusted huff, she kicked the covers off too forcefully, propelling them halfway across her small studio into a heap, half falling off the coffee table. Of course, that also knocked over a glass of water she'd left there overnight, which took it upon itself to spill onto the carpet, as if it, too, were protesting the status quo.

"Not helpful," she grumbled.

But then she remembered the accident from last night, and Talia blinked at her arms and legs. No road rash. Her hip and ankle were perfectly fine, evidenced by the duvet on the floor and the spilled water. Of course, she knew that the watch erased everything, and yet after all these rewinds, it was still difficult for the scientist part of her mind to wrap itself around how her injured body could undo the biological harm to its cells.

Her phone buzzed on the nightstand. As late as it was on Saturday, there were already a dozen or so notifications waiting for her. A new one came in while she was putting on her Omni 3Ds.

Summer Million update: Level 6 live stream starts now!

"Oh my god—Sam!" Talia had forgotten that this weekend was Summer Million, the poker tournament he'd signed up to play in. Was he still in it? He'd said there were two thousand players.

She asked her Omni 3Ds to search the list of current players.

Samuel Chang is playing at table 23 in level 6.

(In poker, they said "levels" instead of "rounds." So Sam had made it through the first five levels.) *Good, good, good.*

The way the Summer Million worked was you paid $5,000 to "buy in" to the tournament. That got you 20,000 chips (everyone started with the same amount, and you couldn't buy more), and then you just kept playing until you lost all your chips.

Out of the two thousand players, only the top 10 percent got prize money. It started at $8,000 for 200th place. But since you'd already spent $5,000 on the buy-in fee, that was really only $3,000 net.

Sam needed to do significantly better than 200th place to make a difference for his bookstore.

Talia pulled up his tournament history and skimmed it to get a sense of how he'd been playing. She was still in her pajamas and her mouth tasted like she'd sucked on an old sock all night, but that didn't matter right now.

In level 1 and level 2, Sam had won some small pots and increased his chip count a little. 250 players eliminated, 1,750 left.

In levels 3, 4, and 5, he'd managed to hold steady by folding most of his hands. A lot of players in open tournaments like Summer Million chased emotions and let their egos lead. Sam, however, let game theory guide him logically, and he finished those rounds with 45,000 chips. The number wasn't equivalent to real dollars, but it still mattered, because the more chips Sam had, the more leeway he had to bet, and the longer he could stay in the tournament.

Now at the start of level 6, there were 900 players remaining. He'd survived the culling of more than half the competitors, but he still had a long way to go to 200th place or better.

"Come on, Sam, you got this," Talia said, opening the live stream to watch. As usual, it was on a thirty-minute delay to prevent cheating, but this was as up-to-date as Talia would get, so she'd take it. She wondered if his parents were watching the tournament, too.

Sam sat at table 23 with the king of spades and the king of hearts. It was a great hand. He slid 1,200 chips into the pot.

But there were eight other players at the table, including Louise Enger, the intense woman who had bested Sam in the tournament in Cleveland a couple of weeks ago. When it was her turn, she paused, then pushed in 3,600 of her chips.

Confidence? Or a bluff?

The right corner of Sam's mouth twitched, his tell that Talia hoped was small enough that Louise and the other poker players wouldn't catch it.

He faced a decision—call the bet or fold his cards.

Unfortunately, he couldn't see Louise's cards, but Talia could.

"Fold, Sam," she urged.

He did the opposite and called.

The dealer spread three community cards: an ace of clubs, seven of spades, and two of diamonds.

"Shit," Talia said. The ace changed everything—anyone holding one would be ahead of his kings.

Louise bet more, and Sam took the bait.

Then Louise pushed forward her entire stack of chips—enough to eliminate Sam if he called and lost.

He studied her for almost two full minutes in silence.

Please, Sam, please . . . Talia's heart was in her throat. He needed to fold. He would be fine if he did. He'd still be in the tournament.

But Sam took a deep breath and said, "Call," while pushing all his chips forward.

Louise turned over two aces.

"Shit!" Talia punched her mattress.

Sam had lost everything. His $5,000 buy-in was gone, which he really couldn't afford to lose, and at 734th place, he was going to have to walk away with nothing.

Talia watched as he stood from the table.

"Seat open at table twenty-three," the tournament director announced, making Sam's exit official.

"No," Talia said. "This is *not* okay."

She got up to retrieve the watch from her nightstand.

But halfway across the room, she stopped. Last night, she had stashed the watch away because she'd made the decision to finally stop this madness of constantly turning back time.

True emergencies only, she'd told herself.

This was *Sam*, though. His future was more important to her than almost anyone else's.

He would hate me using this on him.

But he won't know . . . He never does.

All of her muscles felt too tight, her insides too tangled, but Talia got the watch out of the drawer and rewound anyway.

Back to the beginning of level 6. She had gone back slightly more than thirty minutes before the live stream, since that was on delay.

While she waited to watch, Talia brushed the nasty old-sock taste from her mouth, took a quick shower, and brewed some coffee.

Summer Million update: Level 6 live stream starts now!

"You got it this time, Sam."

Table 23. He had the same cards as before. Louise Enger also had her original starting hand.

Sam put in 1,200 chips.

Louise pushed in 3,600.

Talia sat at the edge of her couch as she watched. Everything so far was the same. She gulped down her coffee and willed the dealer's cards to change.

Ace of clubs. Seven of spades. Two of diamonds. Just like last time.

"Oh no," Talia said.

The rest of the hand happened exactly the same, too. Sam kept calling, and Louise kept escalating.

All in.

Sam pushed all his chips forward.

"Seat open at table twenty-three."

"I refuse to accept this," Talia said and rewound again.

She did it a total of seven times. By the last undo, she was nauseous and her head felt like it was cracking open, and then she fell asleep before the level 6 live stream even started.

When she woke up, level 6—version eight—had ended, and Sam had lost identically.

"Seat open at table twenty-three."

Talia staggered into her bed, so ill that it felt as if every single cell in her body was throbbing, threatening to burst and spill out their insides. Her skull was all migraine and no brain; she'd had to shut down Ideal Life Queen Elizabeth after the second rewind because the royal bee was whirling herself into a tizzy with concern.

Short of rewinding and calling Sam during his earlier break to tell him Louise's future cards, it seemed nothing would change.

Sam would never cheat, of course. She had only hoped that by turning back time, it would have given him an opportunity to make a different decision.

But he hadn't. Why not? Talia tried her best to think through her pounding headache, and all she could conclude from the evidence of all these "microexperiments" was that things didn't change when she rewound, unless *she* was there to effect the change.

Talia buried her face in a pillow.

Sam needed the winnings to keep Lighthouse Books afloat. He was such an earnest person, doing the work of running a bookstore to encourage a love of reading in a world where shallower, more passive entertainment was easier to achieve. People who swam upstream to try to do good ought to be rewarded. It wasn't fair that life was harder for them.

But was this really about Sam? Or was it subconsciously about herself?

Because it wasn't only about wishing that Sam could have made a different decision in the tournament, was it? It was also about wishing that *she* could have made a different choice about signing the acquisition agreement with Omni. But now Talia and Ideal Life were trapped on a path they couldn't veer from, like being locked in on a roller coaster. You couldn't get out once the car left the station. Not unless she magically had a million dollars with which to pay the termination fee to stop the ride and get out of the deal.

Talia bolted upright in her bed, even though a flash of pain shot through her head.

The prize at the poker tournament was a million dollars. And it was only half an hour away in San Jose. It was also an open competition that anyone could enter. Registration had closed only last night, and her recent stock market investments meant she had enough money for the $5,000 buy-in fee.

Sam couldn't win the Summer Million. But maybe Talia could.

Talia

Talia had played poker in college, but it had been years, and she'd never played in a professional tournament. Still, she turned the watch dial back to yesterday, just before midnight when registration closed.

Here she was again, before she went for a run, before Erin hit her with her car.

How many actual hours had it been since the first time Talia was here?

But her brain was so scrambled from going back and forth she couldn't get a grasp on the answer. With all the redos for Sam, she felt lost in time, although ironically, she hadn't made any forward progress.

Talia looked at the clock: 11:50 p.m.

A fog of pain closed in on her mind.

Wait—why was she here? Talia looked around her apartment, her thoughts muddled in the murkiness of her brain.

She blinked. She'd rewound because . . .

Oh, right. She'd come back to sign up for the poker tournament.

And yet, with that clarified, Talia still hesitated. On the morality spectrum, where did this fall between buying BiomeLabs stock before a market surge and sneaking winning lotto tickets into the past? One had seemed acceptable to her (maybe not virtuous, but acceptable), while the other had felt obviously unethical, even though she couldn't put a finger on exactly why they were different.

Talia's breathing sped up.

Had her moral compass broken and been replaced by the watch?

Ideal Life Queen Elizabeth: It appears that you're experiencing stress. Would you like suggestions to calm your mind? How about exercise?

"What? How did you get turned back on?" Oh, wait—Talia had rewound again past the moment she'd shut her Ideal Life app off. She dismissed it again now, and Queen Elizabeth flew away.

Before Talia could change her mind, she created an account on the Summer Million website and registered.

She should probably tell Sam she was going to be there.

No, then he might suspect she was rewinding, since she hadn't shown any interest in playing poker herself during the intervening years between undergrad and now. And Talia didn't have any extra emotional bandwidth at the moment to deal with his concern about her overusing the watch. She had a company to save.

Besides, Sam's phone will be off, she rationalized, *so I couldn't tell him even if I wanted to*. By now, he'd already be in his pretournament meditative-immersion stage. Or, more likely, asleep since it was near midnight.

Speaking of which, she also needed to get some rest, to sleep off the migraine and time sickness.

Tomorrow, there would be a game to play.

Talia

At nine in the morning, Talia was seated at table 11. She had arrived at the Magnolia Grand Hotel and Conference Center in San Jose with only minutes to spare since there had been an accident on Highway 87, so she had been able to avoid Sam in the hallways.

The competition itself was held in two ballrooms. Luckily, Talia had been assigned to a different one than Sam, but when she walked into hers, she froze at the sight of how many players there were. A thousand in this ballroom, a thousand in the other. Round tables covered in green felt tops filled the space, with big numbers on them like wedding centerpieces, except without the frill or flowers. The chandeliers had been dimmed, and instead, spotlights illuminated each table, making the whole endeavor seem so much more intense.

How did she think she was going to win the tournament when she hadn't even touched a card in years?

I've got a secret weapon nobody else has, she reminded herself.

For a room of that many people, though, it was shockingly quiet. Or, rather, Talia could feel the *hum* of silence, if that was possible, as every player got in their "zone," their "flow," or whatever they called their state of extreme focus.

Talia steeled herself with a few deep breaths, then stepped into the breach, weaving herself through the tables until she found hers. She had just enough time to get her chair pulled up to the table before the tournament began.

Despite worrying about not having played poker in a while, though, it turned out that watching all of Sam's tournaments had made Talia sharp enough to get through the morning. And because this was an open competition and not an invitational, there were plenty of amateurs she could outmaneuver.

She played carefully but well during level 1.

In level 2, she gained more confidence and won big.

During level 3, though, Talia got a little cocky and lost a chunk of her chips.

"It's okay—you're still in it," she told herself. She and 1,749 other people.

The tournament director announced the first break of the day. There were only twenty minutes, barely enough time to go to the restroom, wolf down a protein bar, and report to her next table. There was no opportunity to find Sam, and honestly, Talia didn't know if she wanted to yet.

Level 4 at table 1 began well, but then things got a little sticky when the dealer revealed the final card. Talia had been betting aggressively, and now she had to decide whether to bluff or not.

Don't be emotional. Do the math.

The probability of the remaining player having a better hand was not high.

Bluff it is. She pushed 5,000 chips into the pot and hoped it was enough to fool him.

"Nice try," her opponent said. "Call."

Fuck. Talia glanced at her watch.

But she shook her head at herself. She was still in the tournament—no need to cheat. Talia did wish she had her phone or Omni 3Ds, because Ideal Life Queen Elizabeth would surely have had a good suggestion for a mental reset, but of course, devices weren't allowed in the tournament.

Okay, fine, her watch might technically be a "device," but she hadn't turned it in at the ballroom door with everything else, because they hadn't asked her to. It was analog . . . or something.

Talia started the next round with a pair of aces. *Score!* As Sam would experience later today (in version nine of playing against Louise Enger), two aces were hard to beat.

Unfortunately, probability was not on Talia's side for the rest of the cards.

She lost everything.

"What? No!"

"Seat open at table one," the tournament director announced.

Talia gaped at her losing hand.

That was it. She was out of the tournament at 1,244th place.

No winnings.

$5,000 buy-in, gone.

And the $1 million hole for Ideal Life now felt like a bottomless pit.

"Ma'am," the dealer said, when she hadn't moved. "You'll have to vacate that seat now."

She looked up at him.

Then Talia shook her head. "No. I won't. I'm not going anywhere."

"Ma'am," the dealer said, louder. "You must—"

She rewound the watch's crown to the beginning of level 5, and this time, she played it right. She kicked ass in level 6, too.

That'll show 'em.

There was a spring in her step as she exited the ballroom for the second break. They had an hour before competition would resume, so the hotel had set up a small buffet in the corridor. With over 700 players still in the tournament, though, the hall was crammed to the gills with people waiting for food. By the time Talia got anywhere near those steam trays, they would be empty and she'd hardly be able to eat before she'd have to report back into the ballrooms.

So instead, she went out to her car, drove to a sandwich place a few minutes away, and grabbed a roast beef and cheddar on rye—analytically, it seemed like the right balance of protein, fat, and whole grains to sustain her for three more rounds of play before the next break. Assuming she made it to the next break.

Talia looked at her watch.

It's still just in case, she told herself. She knew it wasn't technically fair what she was doing, but she thought of Erin and Jody and Jonathan and everyone else at Ideal Life. Talia was here to save the company so they could keep doing what they believed in. So she could save them from a future under Omni's reign.

She got back to the Magnolia Hotel with ten minutes to spare and stopped into the ladies' room. When she exited, she gasped and retreated, plastering herself inside the door.

Sam was in the main corridor outside the ballrooms, filling his water bottle at a dispenser.

What is he still doing here? Level 6, when he lost, ended an hour ago. He should have been home at Lighthouse Books by now.

Unless he *hadn't* lost? Talia took out her phone and looked up the Summer Million players still in competition.

Samuel Chang was definitely still in the tournament for level 7.

"How?" she asked.

A woman washing her hands at the sink looked up. It was Louise Enger, the woman Sam had previously lost to during level 6 over the course of eight iterations.

"How what?" Louise said. "Do you need help?"

Talia shook her head. "Sorry—just talking to myself. Actually . . . what table were you at in the last level?"

"Table 14 in ballroom B. Why?"

"I thought you looked familiar is all, but I'm in ballroom A, so I must be mistaken."

Internally, though, the cogs in Talia's brain were whirring at full speed. During the earlier rewinds when she'd been trying to help Sam win, both he and Louise had been at table 23. Why had Louise's table changed now?

Maybe because me being here shifted the player assignments for the tournament, and that set off a cascade of little variations in how each hand was played because there were sometimes different people at the table than before? And something in that butterfly effect allowed Sam to make it through level 6, whereas he had lost eight times in a row when the rewinds were identical.

Talia had known that her past rewinds would result in small butterfly effects, but she'd never actively sought out what had changed. She'd only focused on the big revisions and hoped that the other ones were inconsequential. *You can't be sure that any change you make would have made this world better or worse*, she'd reasoned.

But *this* change—Sam still being in the tournament—was okay, right? It was great news that he was still here. If he placed higher, he could win something to put toward the bookstore.

So why was Talia hiding from him in the restroom?

Guilt wrapped its tentacles around her heart.

Not only had she broken her promise (many times over) not to use the watch on him, but she was also cheating. Talia thought the end justified the means—by winning the tournament, she would prevent Omni from merging Ideal Life with CerebraLink and creating a Frankenstein AI capable of brain horrors she couldn't even think about.

But that didn't mean Sam would see her "strategic use" of the rewind mechanism in the same way.

She wasn't even sure if *she* really saw it that way.

It wasn't until Louise opened the bathroom door and left that Talia poked her head out to check if Sam was still there.

The coast was clear.

She slipped back into ballroom A. At least for the rest of today, the tournament would keep the players in their respective ballrooms, just whittling down the number of tables in each. Tomorrow, they would consolidate into one room, and if Talia and Sam were both still playing then, there would be no way to avoid him. But she'd figure out later what to do if that happened. Right now, she had level 7 to concentrate on.

★

Talia breezed through the rest of the evening. Well, perhaps "breeze" wasn't the right word, since she had the benefit of redoing her strategy should any particular hand not go as she'd hoped. At first, she wasn't sure if she should keep using her watch, since it was clearly having an inadvertent effect on Sam's life, too. But Talia decided that because she was working toward a greater good, it was okay. Besides, Sam had lost in level 6 all the previous times; the fact that he had made it past that now was gravy, right?

The only side effect was that headache, nausea, and dizziness were now her constant companions. But for better or for worse, she was getting used to functioning with a baseline of feeling ill. Maybe this was what it was like to have morning sickness. (Was Libby feeling this way? She reminded herself to catch up with her sister once this was all over.)

In any case, if Talia messed something up because of brain fog or otherwise, she simply undid it and tried again. A little sicker, but with knowledge of what the other hands would be and what she needed to do to win.

By the time level 10 concluded, Talia was ranked 82nd out of the remaining 471 players. Sam was doing even better, ranked 16th. Not that the current standings really mattered; all that counted was what you were ranked when you finally lost all your chips, and you'd better be in the top 200 if you wanted to go home with anything.

Still, it was a relief to make it to the second (and final) day of play. Hopefully Sam wouldn't look past the top twenty-five or so names on the leaderboard tonight, and Talia could avoid talking to him about her presence at the tournament until tomorrow.

As she walked out of ballroom A, though, Sam stood waiting with his arms crossed.

"What are you doing here, Tal?"

"Um . . ." A couple of other players stopped, anticipating some drama and hoping to eavesdrop.

Talia crossed the hallway to Sam and lowered her voice a little. "I decided to sign up and play in the tournament."

The right corner of his mouth twitched. "You don't play anymore. You haven't since college. And never in a real tournament." He looked pointedly at her watch. "And yet here you are, ranked in the top one hundred. How curious."

"Sam, I can explain."

"No need. I understand perfectly." He turned and strode away.

"It's not like that!" Talia chased him down the hall and grabbed his arm. Now people were definitely watching.

Sam jerked out of her grasp, turned, and glared straight down at her. Talia shrank. Never in their years of friendship had he looked at her with so much anger. So much disappointment. "It's not like what?" Aware of the onlookers, his voice was a furious whisper now. "Not like you using that watch to go back in time and redo any hands that didn't turn out the way you wanted?"

"I swear the money's not for me. Come on, Sam—you know me! I have to do this because I found out something awful will probably happen if I let this deal with Omni go through, so I have to kill the acquisition, but there's a one-million-dollar termination fee in the agreement."

He kept staring at her.

"The company doesn't have that kind of money to spare, so if *I* don't come up with it, Ideal Life goes bankrupt. All my employees lose their jobs. Everything we've worked hard to build—a really amazing technology that could be helpful to the world if it's in the right hands—will go up in flames."

Sam bit his lip. She hoped he could understand. "And what about me?" he asked.

"What about you?"

That was the wrong thing to say, though, because he clenched his fists and turned to walk away.

"I'm sorry," Talia said. "That didn't come out right."

"My parents are waiting at the lighthouse to take me out to dinner. I have to go."

"Sam, please."

He turned back around slowly. "You promised not to rewind my life without telling me. But I've been here at this tournament, too, apparently replaying every level whenever you decided to undo it and try again. Were you even going to tell me? Did you think I wouldn't notice at some point that the woman I love was on the leaderboards?"

Talia's mouth fell open.

"The . . . the woman you love?" Talia frowned. "But when I kissed you, you didn't kiss me back. I thought—"

"When you *kissed* me?" Sam's brows knit in confusion for a split second. And then his eyes went wide as realization dawned.

Oh, fuck.

Talia reached for her watch.

"Don't you dare." Sam wrapped his fingers around her wrist so she couldn't wind the crown. "So today isn't the first time you've undone my life?"

"Sam, I—"

"Who are you anymore, Talia?"

She looked at the ugly carpet at her feet and shook her head. "I'm the same person you've always known. I'm just . . . I'm trying to make things better, but sometimes I do it wrong! Let me rewind today. Please, Sam." She looked up at him now. "Let me go back to the beginning and tell you that I'm going to play in the tournament. Let me make it right."

He closed his eyes for a long moment.

When he opened them again, the light that usually danced in them was gone. He let go of her wrist and said quietly, "Ideal Life made you obsessed with the future, but the watch opened up that same addiction to the past, too. And now you're suspended in the middle."

"I don't know what you're talking about."

Sam sighed. "You can't move forward, because you keep rehashing the things that just happened. And even when you aren't, you're incapable of being in the present, because you're always thinking about how you can be better in the future. But when are you going to stop trying to optimize every situation, Tal? When are you going to stop rehearsing for life and actually *live* it?"

"I am. It's just . . . wouldn't you want the *best* version of your life if you could have it?"

Sam shook his head sadly. "I liked my life exactly the way it was."

And with that, he finally did turn and walk away.

Sam

He hadn't meant to let it slip that he loved her.

But if he hadn't said it, he wouldn't have found out that she'd been rewinding his life.

Sam's knees almost gave out as he left her; it was difficult even to stand when the one person in the world that you thought you could believe in turned out to be a lie. The Talia he thought he knew was really just a story he'd told himself, a version of a woman who no longer actually existed.

And yet, that wasn't the worst of what Sam felt. No matter how Talia had deceived him, he couldn't simply turn off a switch and stop loving her. He'd loved her quietly for his entire adult life. And now she was losing her way, and it hurt him to watch it happen.

Every night at 11:11 p.m. for the last couple of weeks, he'd wished for that watch to disappear.

But it hadn't.

Sam cursed himself. He should have tried harder to intervene, rather than relying on a fickle wish. Maybe you only got one wish granted your entire life, and he'd gotten his when he was eighteen, when Talia had shown up at his dorm room door.

How could Sam have stopped Talia from using the watch, though, short of ripping it off her wrist?

Halfway through the Magnolia Hotel parking lot, he stopped short. A car honked and swerved to avoid him.

Maybe there *was* something Sam could do.

He hurried to his car, turned on his phone, and called the only other person he knew who might be able to make a difference, the one whom Talia would do anything for.

The phone rang.

"Hello?"

"Hey, Libby? It's Sam. I need your help."

Talia

On Sunday, Talia showed up again at the Magnolia Grand Hotel and Conference Center for the second and final day of the Summer Million tournament. The field was currently 471 players in level 11.

But even though prize money started at 200th place, the payouts didn't get big until the final table of nine players—level 20—and a screen at the registration table showed what those amounts would be:

1st: $1,000,000
2nd: $615,000
3rd: $450,000
4th: $335,000
5th: $250,000
6th: $188,000
7th: $142,000
8th: $108,000
9th: $82,000

"Well, I know what my goal is," Talia said.

The man behind her in line at registration chuckled. "I think it's all of ours. Good luck."

She nodded. "Good luck to you, too."

Talia reported to her assigned seat at table 2 in ballroom A, where everyone would be today. Sam was supposed to be across the room at table 10.

But he wasn't there.

When play began at noon, he still hadn't arrived.

Talia frowned. Was he okay?

She couldn't send him a message, though, because she'd left all her devices at registration.

Then her stomach sank. Sam hadn't come back today because of her.

Play started, and Talia lost a lot of chips early. The pace of the second day was much faster than the first, and she was also getting antsy about being away from the office for so long since she usually worked weekends. Yes, she was here to save the company, but still, the rest of her team was buried in due diligence . . .

Screw the due diligence, she thought. *If I can focus and win the money here, the merger stuff won't matter*.

Talia powered her way through levels 11, 12, and 13. All the playing yesterday had buffed off the rust on her game, and she felt like her old self at the Stanford physics department poker table.

But *not* the same. Because Sam and Libby weren't here with her, like they had been back then.

Focus now, feelings later, Talia thought. Ideal Life was at stake.

But in level 14, Louise Enger sat down across from her at table 2.

The hand started out okay. Talia was dealt the king of clubs and the king of hearts, and she raised her bet.

Then Louise, clearly feeling confident, tripled the stakes.

Talia went all in.

Louise revealed a pair of aces.

Just like how Sam had lost to her in the previous versions of this tournament.

"Seat open at table two."

Talia was done. She finished the tournament at 199th place with a prize of $9,000.

She was $991,000 short of what Ideal Life needed.

★

Talia sat in the hotel hallway, stunned. It had all happened so fast, from the high of killing it to the sudden crash down to earth a few minutes later. She had her fingers on the watch's crown, but her hand shook, and she needed a minute to calm her nerves before she went back to play again. Besides, rewinding reliably made her nauseated and migraine-y now, so she had to be in top mental shape prior to undoing the last round. Otherwise, she would just lose right away again.

But now that the adrenaline of the tournament had died down, the compartment she'd stuffed Sam into reopened, and their conversation in this very hallway yesterday spilled back into her thoughts.

Who are you anymore, Talia?

She slumped farther down against the wall, onto the well-worn carpet.

They say you don't know a person's true character until they are standing at a crossroads. Talia remembered Sam telling her a story in college, about Hercules before he was famous and had done any grand deeds. He'd been at a fork in the road, and two goddesses were tempting him in different directions. One offered him an easy life where everything went his way. Another offered him a noble life, where he would have to make hard decisions, but he would be given the opportunity to do the right things.

Talia looked at the watch on her wrist. Was it the goddess offering her the easy way out?

But life wasn't as simple as a Greek parable. The crossroads Talia stood at wasn't about only herself. Her choice was not about whether she took home a million dollars to keep or whether she let someone else have it. Her choice would steer the direction of her company and, in turn, potentially the fate of billions of people.

God, that sounded self-important and melodramatic. But in a world where a handful of big technology companies like

Omni really could put their thumbs on the scale and affect the opinions and decisions of entire populations, didn't Talia have a duty to do her part to make sure that *her* contribution, *her* technology, was used responsibly?

And yet, if she believed in fairness, if she believed in being an upright person, how could she continue to rewind and cheat to win this tournament? Her past stock investments had already teetered on that moral line. Now it seemed Talia had *moved* the line so that she could conveniently stay on the "right" side of it.

If she hadn't had the watch, would she ever have condoned cheating?

Absolutely not.

So then why was it acceptable now?

I didn't ask for this watch to be given to me, Talia argued with herself.

But even as she thought it, she knew it was just a deflection from the hard truth that she *had* bent the rules of morality to suit herself.

She could rewind time over and over until she won the tournament, and no one would remember any different.

Except her.

Talia would remember. And she would have to live with the truth of the kind of person she'd become.

Who are you anymore, Talia?

She got up and walked to the payout area, where she was supposed to fill out paperwork to claim her prize. But when she arrived at the table, Talia handed over her tournament entry receipt and said, "I'm forfeiting my winnings. Please give them to the next-ranked player who actually deserves it."

Talia

Omni's product development engineers descended on Ideal Life's offices on Monday, taking over all the free space on the third floor. Due diligence for the acquisition had reached the phase where Omni now wanted to talk to their counterparts here. Talia had thought that Ideal Life had plenty of room, but with ten Omni engineers here, it was a bit tight.

The mood was lively, though, because if you got a bunch of tech nerds together and encouraged them to talk about their hopes and dreams for what they could build together, it was like Christmas Day, Silicon Valley–style.

Ostensibly, Talia was camped out with her laptop on the third floor in case anyone had questions for her. But the real reason was she hoped she would overhear something from the Omni team that would prove her fears and suspicions wrong.

Especially since she had failed to win the top prize at the Summer Million. Sure, she had the investments she'd made recently, but that was only $20,000 (after the poker buy-in). It was a lot to her, personally, but nowhere near enough to pay the termination fee to end the deal with Omni.

Two of Omni's engineers, Sheila Jiménez and Lucas Williams, sat at the desk closest to Talia, where they were looking at product schematics.

"So, the Temple Dots," Sheila said. "Is skin contact necessary, or do you think it would be possible to measure brain activity remotely?"

"Not from super far," Lucas added. "But yeah, could we do it remotely?"

Yan Kristiansen, Ideal Life's head of engineering, nodded.

"I think I understand. You're wondering if we need the Temple Dots, or if we can eliminate an extra accessory and roll all of the Temple Dots' technology into Omni 3Ds, which you think is the future—no one's going to be using phones or earbuds in a few years. Like, if we could put the sensors into the arms of the glasses, close to the customer's temples but not touching them."

"Precisely," Sheila said, grinning. "The goal is always less friction for the consumer. We want to make it as easy as possible for them to use our entire suite of Omni products. If we can get rid of Temple Dots, that's one less thing they have to deal with or remember."

"Well," Yan said, "as of right now, the Temple Dots do require direct contact to the skin in order to pick up on brain signals. But I can envision a near future where we can engineer that away, especially with the financial resources that Omni has at its disposal."

"Maybe this is a crazy idea," Lucas said, "but what about . . . Nah, never mind."

Yan leaned forward on the edge of his seat. "Tell us. No ideas are bad ideas in brainstorming, you know."

Lucas laughed. "Yeah, you're right. Okay, what about the reverse of what we were just talking about? What if someday we could actually get rid of our glasses and put all of it into Temple Dots? Not only brain-activity sensors, but *all* of the functionality that currently has to sit inside the Omni 3D hardware."

Sheila's jaw dropped open. "Oooh, yes! No need to wear glasses. Everything would be available in two unobtrusive stickers on your head . . . I love it. Talk about visualizing success!"

The three of them laughed at her pun.

Talia was thinking about what they'd said, though.

But all this was just fantasy for the engineers. It wasn't evidence that Omni had an evil grand plan to unite Ideal Life's technology with CerebraLink. Talia slipped away to walk around the third floor to see what other due diligence conversations were going on.

There was one about open-source software.

A debate over how best to integrate Ideal Life's suggestions into Omni's many notifications on their social media platforms and chat applications.

A tangential—mostly irrelevant—discussion of living in a virtual augmented reality world.

Then Talia slipped into one of the conference rooms, which several Omni and Ideal Life engineers, including Jody and Jonathan, had taken over to talk about the guts of the Ideal Life AI system. Their laptops and papers littered the long glass table.

"How much effort would it take to change that?" one of the Omni guys asked.

"I mean, we'd basically have to retrain the whole system," Jody said.

"How long would it take?"

"Depends on how much compute you have," Jody said.

Talia sat down in a chair near the conference room door. "What are you discussing?"

Jonathan said, "We were talking about how we trained our underlying AI with a base principle that all suggestions had to be for the good of humanity overall. Of course, they also have to be beneficial to the individual customer. But any recommendations that are likely to be good for just one person but at the detriment of society in general would be suppressed."

Talia nodded. "That was part of our founding mission—to make life better for everyone. It was tricky to align our AI systems to something that was, by definition, subjective, but Jody and Jonathan did a superb job. Like, if customer A is feeling a little down and needs to be entertained, and his profile says that going fast often lifts his spirits, Ideal Life still isn't going to suggest that customer A race his car down the freeway at a hundred miles an hour. That might improve his life temporarily, but it obviously comes with societal risks."

"Sure, of course," the Omni engineer said. "Oh, I'm Mike, by the way. And this is Bonnie, Phil, and Marya. It's an honor to meet you, Talia. But getting back to the discussion, what we're trying to figure out is if we can make adjustments to the Ideal Life AI without having to rebuild it from scratch. Not for telling customer A to speed illegally, but for more innocuous things—like can Ideal Life read a dip in blood sugar and then recommend a suggested product from one of our partners?"

Talia froze in her seat.

Jonathan frowned. "Are you saying integrate advertising into suggestions?"

Jody had the strongest reaction, rising up from her chair and throwing her pen down onto the conference table. "That's completely against our philosophy! Even by framing the question the way you did, you're acknowledging that feeding a 'suggested product' to a customer is not good for society overall. It's good for advertisers and corporations."

"It's *useful* for the customer, though," Phil, one of the other Omni engineers, said calmly.

"But in the grand scheme of things," Jody said, "you'd be making the world worse."

"Whoa, hold on," Mike said. "That's a bit harsh."

Jody crossed her arms. "I get that you guys have to make a profit for the shareholders. That's the way companies work, and I don't begrudge you that; if you don't make money, people lose jobs. And it's true that Omni has made a lot of innovative tech. But there's a line I think Big Tech companies should draw, and that's *not* to do things that you can foresee will have a negative impact on humanity. I don't think we need to be told to buy more stuff."

"From another angle," Jonathan said, "if I'm that customer you mentioned and my blood sugar is low, and I ask Ideal Life to search for something that is of optimal nutrition for me to eat, I want to be given unbiased options and then get to make that decision myself. I don't want advertising dollars to make the decision for me, and especially without me realizing it's happening."

Talia, finally recovered from Mike's reveal about their intention to serve ads to Ideal Life customers, wanted to know more. But to avoid putting him any more on the defensive, she pretended to play devil's advocate.

"Let's say," Talia began, "that we did allow sponsored suggestions if they were labeled clearly. What is Omni's plan? I feel like just having a pop-up notification saying, 'It looks like you're hungry. May I suggest shrimp nuggets from our partner Luigi's Seafood Drive-Thru? It's delicious, convenient, and only two dollars right now' is, like Jonathan pointed out, a quick way to lose the trust of our customers. And if they don't trust you, they'll eventually dismiss your ads, and then you've not only tanked Ideal Life as a product but also the space for your ad revenue."

Mike, Bonnie, Phil, and Marya looked at each other.

"What?" Jonathan asked.

"Well . . ." Mike said. "Omni has some plans for synergizing Ideal Life into our ecosystem."

Jonathan rolled his eyes at the corporate speak. But Jody, who was still hovering over everyone seated, was a lot less composed about it. "You think using fake MBA words will create a smoke-and-mirrors effect that will distract us? Do we really seem that obtuse to you?"

"There *is* a plan!" Phil said, standing so he was now at eye level with Jody.

Talia wouldn't get any information if the temperature in this conference room kept rising. "Hey, it's okay, everyone. I know Omni has a plan. I met with their executive team not long ago, including their CEO, and it's brilliant."

Phil's indignance deflated and he sat back down. "Oh. Good. So you already know."

"Of course," Talia bluffed. "We're going to be part of Omni in a matter of weeks anyway. There's no point in keeping secrets."

Mike exhaled. "Yeah, good, good. I completely agree. With our acquisition of Ideal Life and CerebraLink, we're all going to get to work on stuff that seems like science fiction. Combining

Ideal Life's understanding of psychology and behavior with CerebraLink's implant communication technology . . . Advertising is small potatoes. We're going to have so much fun. And you're all getting Omni stock options as part of this deal, right? We're going to get really rich integrating all this together."

The scowl on Jody's face could have melted the glass of the conference table. Then she stomped out of the room, and Jonathan—less volatile but just as disgusted—followed.

Mike's brow furrowed. "What did I say? Isn't the main point of working at a startup to hit it big and make a shit ton of money?"

"I'll, um, go talk to them," Talia said, although it was really an excuse for her to exit, too. She'd heard all she needed to know.

She found Jody crying softly at her workstation. Jonathan had his arm around her.

"Talia," Jody said, "tell me it's not true. Tell me you didn't sell us out to an evil empire. Jonathan and I joined Ideal Life because we thought we were contributing to something good." Her voice cracked on the last word.

"I swear I didn't know that's what they were up to," Talia said, kneeling to be on the same level as Jody and Jonathan. "I was just bluffing in there to see what they would reveal."

"So we don't have to do it?" Jonathan asked. "Can we decide not to let them buy Ideal Life?"

Talia ran her hand through her hair. "We'd have to pay them a million dollars if we're the ones to terminate the deal. That would bankrupt us."

Jody blew her nose and wiped away some of her tears. "Too bad none of us have big social media accounts. We could've used one of Omni's own networks to go viral about how they're trying to use us to screw over humanity. I can imagine the public outrage, if only they knew."

"Hey . . ." Jonathan said. "What about your sister, Talia? Isn't she famous?"

But Talia shook her head. "I don't want to use Libby like that.

And besides, if it's my sister who posts a video about this deal, it's kind of obvious that the information came from me. Omni's lawyers would be all over that to say it was my fault if the acquisition died because of it, and then we'd still need a million dollars to cover the termination fee."

"Then we're stuck." Jody slumped in her chair, and Jonathan slouched, too, his head on her shoulder.

Talia, however, gasped and shot to her feet. "I have a different idea. But I'll need your help."

"Just tell us what to do," Jonathan said.

"Mention on our internal Slack channel what you heard in that conference room. Don't get too involved in the conversation—just seed it. I think it'll spread pretty fast among our people."

"And then?" Jody asked.

"Cross your fingers that the rest of my plan will work."

Upstairs in her office with the door closed, Talia dug around in her purse until she found the card from the Techie Singles Mixer:

Evangeline Gray
Journalist

"I hope I'm right that you're the anonymous writer behind *Your Gossipy Tech BFF*," Talia said as she composed a message to invite Evangeline out for coffee.

Within a minute of hitting Send, a reply came in.

Not in Palo Alto. Too many eyes and ears. Meet me at Coffee Kitten in San Carlos at 1 p.m.?

Heart in her throat, Talia fired back an answer.

See you then.

Libby

Libby and Jacob landed at San Francisco International Airport refreshed, despite the eleven-hour flight from Seoul. Flying business class on your sponsors' dime meant sleeping most of the way across the Pacific, which, as a pregnant woman, Libby really appreciated. The little bean of a baby inside her was an energy vampire, and Libby needed all the nap time she could get.

Sam was going to meet them at the airport because his parents—who had been visiting—were leaving today to go on a world tour. Libby still didn't know why he'd needed her to come home, but Sam would never call her like that if it weren't important. Still, he'd assured her that whatever the situation was, it wasn't life-threatening and the explanation could wait for them to be in person, and that had been enough for her. She'd known Sam for so long that he was a surrogate big brother; she trusted him and his judgment.

As soon as Libby spotted him in the arrivals hall, she ran to him and threw her arms around him. "Sam!"

"Aw, Libby, hi!" He gave her a hug, and Jacob, too. "Thanks for coming, both of you. Oh, and Libby, you remember my parents, Jenny and Roger, from my college graduation. They're about to head off to Europe."

"So nice to see you again," Jenny said, "and to meet you, Jacob." She immediately pulled them together into a maternal embrace. When she released them, she said, "We very proud of you, Libby. Roger and me, we big fans of your YouTube."

"Oh my gosh." Libby blushed. "You watch our channel?"

Roger nodded as he shook their hands warmly. "She follow all your advice."

Jenny patted her purse, where a bright yellow folder with their itinerary was sticking out. "Europe vacation, all hotel, activities . . . We do just like you say."

"That's incredibly flattering, thank you," Jacob said. "Please let us know how you like it."

"We will love it," Roger said. "Guarantee."

"Sam," Jenny said, "we treat Libby and Jacob to coffee and cake before we check in and before they go to hotel, okay?"

He turned to Libby. "Does that work for you? I'll explain everything."

"Sounds great," Libby said. "I love cake."

Jenny radiated joy. "I love cake, too."

There was no need, though, for Jenny and Roger to treat them at Starbucks or Peet's. Instead, Libby and Jacob led them to a supersecret VIP club that was tucked away in a corner of SFO no one knew about except the highest-status frequent fliers. It was an elegant salon of velvet and polished wood on the top floor of the airport, with one-way windows that gave them a view of the busy terminal below. Anyone outside would only see frosted glass panels.

By design of its exclusivity, all the seating was in secluded, closed rooms like small private dining rooms. The lounge's host settled them into one decorated in pale-blue wallpaper with a gold floral pattern, a white marble table, and deep armchairs upholstered in a plush, soft gray. Hardly a beat after Jacob ordered coffee, it appeared, along with a selection of cookies.

Jenny, Roger, and Sam put on their earbuds.

"Simultaneous translation," Sam explained to Libby and Jacob.

"Oh, of course!" Libby said. They had recently started using earbuds like that, too, during their travels. She rummaged in her purse and retrieved hers. Jacob was just as quick with locating his.

Jenny reached into her own purse but came back with an unwrapped box decorated with two happy pineapples holding hands, one wearing a chef's hat and the other, glasses.

"Oh my gosh, Sunshine Cakes!" Libby clapped her hands.

"You know them?" Jenny asked.

"Of course. You used to send boxes of your pineapple cakes to Sam in college, and I'd steal half of them when he wasn't looking."

Sam laughed. "It's true. But I actually knew you were doing it and let you."

Libby wrinkled her nose at him, but in an affectionate way. She'd always liked Sam and secretly hoped he and Talia would get together. Her sister was far from perfect, even though she tried hard to be, but Sam would leap in front of a train for her if she needed him to. And he'd loved her steadily in the background for years and years. Everyone could see it, except Talia.

Which is why when he'd called to say that Talia needed Libby, Libby had jumped on a plane without question.

"So," Libby said, "you wanted to wait till we were here in person to tell us what was going on with Talia. What's happening, and what can we do?"

Sam sighed and shook his head. "It's kind of an unbelievable story."

Half an hour later, Libby sat back in her armchair, dazed. Sam had told them about Talia's watch, from the night it appeared until recently, and how Talia had gotten addicted to the ability to redo her life over and over. It was taking a toll on her, too—not just physically, but also mentally. Sam worried Talia's obsession over creating the perfect life was preventing her from actually living one.

And then there was the problem with the Omni deal.

"I don't know what to do about any of it," Sam said. "I tried talking to her, at least about the rewinds, but I don't think I'm getting through to her, and I'm out of ideas. So I called you."

Libby's mouth had been hanging open almost the entire half hour he'd been talking.

"I'm still stuck on the part about my sister being able to turn back time. How is that possible?"

"Possible," Roger said. "But time is . . . complicated."

Jacob, who had recognized that Roger didn't speak much so maybe this was important, leaned in. "Can you explain more?"

"With the help of these earbuds my amazing son bought for me? Absolutely." Roger took a moment and looked at Sam, so clearly happy and proud that it made Libby tear up a little. She knew that Sam had been lonely in college, and he'd said more than once to her and Talia how he admired their closeness and how he wished he'd had family like that. It seemed like maybe he and his parents were starting to find their way to each other now, too.

"Western thinking," Roger began, "views time linearly, as a discrete past, present, and future. However, Eastern philosophy sees it differently. It is consciousness itself that shapes our experience of time, making it more fluid than fixed.

"For example, the Taoist concept of time is cyclical, rather than a straight line. This view sees time as rhythmic patterns that repeat but also transform, like seasons changing or day becoming night becoming day again."

"Yeah . . ." Sam said. "I remember studying the *I-Ching*, and there was something about how all possibilities exist simultaneously. Each moment actually contains potential futures that branch out, which I guess could explain how Talia can rewind to access different branches. But does that conflict with what you're saying?"

Roger shook his head. "Perhaps, perhaps not. These ideas about time are, themselves, not linear. They are not necessarily mutually exclusive. But I don't think we will solve *how* Talia's watch works. Regardless, it is enough to know that there are potential explanations. And as long as there is a possibility, we cannot rule out that that is the reality."

Libby chewed on her lip. This was all so improbable. But Sam wouldn't drag her into something that was just a fantastical conspiracy. What Roger said made sense, too . . . sort of. Just because Libby had grown up thinking time worked one way didn't mean it was the only way.

"I also know for a fact that Talia has gone back in time," Sam said. "She proved it to me once. Hell, she could have rewound you and Jacob, and you wouldn't know it if she didn't tell you."

"She wouldn't do that," Libby said.

Sam made a noise in the back of his throat that sounded like a noncommittal "hmm."

Libby poked at the crumbs on her plate, all that remained of her pineapple cake. "Part of me still can't wrap my head around the watch, but a bigger part of me says, *Who cares*? Whether the watch actually works or not, Talia's problems *are* real. And that's what I need to focus on."

"What should we do?" Sam asked.

"You've already done so much for her. Now it's my turn. And I have an idea . . . I just need to think on it a little with Jacob."

Sam took her hand and squeezed it. "Thank you, Libby. You have no clue how much this means to me."

But Libby was pretty sure she did—to Sam, Talia meant everything.

They soon parted ways when Sam took Roger and Jenny to check in for their flight to London. Libby and Jacob headed to their hotel.

It was nice, nothing special, but they realized they were pretty spoiled by where they usually got put up.

"Guess we should get used to it," Libby said. "If we give up being travel YouTubers, no more ocean bungalows in the Maldives."

Jacob shrugged and sat on the edge of the bed. "You know, we *have* done an amazing job with saving what we've earned in the past, what, decade that we've been doing this? We can pay for ocean bungalows in the Maldives on our own. We can take our baby with us all over the world on our own dime, without putting her on camera, if that's what we decide we want."

"I know, and I love you for that, hon." Libby put her arms around him and sat next to him on the bed. "But we still need something to work toward. I'm not the kind of person who wants to 'retire' at thirty-three. I'll drive you crazy if I don't have some kind of job or goal to work toward."

He laughed. "Yeah, I'm happy being a stay-at-home dad, but you would be like a tigress pacing in a cage within two weeks of not having some kind of job."

Libby kissed him. "So, about that . . ."

A few hours later, she arrived at Ideal Life's office. Libby had thought about just showing up unannounced, but she was glad she'd decided to call her sister first, because Talia had been out at a meeting earlier.

The elevator arrived in the lobby, and Libby moved to step inside, but Talia burst out from it.

"What are you doing here? I didn't even know you were in the country!" Talia enveloped Libby in a hug, and Libby let herself melt into it. There were many times, growing up, when she'd needed the comfort of her big sister's arms, and being here with her felt so right.

Libby squeezed her sister for a second longer before letting go. "I wanted to surprise you."

Talia raised a brow, assessing her.

"What, I can't fly halfway across the globe because I miss my big sister?" Libby said.

"Of course you can, but I know you too well, and the way you're shuffling your feet means there's something else on your mind. Is the baby okay?"

"Don't worry; the baby's great. But you're right—there *is* something else I wanted to talk to you about. Can we go upstairs?"

When the elevator opened on the Ideal Life offices, a young woman with red hair stood waiting, bouncing on her toes.

"Oh my god, Libby, it's really you," she gushed. "I am *such* a fan. You and Jacob are living the dream. I want my future to be a combination of Talia's and yours. You are, like, the most successful sister duo ever."

Talia smiled. "Libby, meet Erin Berg, our intern. She's whip-smart and has been such an asset to us this summer."

Libby shook Erin's hand. "It's nice to meet you, Erin. And you must really be excellent, because Talia tends to attract the best people to work with her."

Erin blushed. "Thank you. Um, sorry to bother you, I know you two probably have a lot to do, but could I beg you for a selfie? My roommate loves you, too, and she'd die to see a picture of us together."

"Of course!" Libby was so used to posing with fans it only took a few seconds for Erin to get a variety of great shots.

They left her in the reception area furiously sending the photos to her roommate.

As soon as they reached Talia's office and the door closed, though, Libby shed the public version of herself and got down to business.

"So, Sam called. He said you needed me."

Talia sighed and flopped onto the purple couch. "I'm sorry. We're . . . going through some stuff. But he really shouldn't have done that."

"No, actually, I think he did the right thing." Libby sat down and took both of her sister's hands. "He's worried about you. He told us everything, including this"—she tapped the watch face—"and about the Omni deal and that you need to get out of it. And Talia . . . honestly, you look like shit run over by a truck five times. Maybe ten. Only your sister can tell you that to your face. So it's not just Sam who's worried. I am, too."

"I'm—" Talia began.

"No, please, let me finish," Libby said. "All my life, you've been the one who was fine. It didn't matter if you really were or not; for my sake, you had to be. It's impossible to count the number of times that you've been there for me, whether saving me from our parents forgetting they had to feed us, saving me from *myself* when I said yes as a freshman to prom with that asshole senior, or always being the first to like my and Jacob's videos from the very start of our careers when we filmed grainy, shaky footage and didn't know a thing about what we were doing.

"My point is, let me have *my* turn to help *you*. Sam said there's a termination penalty if you walk away from Omni's acquisition of Ideal Life. Jacob and I want to help pay it. I know, I know, you're surprised your baby sister has so much money, but being a creator can be shockingly lucrative, which is why it'll be hard to walk away . . . but I'll get to that. We don't quite have the million dollars to kill the Omni deal, but we have half. And if you're okay with it, we can start a fundraiser with our followers to get the rest?"

Talia stared at her, unable to speak.

"Consider it an investment in Ideal Life. There's no one I believe in more than you, Talia. You've always had such a good heart, on top of being smart. If there is anyone who can actually make a positive difference in this crazy world, it's you. Also, this can be my first foray into tech startups. It's something I'm interested in learning more about."

"You want to be an angel investor?" Talia said, still clearly trying to catch up in the wonderfully upside-down version of the world where *Libby* was saving *her.*

Libby nodded. "Jacob and I have decided to quit the creator life. It was a hard decision, but the industry has changed a lot from when we started, and we don't want to compete with AI personalities anymore. Plus, we want to raise our family here, near you and Mom and Dad."

"I would love if you were here," Talia said. "But Libby, you don't have to invest in Ideal Life. I-I took care of the problem, without using the watch."

"You did? Where did you get a million dollars?"

"I didn't. I figured out another way."

"How?"

Talia got up, swiveled her computer monitor toward the couch, and pulled up a newsletter site called *Your Gossipy Tech BFF.*

Breaking News: Is Omni Auditioning to Be the Next Bond Villain?

Palo Alto, CA—If you could make a Hollywood film about a dastardly tech company trying to take over all the minds of humanity, what would it be about? If you guessed a plot where the tech giant snaps up neuroscience startups and then combines them all into a mind-control app that hypnotizes you into buying boatloads of stuff you don't need, manipulates your dopamine receptors into staying online longer than you want, and sells all your brain data to Big Brother, you're right!

But you don't need to head to theaters to watch this story unfold, my friends, because it's happening in real time right here, right now, in our very own Silicon Valley. OmnisZcience's engineering team descended on Ideal Life's offices today and—gasp!—revealed their plan for total brain domination. It's no secret, either—it's all over the startup's internal Slack communications, and I have confirmed it with multiple sources.

So what do you think, Court of Public Opinion? Should we just sit back and let this happen?

Or should we speak up and stop this idea that nobody asked for, like how we put a stop to Omni's ridiculous plans to plug us all into the Matrix to live out our lives there like we're eternal Sims?

Let me know in the comments!

Libby whistled. There were already over three thousand comments in the less than one hour since the story had been posted. And Libby knew from her own posts online that that was a ton in so short a time.

"Other media have picked up the story, too," Talia said. "It's on *Forbes*, *TechCrunch*, everywhere. And the overwhelming public sentiment is that letting Omni acquire us and CerebraLink is bad for humanity."

A notification chimed for Talia. She opened the message.

"Oh my god," she said. "I didn't think it would happen this fast."

"What is it?" Libby asked.

"Raj Banerjee, head of Omni's artificial intelligence division, wants to talk to me ASAP."

"Well, call him!"

Libby watched as her sister sat down behind her desk and went into CEO mode. Sometimes, tech industry people got a bad rap. But there were also truly good people who worked here, who wanted to make the world a better place. Talia was one of them; she'd just gotten a little derailed.

When Talia finished talking to Raj, she was shaking. Libby hurried over to her side. "Are you okay?"

Talia nodded slowly. "Raj said that Omni is backing out of our deal. It's not worth the PR headache for them."

Libby squealed. "You're free!"

"There's more . . . Since Omni is the one choosing to walk

away, it's going to trigger the termination penalty in the contract for *them*. For five million dollars. They have to pay *us*."

"Holy. Shit."

"Yeah . . . Ideal Life can be independent for a lot longer."

"Okay, but Talia?"

"Hmm?"

"Jacob and I would still like to invest."

A grin broke out across Talia's face, lighting up even the dark circles beneath her eyes. "Then welcome to the family business."

Erin

Word spread like wildfire through the office about what had happened—not only how Talia had outmaneuvered Omni, but also how her sister had offered to step in to save Ideal Life. Erin had been impressed by the Morgan sisters before, but now she was even more awed by their ability to bounce back, even when the odds seemed impossibly stacked against them.

Feeling inspired, Erin drove over to the dorm Georgia was staying in for the summer. Because if Talia could come back from her dream company almost collapsing, maybe Erin could recover from something much smaller. After all, if she couldn't be resilient enough to try again after a flubbed date, she had no business thinking she could someday become a tech founder and CEO herself.

Outside of Georgia's door, Erin took a deep breath. She could hear music playing inside the room, and she hoped that meant Georgia was home (although part of Erin hoped it was her roommate, and Erin could postpone this act of bravery until later).

Just as she was about to knock, the door opened, and pop music, no longer muted, blasted into the hallway. Georgia stepped out, nearly bumping right into Erin.

"Oh god!" Georgia, startled, jumped backward.

"Crap," Erin said. "Why can't I do anything right?"

Georgia, having recovered herself, snorted. "You? What about me? I'm the one who force-fed you something that could've killed you. If one of us here can't do anything right, it's me."

"Wait," Erin said. "You blame yourself for our disaster of a date? *I'm* the one who was so nervous about it that I didn't keep track of my own allergies and ended up ruining everything by turning into a gasping, swollen red monster who needed an ambulance."

"It's not your fault you didn't know there were candlenuts in the laksa."

"And it's not yours that you didn't know I had an allergy to candlenuts," Erin said. "Honestly, I still don't know what the heck they are."

Georgia pulled her phone out of her pocket and showed Erin the lock screen. It was a photo of little beige nuts, like if chickpeas and macadamia nuts merged. "I've had this picture of candlenuts here ever since that night, as a reminder of what an idiot I am."

Erin started laughing then. Georgia, looking hurt, began to retreat into her room.

"No, no, stop—I'm sorry," Erin said, still giggling. "It's just that . . . look at us. We've both been beating ourselves up, when we could have been happier if we'd, I don't know, *communicated*? I mean, maybe that part *is* our faults, but . . ." Her smile softened into something more serious. "Well, I'm sorry. I'm sorry for the way our first date went, and I'm sorry I was too chicken to call you after, and I'm sorry you thought it was your fault. That's why I came today. And also, hi, since we seemed to have skipped that part."

Georgia hugged her arms around her own chest, but she laughed a little. "Hi. And I'm sorry for all that, too."

"I'm also sorry I didn't do this earlier." Erin stepped up and leaned in to kiss her. "Oh, hold on," Erin said. "You haven't eaten any candlenuts recently, have you?"

Georgia broke out into a full smile then and shook her head. "I will never eat nuts again if you'll just hurry up and kiss me."

"Consider it done," Erin said. And then she pulled Georgia to her and their lips met, and Georgia's mouth was every bit as delicious as she'd imagined.

Talia

Over the next week, Omni's lawyers finished the deal-termination paperwork, and Ideal Life's bank account had five and a half million more dollars in it from Omni, Libby, and Jacob.

Talia could still hardly believe that her baby sister had swooped in to rescue her and was now part of the startup. Life could be delightfully surprising when you didn't try to control and plan every moment of it.

That was a lesson she'd realized she needed to impart to Erin, too. All summer, Talia had watched Erin emulate her. But Erin was too bright a candle to allow to burn out so young.

So Talia had called her up to the rooftop garden for another performance review, but this time, in reverse. Talia had written up a scorecard of her own work and behavior over the past weeks and pointed out to Erin how all of Talia's striving for perfection had driven her a little mad (without mentioning the watch, of course) and that she'd ended up leaving no space in her life for friends or even for taking care of herself.

There was no easy answer to how women were supposed to move in the world, but Talia wanted Erin to know that "having it all" was a myth. Not in a bad way. Just that life required compromises, no matter who you were. And it was up to Erin—and each individual person—to decide what to give and what to take.

"You know, boss," Erin had said when Talia was finished with the reverse performance review, "I learned something else new recently."

"What's that?"

"It's that I don't have to do everything right the first time. I was really inspired by how you and Libby came up with a way to rethink Ideal Life and your own careers. I mean, my revelation was smaller; I'd totally screwed up a date with a woman that I really liked. But then I got a second chance by simply apologizing. And now we're together."

"Wow," Talia said. "That's wonderful—congratulations!"

After that talk, it was very apparent that Erin had begun recentering herself. She even started coming into the office at a normal hour, rather than way before anyone else. It was a great first step.

So now it was Talia's turn.

On Sunday, she drove out to the coast. She hadn't spoken to Sam since the Summer Million tournament last weekend and didn't know if he'd be willing to see her after how she'd betrayed their friendship, but she had to try. Because it turned out that mentoring was a two-way street, and she had learned something from her own intern—sometimes, you can get a redo in life just by communicating better. No watch needed.

Talia hoped that a peace offering from Taco Bell for Sunday Lunch would be a start.

Weekend traffic to the beach during summer was a bit of a bear, though, so Talia had plenty of time to think while she inched along Highway 92, and right now, she was pondering something Libby had said: *You've always had such a good heart, on top of being smart. If there is anyone who can actually make a positive difference in this crazy world, it's you*.

But had Talia achieved that? Or had Ideal Life started veering off course, caught up in the momentum of its own success? Her initial concept for Ideal Life had sprouted from good intentions, but Talia hadn't paused since then to ask herself whether it was still achieving what she wanted—to improve other people's lives, not make them worse.

She could see now that too much focus on self-improvement could sometimes grow into a burden rather than a boon. People weren't video game characters who constantly and eternally had to level up.

Sam had tried to warn her that she was stuck in a cycle like that, never able to be happy with how her past had unfurled or always apprehensive about how she would act in the future. There had been no space for Talia to be just Talia. To let life simply be what it was going to be.

So maybe Ideal Life, the company, needed to shift gears to match this revelation.

Big Tech and Silicon Valley were sometimes painted as soulless capitalistic machines. But Talia knew there were a lot of wonderful, truly morally upstanding individuals who worked here. Like in any field, though, it took effort to remain dedicated to being good. And Talia wanted to be that person, the woman that her sister believed she could be.

What if, instead of trying to "improve" ourselves, we use Ideal Life to help map and reinforce existing positive *neural pathways?* she thought as she reached the end of Highway 92. The beach opened up in front of her, and she turned onto Highway 1 to head up the coast to Taco Bell.

When Talia was a doctoral student, she had read a study about the amygdalas of young people and elderly people. Those who were young focused on both the good and the bad, but the older study participants had trained their brains to focus on the positive aspects of their lives and memories, and they reported higher levels of satisfaction and happiness than the younger participants. It was scientific verification that what you pay attention to creates the world you live in.

Ideal Life could encourage that for more people—it could help identify the moments when people felt content or happy, when they were satisfied with who they were or enjoying what they were doing. No need to think about what else they *should* be doing or needed to be.

You are already enough.

Talia smiled.

At Taco Bell, Talia asked the cashier to push three random buttons for Sam's order, in hopes that he'd be amused by the surprise. But then, before she was about to recite her own order of the same soft taco, nachos, and cinnamon twists that she'd gotten for Sunday Lunch over the course of the last fifteen years, she hesitated.

This had been her go-to meal because she knew it was optimized. But today, she wanted to loosen the tight hold she'd tried to keep on every aspect of her life.

"Push three more random buttons, please," she said to the cashier. "I'll eat whatever comes up."

At Lighthouse Books, Kenneth told her that Sam wasn't in, that he'd gone to the beach.

"Do you know which beach?" The coast stretched on for ages.

Kenneth shook his head. "Sorry . . . He just said he wanted some peace and quiet where there were no other people."

"Ah . . . then I think I might know where he is."

Talia

She wedged herself into the narrow crevice in the cliffs, scooting herself deeper into the rock.

A couple of meters in, the space angled right and opened up into a small cave. Sam sat on the far side, reading, his back propped against the wall with a blanket as a pillow.

Talia's chest clenched, and she hovered in the entrance. Would he want to see her?

"Hey," she said quietly.

Sam looked up at her.

"Mind if I join you?" she asked. "I brought Sunday Lunch, although it's probably cold by now—sorry."

He didn't say anything. But he didn't ask her to leave, either.

Talia crossed the small cave and handed him the bag. "I don't even know what's in there. I took a leap of faith and ordered random stuff." She laughed nervously. It was strange to feel jittery around Sam. He'd always been a calming force for her, a safe place to come to when everything else out there felt like too much. But of course, she didn't know if she had the right to want that from him anymore.

"Sam, I'm so sorry—about the rewinds that I didn't tell you about, for kissing you and erasing it, and for not listening when you tried to keep me from getting sucked into the seduction of this thing." She toyed with the band of her watch. "You've only ever cared and worried about me, and I've taken you for granted. I am more sorry than I can ever express."

He only looked at her, his expression blank.

Talia stumbled on. "I wish I could undo it all. No! Not like that! I just mean that . . . I'm sorry a million times over. I broke your trust by manipulating your timeline. Those weren't my choices to take away from you or to make for you, and even worse, I'd made you a promise and didn't keep it.

"I know now that what I really should have done was simply *talk* with you. Rewinds can actually come from open, honest conversation and making different choices and not just the watch. I should have chosen that path—chosen *you*—over a magical watch.

"I'm not sure if you can forgive me. But if you can, I'll buy you Taco Bell forever. I'll be less selfish, more considerate, and I'll be better about not using technology all the time, because I see clearly now that it's not a substitute for real friendship or real life.

"And most importantly, there will be no secrets between us. But . . . but if this apology is too late or not enough, I get that, too." Tears brimmed over the rims of Talia's eyes. "I hurt you, and you deserve so much better. I'd understand if you never wanted to see me again.

"Just know that you're my best friend, Sam, and . . . I think I might love you, too."

The right corner of his mouth twitched, but still he didn't say anything. The sunlight filtering in through the cracks in the cliff faltered. And the sound of the surf hitting the shore seemed to go silent as this moment stretched on and on.

Talia unbuckled the watch and offered it to him. Sam didn't move, though, so she laid it on the sand at his feet.

"Okay, then . . . I'm sorry."

She swallowed the lump in her throat and turned to go.

Sam

Sam rose and put his hand on her shoulder before she could leave. He'd been letting her talk, to get it all out, but he'd already forgiven her from the second she entered the cave. Because that's what love was—seeing the person for the entirety of who they were, not only the good moments or the bad ones. *All* of them.

"Talia . . . if you had given me a chance when you kissed me, instead of rewinding right away, I would have kissed you back." He sighed. "I've loved you since you showed up at my door freshman year. But I think my reaction time to your kiss was just a little delayed, since I'd been waiting for seventeen years."

She turned slowly to face him. She was crying a little now, but she braved a tentative smile. "Then you forgive me?"

"You had me at 'I'll buy you Taco Bell forever.' "

Talia laughed.

"Well," Sam said, "are you going to kiss me or what?"

She looked at the watch on the sand. "Just one more thing."

Talia

Talia grabbed the watch and led Sam out of the cave onto the beach.

There, she picked up a jagged rock, held the watch against the cliffside, and smashed the watch to pieces.

Sam jumped at the suddenness. But Talia already felt lighter.

She scooped up the shattered watch parts and put half in Sam's hand. "On the count of three, okay?"

He didn't have to ask what she meant.

"One, two, three!"

As the tide rolled in, they hurled the remnants of the watch into the ocean together. And when the wave rolled out, it took everything with it to sea.

Talia turned to Sam and stood on her tiptoes.

And then—finally—she kissed him.

The wind tangled horrible knots through her hair.

The sunlight glared in her eyes.

And a fresh, bigger wave roared in and soaked them.

But Talia and Sam stayed right where they were in this perfect, messy, unplanned moment.

No rewinding. No worrying about the future.

Just here, right now.

An ideal life.

Acknowledgments

The funny thing about *Ideal Life* is that I hadn't meant to write another book yet. I wanted to take a bit of a break after *The Incredible Kindness of Paper*. But then Talia and her startup ambitions and the mysterious watch appeared unbidden one day, and when I shared the idea with my wonderful editor, Lara Jones, and my talented agent, Thao Le, their overwhelming excitement (and mine) meant that I dove right in to writing it. So thank you to Lara and Thao . . . Or maybe I *shouldn't* thank you, because if you'd hated *Ideal Life*, I would have taken a nice vacation after all.

I am in awe of my amazing publicists, Brittani Hilles at Lavender Public Relations and Holly Rice-Baturin at Atria. Thank you also to the rest of the incredible crew at Emily Bestler Books and Atria, from the art department to production to the audiobook team and everyone in between.

Thank you to Rose Bloomin for talking to me about what it's like being a woman tech founder in Silicon Valley, especially one who is driven by a mission to do good. Here's to more bold, brilliant women aiming to make the world a better place!

This book begins with quotes from Oliver Burkeman and Marie-Louise von Franz, both of which I borrowed from Burkeman's *Wall Street Journal* piece, "'New Year, New You' Doesn't Work. Here's How You Can Actually Improve Your Life." The way he wrote about not postponing your real life resonated with me and coincided with my writing of *Ideal Life*; as an homage, this sentiment is echoed by Sam in my book. Thank you to Oliver Burkeman for that lovely, thought-provoking essay.

To Mom and Dad, I've said this before, but I'll say it again and again: Thank you for believing that I can do anything I set my mind to. From when I scribbled my first "book" in first grade to when I decided in college to major in Russian literature to when I ditched law to become a novelist, you've been unerringly proud and supportive. I love you.

And last—but really, always first—thank you to Tom and Reese. You are sunshine and laughter and chocolate chip cookies, Target and gelato and math puzzles I don't understand. You are vibrant and so different from me, and yet, we are the same, because you are mine, and I am yours. I love you both—thank you for this perfectly imperfect life.